Panda Books

Catkin Willow Flats

LIU Shaotang, a native of Tongxian in the suburbs of Beijing, was born in 1936. He began publishing short stories when only thirteen and his first collection appeared in 1953. In 1954, he entered Beijing University where he studied Chinese literature. He subsequently published several collections including *Songs from Hawthorn Village* (1954) and *Mid-Autumn Festival* (1956), and the children's book *The Melon Shed* (1957).

He was sent to the countryside during the political upheaval in 1958 where he continued to write in his spare time. During this period he wrote three novels, *The Earth's Fire*, *Spring Grass* and *Flames of War*. Liu Shaotang now lives in Beijing with his wife and three children.

Catkin Willow Flats

Liu Shaotang

Panda Books

Panda Books
First edition 1984

ISBN 0-8351-1166-0

Published by CHINESE LITERATURE, Beijing (37), China

Distributed by China International Book Trading Corporation (GUOJI SHUDIAN) P.O. Box 399, Beijing, China

Printed in the People's Republic of China

CONTENTS

Catkin Willow Flats

THE mid-morning July sun blazed down.

Manzi was bound firmly to an upright of the vine trellis by his grandfather. The knot was a complicated one used for tying up a thief.

That was in 1936, when Manzi was six, his head shaven clean except for a tuft on his crown. He was burnt brown as a berry, for he had gone about stark naked ever since summer came. Only two patches under his brows showed white where the sun had not touched him. The bridge of his nose was black and cracked. It was as if he had just crawled out of a chimney. Even his eyeballs seemed blacker than before the summer.

His granny had asked Wang Ri Lian, the neighbour on the east side, to make the boy an apron-diaper of the brightest red cloth, lovingly embroidered with a colourful floral design. People must wear clothes as horses must wear a saddle. If Manzi had worn his apron-diaper, he would have been the star attraction among all the other boys. However, Manzi refused to wear it, even for a day.

He went about in his birthday suit, running wild all over the canal flats, no matter how fiercely the sun beat down on him. If he had deigned to wear the apron-diaper it would have made him sweat and within hours his whole body would have been covered with an irritating, itching heat rash. Not one of the girls of his age had an apron-diaper to compare with his in splendour, so he would have felt a little sissy, neither a boy nor a girl. The girls would have ridiculed him until he would have wished to find a hole to crawl into in embarrassment. Even the smallest boy in the village would have laughed and jeered. He would never live it down for the rest of his life. Manzi's granny was, of course, furious. She threatened to whack him with the long rolling pin if he didn't put on the bright red apron-diaper and to starve him for three days. This apron-diaper had a very special significance. Manzi was the darling of the whole family, and his granny was always afraid that the King of Darkness would carry him off one day. It was said that the King of Darkness snatched little boys away but never little girls. So if Manzi wore the bright red apron-diaper making him not look too much like a boy, he might escape the rheumy old eyes of the King of Darkness.

People addressed Manzi's granny as Aunt Yi Zhang Qing. She was tall and bronze and had large, unbound feet and a very penetrating voice. When she bawled anyone out, she could be heard fifteen kilometres away. Few could match her in this respect. When she cussed, the words came tumbling out loud and clear like rain beating down on wide banana leaves. She had no need to stop for breath. Abuse poured out of her mouth in one long endless stream. She could also fight. She was well into her fifties, but it would have taken more than half a dozen strapping young men to get the better of her.

Her home was on the bank of the Northern Canal and the house opened out on to it. Once a large junk from other parts of the country happened to pass her door. It was almost noon, and Aunt Yi Zhang Qing was sitting in the shade of the willows tending ducks when several boat-haulers came trudging past, naked as the day they were born except for a piece of cloth about their waist, their trousers rolled up like a turban high on their heads. Suddenly, they heard someone shout, "Hold it!" Now these were tired men, bone weary. They had been towing upstream against the wind under the broiling sun for the last hundred *li* and had not had so much as a moment's rest. Their stomachs were rumbling angrily for lunch. They ignored Aunt Yi Zhang Qing's shout. When she saw this, fury seized her and she shouted again, louder, "Put on your trousers!" One young hauler, who ought to have known better, looked up and said surlily, "You're old enough to have seen most things. Shut your eyes or turn the other way if you don't like what you see!" That got Aunt Yi Zhang Qing's dander up. Rolling up her sleeves to expose a pair of big bronze bangles, she rushed down on him. "I'm not going to have you insult women-folk like this!" she yelled, shaking a finger at him. The young hauler brushed her hand aside. "Out of the way, you bitch!" That did it! Aunt Yi Zhang Qing landed him a blow that sent the young fellow reeling, his ears ringing and blood spurting from his nose. He staggered and fell on the hot white sand, fighting for breath. His mates rushed to the rescue. They heard Aunt Yi Zhang Qing break off a branch about as thick as a bowl and saw her come at them, flaying wildly. She drove them all into the water like so many dumplings sliding into the pot. Aunt Yi Zhang Qing stood on the bank cursing them, driving each back into the water as he tried to clamber up out of it. They were all stuck in the canal. The helmsman tried in vain to control the junk which kept twirling along with the current. Finally, the owner of the junk persuaded Liu Guandou, the ferryman, Ji Laocheng, the blacksmith, Zheng Duanwu, the carpenter, and Du Si, the shopkeeper, to come and intercede for him. It took all of them a couple of hours to persuade Aunt Yi Zhang Qing to relent and let the men back on dry land.

Aunt Yi Zhang Qing's hands were calloused. She could work in the field, handle a boat and fish as well as any man. She also cured people's afflictions with acupuncture and cupping. She was the local midwife, surgeon and bone-setter, and old and young in the village sought her when they needed help. Every man, woman and child in the village under thirty had come into this world with the assistance of her able hands.

Though she was such a capable person, yet she could do nothing with her only grandson, Manzi. The He family for generations had always produced only one son and then always late in life. Manzi's grandfather was an only son, born when the parents were getting old. The boy's own father was not born until Aunt Yi Zhang Qing was almost forty. But Manzi was different. He was the first-born, and a boy. When Yi Zhang Qing heard her grandson's first whimper, she shed abundant tears of joy. She burnt incense and gave thanks, praying to Buddha and making many vows. On the boy's third day, Aunt Yi Zhang Qing slaughtered a sheep and three chickens and held a little banquet to mark the event. When the boy was a month old,

Manzi's grandmother butchered a pig and six chickens. She invited all their relatives to the celebration. She then scoured all the neighbouring villages for pieces and scraps of coloured cloth to make a multi-coloured garment, "a hundred family garment", for Manzi. On the boy's hundredth day, it was ready. She dressed her grandson in it to receive the guests, who were each and all very impressed and who loudly praised the work and showered their felicitations on the boy. On the boy's first birthday, his grandmother had a shiny, gilded bronze lock cast to hang around his neck. The heavy amulet almost strangled the infant before he was another day older. Manzi was his grandmother's joy and delight, her hope and her life. This led her into conflict with the boy's mother.

Manzi's father had been apprenticed at the early age of thirteen to a bookseller in Tongzhou to learn the art of lithography. He learned to write a good script and paint a passable picture. His employer liked him for his looks and willing docility, so he promised to let his daughter marry him. Manzi's father was a vain man and keen to get ahead. He was very pleased and accepted the offer. His mother Yi Zhang Qing, however, was not particularly pleased. She was prejudiced against townspeople. She wanted her son to marry a farmer's daughter or a fisherman's daughter, someone who could help her with the work and support a family. However, she could not talk her husband into opposing the match, and she was also afraid of breaking her son's heart. Although much against it, she finally went along with it. It would be wrong to think that Manzi's mother was a pampered young lady, for her father's shop could barely support the family. Still, she had been brought up in a fairly well-to-do house of a literate family. Though she was never taught to read and write, she had learned to read some characters and write a few. She was, moreover, quite beautiful, of slender build, soft-spoken and mild. In Aunt Yi Zhang Qing's eyes, her daughter-in-law was a beautiful paper flower, good to look at but useless. In her heart, she did not like her. Conversely, Manzi's mother did not like her mother-in-law, for she thought her coarse and uncouth. She was not used to life in the countryside either and no sooner had she crossed the threshold than she wanted to go back to her mother's house. After Manzi was born, the father wanted to set up house in town. Now Aunt Yi Zhang Qing was a proud woman and would not hear of it. It would shame her in the eyes of her neighbours. But living together under one roof and squabbling like geese all day made one a laughing stock too.

She was terribly upset and shed many silent tears. She debated with herself a long time and finally agreed, deciding to bow to the inevitable. The break had to come, sooner or later. But she fought a rearguard action. She did not let her daughter-in-law have it all her way. She insisted that the child stay with her. The boy's mother was very unhappy and cried her eyes out. The matter was settled by calling on Liu Guandou, the ferryman, Ji Laocheng, the blacksmith, and Du Si, the shopkeeper, to mediate. They spent several days and several nights before the matter was settled between the two women. It was decided that the boy would stay with his granny until he was old enough to go to school, when he would join his mother and father in town.

While Manzi was with his granny he had everything he wanted. She would have plucked stars from the night sky for him had he asked. By the time Manzi was four or five, he was living as free as a bird, hardly ever at home the whole day, running wild along the flats. His granny was for ever worrying and fretting, afraid a dog might bite him, an eagle carry him off, or that he might tumble down a disused well, or a child-snatcher abduct him. Her fears were endless. The old lady was always running out of the house after the boy, yelling for him in her loud voice which could be heard all over the village. Manzi would hide himself in the willow bushes, burrowing deep into the reeds or in the bean vines playing hide-and-seek with his old granny, chortling to himself all the while. When the sun set he would return to find his granny waving the stick of wood that propped open the door, threatening to "smash his shiny young head". Manzi never even batted an eyelid. He just stood there until his granny tossed away the prop in exasperation, crying, "You'll be the death of me yet!" Then she would go inside to prepare something good for him to eat, a poached egg or pancakes of the finest white flour.

One day, the boy's grandfather returned home from his frequent trips outside the county. His wife grumbled about this and that, which her husband nonchalantly answered with a few mumbled words. He appeared to have heard, yet he hadn't. The exasperated grandmother escalated her voice and complaints. She complained long and loud about their grandson's escapades. The grandfather was a hot-tempered man. He seized the boy and dragged him yelling to the trellis and tied his leg to an upright, knotting the rope with a clever hitch that even a hardened thief would not have been able to untie, let alone young Manzi. The grandfather tossed a paper box full of characters on square pieces of paper, a slate and chalk and ordered the boy to copy out all the characters before lunch.

Manzi was not dismayed. He felt confused and wronged. This was the first time in his young life he had been deprived of his freedom. He stared at the characters in the box, his hands idle, without the slightest inclination to write.

2

It was difficult to trace the personal name of Manzi's grandfather, but he had won renown by his nickname on the two banks of the Northern Canal, along the entire old caravan route inside and outside the Great Wall, among those who sweated and toiled, among itinerant artists. They all knew him as "Great Learning" or just "Learned" for short.

Learned was tall, sturdily built, barrel-chested, dark complexioned and with bushy eyebrows. His countenance was like Guan Gong, a legendary character. He had been a member of the Yi He Tuan (Boxer) Movement in his youth and was a good swordsman as well as skilled in unarmed combat. Later, he drove carts for landlords for he could handle animals well. He was an expert with the whip, which he seldom used. He loved to exaggerate, and one of his boasts was that the crack of his whip could be heard as far away as Tianjin. Besides being fond of the bottle, this hot-tempered man was addicted to righting wrongs done to others. He would risk life and limb for the sake of a friend. This explained why he never remained long working for one landlord. Finally, he found a job as a drover for a horse dealer. For seven or eight months each year, he was busy herding horses from outside the Great Wall to the various horse fairs along the old caravan route. Several hundred horses would move tamely under his whip like so many docile sheep. The men who preyed on the horseherders en route took care to stay clear of Great Learning when they heard the crack of his whip echoing in the ravines. His ability at handling horses and in keeping horse thieves away made his services highly sought after by horse dealers. He was very proud of this and if he wasn't asked very courteously, he would not work for them. He didn't spend time bargaining over his wages, but he insisted on being treated with deference.

He also did not seem to know the value of money. His wallet was readily open to needy friends. He gave generously to the old, the infirm and the disabled, never counting but just seizing a handful of money and giving it away. So he never had very much left when he got home.

In this little village, he was the most travelled and was recognized as having seen a lot of the world. He loved to boast and do things in a grand style. He earned a fortune on each trip, but had problems when he went home. Still he would act as if his money-belt was stuffed with coins. He would borrow freely from the cattle-dealers at crippling rates and throw banquets and invite all his cronies to come to listen to his wildly exaggerated stories about his travels and adventures. He had a tremendous imagination and the tales he spun were gripping and absorbing about fights and hair-raising adventures. The plots were complicated and the stories were told convincingly and with gusto. This earned him the title of "Great Learning", given partly in jest and partly in respect.

In the past, he had loved to hear the itinerant story-tellers tell their stories, which he would later recount with embellishments of his own. But after he was given this honorific, he began to study in real earnest. He kept in his waistband various librettos put out by a publisher in Beijing. He would be found diligently memorizing them, reciting in a singsong whenever he stopped for the night or when he rested. He was not ashamed to ask others words that he did not know and he would reward them handsomely for their pains.

He would pay for a man's dinner for explaining a word or a passage to him. Since he was a learned man, he began to speak and move with decorum as befitted a scholar and he took to wearing long gowns and enunciating his words slowly and clearly in a refined sort of way. People inside and outside the Great Wall along the old caravan route encountering him riding bareback, a bag of books slung across his left shoulder and a yard-long whip across the right shoulder, were awed and amused. Whenever in his travels he came across a Confucian temple dedicated to learning, he would dismount and reverently make a deep bow with both hands clasped and burn incense. Even in those days, the temples were already in disrepair, with eight out of ten in the smaller towns in very bad shape, walls half demolished and buried behind a tangle of bushes and grass, the haunt of birds, beasts and insects. When Learned made his obeisances and burnt his incense, startled sparrows would dart out in fright and hares would dash away to cover.

In the deep silence of the night, sometimes when he could not find sleep, Great Learning was frequently racked by dismay and troubles. He recalled that for eight generations, his family had owned no house, neither a brick nor a tile, not even a furrow of land. They had always been poor. He himself was already in his sixties, and had only managed to build himself a three-room adobe hut and acquire eight *mu* of sand flats. Although he was popularly addressed as Learned, he had never been to school and could only read a handful of characters, but could not write any of them. His son was quite studious, but he had only had three years of instruction from a private school before being apprenticed to the bookseller. So, apparently, if the He family were to produce a real scholar, it had to be Manzi, the grandson. However, he could only put the boy through primary school with his resources and even then it would be quite a strain. As to middle school and university, they were heights beyond his reach, and each step of the way up had to be paved with silver. Even if his old bones were squeezed of their last drop of marrow, he would not have enough to put the boy through university. Would his little grandson end up herding horses too, or as an apprentice to a bookseller like his dad?

Manzi was a clever boy, nimble of mind and endowed with an excellent memory. He loved to listen to stories and never forgot what he heard. He liked to ask what this and that character meant and he never forgot what he was told. The grandfather masqueraded as a learned sage before his grandson and taught him what he had learned from the opera librettos he always carried with him. The boy devoured them, as hungry silkworms did mulberry leaves. One libretto was not enough to last him a few days. The grandfather was delighted and decided to seek the assistance of a teacher. By chance, he ran into an old scholar of the Qing Dynasty, who was keeping books for a large staging post. He could write passable characters. Business was slack and the owner of the post was thinking of sacking him. Great Learning hired the man on the spot, promising him a copper coin for every word he taught his grandson.

The scholar came to the He household and began giving lessons under the vine bower. He sat on a high chair, a long-stemmed pipe in his hand, which he used freely on Manzi's head as the boy sat on a low straw cushion on the ground at his feet, a small table before him. The elderly scholar maintained a grim and forbidding countenance. Every time Manzi dared look up, he felt overwhelmed by a heavy cloud of gloom. The old scholar recited lines from the classics in an unintelligible singsong mutter. Manzi was bored and restless. He was used to running wild all day and now he was restrained. His bottom burnt and itched and his back ached. When he heard the twitter of birds among the willows outside the fence, he would instinctively try to imitate their call and forget all about learning. When he heard the rhythmic chant of the men along the tow-path, his heart beat faster and he would long to rush out to look and forget what he was supposed to study. But the beady eyes of the old teacher were sharper than an awl. Whenever he caught sight of the slightest twitch of excitement in Manzi's body, out flew the copper-headed long-stemmed pipe to thwack the boy's bald head, leaving a lump the size of a jujube date. How the boy hated the teacher! Moreover, every blow of the pipe was felt by the boy's granny. The grandfather, however, stoutly maintained that beating produced talent and he backed the old scholar. He encouraged him to uphold discipline. Great Learning guaranteed the teacher three meals of white, polished rice, or of white flour, and also a flask of wine each day. He couldn't, of course, keep this up for long, and within a month, Great Learning was broke and had to hurry away to herd horses again to pay the debts he had incurred.

With the grandfather away, the boy became an unbridled horse. Even before the stars had all disappeared, before the sun's appearance, he was off and away, trampling the dew on the grass, away from the confining house and the detested lessons. His granny had taken a strong dislike to the scholar long ago. First, she stopped the daily flask of wine and then ceased providing three meals a day of white polished rice or white flour. Finally, the old scholar could not stand it and indignantly stamped away with several hundred coppers of cash, leaving behind him several hundred squares of characters.

About this time, Zhou Qin came back from school for the summer holidays. He was a pupil in the Luhe Middle School in Tongzhou and lived in the house on the western side of Aunt Yi Zhang Qing's. Manzi attached himself to this neighbour's son. When Great Learning returned and found the scholar gone, he thought it was a great pity and blamed his wife for being so undiscerning. "Long of hair but short of sight!"

he exclaimed. But when he saw his grandson following Zhou Qin around all day long and picking up characters faster without even spending one copper, his anger melted and he rejoiced.

It was not that Great Learning did not love his grandson. Every time he set off for home, his heart always went ahead of him, eager to be home to see his grandson again. His stubbled chin and cheeks would scrape against the boy's soft skin, making him squeal with delight and feign pain until they were laughing together. He always brought back with him a saddle bag of good things to eat for the boy, too.

But this time, when he returned, he looked much older, his face set and grim and his brow dark. When his grandson ran up shouting in delight to welcome him home, he showed no joy. He did not pick the boy up as usual to embrace him or kiss him and the bag was empty too.

Manzi was puzzled and unhappy and he went and sat under the window, wearing a grumpy look, showing the whites of his eyes, lips curled in displeasure.

Later, he heard his granny berating his grandfather, "You come home like some malevolent spirit. Not even a smile! If you dislike us so much, then stay away and take care of your *niang niang* (goddess of fertility) and leave your corpse on the road unattended!"

In the last year or two, Manzi had begun to understand some of the things adults talked about among themselves. From what his elders said, from snatches of their conversation, he knew that his grandfather was on good terms with another woman outside the Great Wall, who was a dozen years younger than granny and who lived in a tent and who herded horses. Every time the grandparents quarrelled, his grandfather would back away when his grandmother began cursing "that herdswoman". How Manzi wished he could go with his grandfather and stay a few days with that younger granny who lived in a tent! He was sure that granny, too, would be nice like this granny who spoiled him. The more who loved him the better.

"Damn it all, I almost lost my life and you still curse me." This time, his grandfather did not back off and hold his peace. "Those Japs are carving our country up into little pieces. They've set up some tinpot Manchukuo Kingdom in our three northeastern provinces and now there is some bloody 'Mongolian Border Government' outside the pass. No one is allowed out through the Wall without a special permit from Yin Rugeng. Those Mongolian soldiers arrested the boss and me. Said we were Communists. Did that just to steal all the hundreds of horses we had. The boss hanged himself. They let me go only because they saw that I was a penniless bum and getting a free meal out of them each day."

Manzi did not entirely understand all of this, but he had heard of the name Yin Rugeng before. It was the winter before, one day when the snow was falling heavily. There was a rumour that in Tongzhou, a Yin Rugeng had set himself up as a king. That had made heaven and the people indignant and the whole earth was put under white in mourning. When Zhou Qin returned for his winter holidays, he had cursed Yin and had said his real name was Shi Jingtang.* He had also

* Shi Jingtang (AD 892-942) was an official of the Latter Tang Dynasty who became a traitor.

told Manzi a story about the last days of the Tang Dynasty.

So his grandfather had been in jail and had nearly lost his life. Manzi's heart warmed to the old man. He was about to go inside and tease and comfort him, when his grandfather had suddenly poured out his pent-up wrath on Manzi. He had not only tied him to the upright and had knotted it so that even a hardened thief could not escape, but had also told him to copy out a hundred characters on his slate. When Manzi saw again the handwriting of the old scholar, he immediately remembered the man's long face and his longer pipe and his little heart was filled with rage and hatred.

His grandfather had finished off the flask of wine and was now sprawled on the brick bed snoring loudly, dead to the world. Grandmother sat in the kitchen on the brick stove twisting a piece of rope, still fuming.

There was now only one person who could help, Manzi concluded, and he waited anxiously for his expected saviour to appear out of the east. But there was no sign.

3

Manzi felt that his home was like a cage, and he was the little willow green bird inside it, or a cricket inside its cage of plaited wheat stalks.

The four sides of the He compound were fenced in by willow stakes festooned with climbing bean vines intertwined with convolvulus, which made the walls even stronger and more impervious. Inside, around the walls stood apricot trees, peach trees, hawberries and crab-apple trees. Outside were poplars, willows, elms, locusts, mulberries, jujubes and birch-leaf pears. The two lines of trees ringing the walls inside and outside seemed like two rows of strong stakes holding the whole wall tightly together. Granny seemed to abhor empty space. She had filled the whole yard with sprawling cucumber trellises and things. Even the space above the ground in the yard was used. She had pumpkin vines climbing up frames and their heavy fruit and large leaves blotted out the light and weighed down the roof of the three-roomed adobe house, threatening to crush it. The pumpkins were almost the size of the stone rollers on the threshing floor.

The heat grew more and more oppressive. There was hardly a breath of wind. It was like the inside of a steaming basket for steamed buns. Although the grape-vines gave relief from the blazing rays of the sun and Manzi was stark naked, he nevertheless sweated profusely. He looked at the rope about his ankle. He could not untie it, no matter how hard he tried. He struggled in vain, sweat breaking out all over him and running down in rivulets.

Suddenly, there was a movement among the shrubs and leaves on the east fence of the compound and a face appeared amongst the greenery and a voice called gently, "Manzi!" He looked up and saw the shining face of Aunt Wang Ri Lian. His rescuer had appeared at last.

"Aunt Wang Ri Lian!" He gave a cry and all at once the flood of tears long held back burst and he let out a long, loud wail of pain and grief.

His granny sitting in the kitchen dropped what she was doing and rushed out. "Manzi! What's the matter?"

Manzi caught the note of concern and love in his granny's voice and, realizing he could capitalize on it, howled even louder.

There was a sharp cluck outside the fence where Aunt Wang Ri Lian was standing. "What has Manzi done to get himself trussed up ready to be exiled?" she asked.

Manzi's sobbing instantly grew louder.

"That old good-for-nothing ran into trouble and has been taking it out on us since the moment he came home. He wants to get rid of this little one first and then drive his old woman to death, so he can bring that slut of his outside the Great Wall into our house!"

Aunt Yi Zhang Qing let loose a stream of abuse about her husband.

There was an angry roar from inside the bedroom and Great Learning charged out bellowing. He was stripped to the waist and barefoot, clad only in his shorts. His whiskers were bristling stiffly like needles.

"If it weren't for that blasted long tongue of yours, would I have tied Manzi up? You got me to do it."

"Did I tell you to tie him up?" she hurled back at him, her voice drowning out Manzi's wailing. "I only wanted you to give the boy a scare and you, you black-hearted beast, did this to him!"

"But I didn't really tie him up."

"No? You nearly strangled him!" She clapped her hands together in anger and despair.

"One day, I'll cut off that bloody long tongue of yours!" Her husband ran over to the boy and with a flip of his finger, the rope slackened and fell to the ground. "See! Did I really tie him up?"

Aunt Wang Ri Lian, a basket on her back, ran into

the yard. "You are a one for a joke," she said, laughing.

"Now, everyone knows this trick of mine!" the grandfather said with a chuckle. "And now this young scamp is going to be even more unruly."

"Why don't you go back and finish your nap. I'll take Manzi along with me to collect some firewood by the canal," Wang Ri Lian offered.

"Wait a moment," said Great Learning. "First, let his grandmother fix him up with something to eat."

"I will not!" his wife flung at him, her anger still unabated.

"Then I'll have to stick my neck out and intrude into the old she-devil's kitchen," Great Learning heaved a loud sigh. "I'll be a big-footed old woman and cook up something for your darling."

"I won't eat it," Manzi said with a shrug. "Give me those snares from the west room. I want to catch birds."

"Yessir!" Great Learning promptly answered. "What a filial grandson you are! Going to get a bird or something nice to go with his grandpa's wine, eh?" The old man hurried inside to do as he was bid.

The boy took the snares his grandfather gave him and walked hand in hand with his Aunt Wang Ri Lian, undried tears still glistening on his eyelashes. But he was already mimicking the cry of the cuckoo as he left the compound.

"You're my pet, too. I'll give you a ride." She crouched down on a slope so he could climb into the basket on her back, and they headed towards the canal.

Aunt Wang Ri Lian was nineteen, and her baby name was Ke Lian Er (Pity). She was the child bride of the family living on the east side of the He family. Twelve years ago Du Si, the shopkeeper, had bought her from a refugee family as a bride for his seventeen-year-old idiot son. The lad was nicknamed No. 2 Monk, ugly and simple-minded, who only knew how to busy himself sweeping up horse dung outside his father's shop. Du Si was a lecherous ne'er-do-well and his wife, Beangreen, was a notorious slut in the small village. Though reasonably good-looking, she was a black-hearted brute of a woman. Her bite and bark were deadly. Ke Lian Er, after she joined the family, did all the chores about the house, right from the very day she was bought, getting up before cock-crow, cooking, fetching water, feeding the pigs, spinning and weaving, foraging for edible wild herbs and collecting firewood. Her work did not end when the sun set. She had to weave baskets by the light of the moon and if she so much as nodded, Beangreen would beat her black and blue.

When the girl was ten, Zhang Zuolin's army was fighting the soldiers of Wu Peifu. They were shelling each other across the canal one day when one of the shells fell close by Du Si's shop and buried the girl in a shower of earth. The husband and wife ran for their lives. Yi Zhang Qing's kind heart drove her to dig the girl out, despite the danger and the choking sulphureous fumes. Aunt Yi Zhang Qing put the unconscious girl in a basket and carried her to safety. A bullet grazed Aunt Yi Zhang Qing's temple, but she refused to abandon the girl and run to safety alone. She hid in the fields amid the growing crops for three days until the fighting was over and then found that No. 2 Monk had been carried off by the troops. No one knew where.

Beangreen cried and wailed and hurled herself on Ke Lian Er, abusing her as a person who attracted bad luck. She bit her and kicked her. The poor girl screamed and rolled on the ground. Aunt Yi Zhang Qing could not stand it. She leaped over the fence, picked up Ke Lian Er and carried her home, with Beangreen screaming vile abuse at her. Aunt Yi Zhang Qing could give as good as she got in a slanging match, but even she was no match for Beangreen for viciousness and vileness. She walloped Beangreen. Beangreen crawled to the doorsteps of Aunt Yi Zhang Qing's house and declared that she would die there. Her husband was not going to let anyone get away with beating his wife. He came with a butcher's knife and said he would set fire to Aunt Yi Zhang Qing's house. Aunt Yi Zhang Qing came out with a fish harpoon and took on the aggressor. Just as they were fighting tooth and nail, Great Learning returned and cracked his terrible whip. He sent the whip snaking towards Du Si stripping the flesh off his bones and would have killed him had Du Si not fled. Du Si thirsted for revenge. He knew someone who knew the local magistrate. A police sergeant of the canal patrol was sent along to arrest Great Learning. Finally, the matter was settled through the good offices of mediators. Great Learning had to throw a two-table banquet and promise to pay the couple's medical expenses. However, Great Learning and his wife insisted that Ke Lian Er become their adopted daughter. Beangreen agreed, on the condition that their child bride's new foster parents paid the dowry when the girl married. The two feuding families signed a pact and Ke Lian Er thus became the adopted daughter of the He family.

Aunt Yi Zhang Qing thought the girl's name was inauspicious and changed it to "Guilian" (Precious Lotus). Although she was no longer beaten and abused, she still worked the whole day, every day of the year without a day's rest. When she went down to the canal to cut brush for firewood, Zhou Qin, who lived in the house on the western side of Aunt Yi Zhang Qing's, also frequently happened to be cutting brushwood for fuel after school. They became good friends and often joked with each other. Zhou Qin called her "Wang Ri Lian", meaning "Sun Craving Lotus". As nothing precious ("gui" means precious) had ever come into her life, she liked and adopted this new name, and so she became known as Wang Ri Lian.

The canal was a riot of flowers of all colours. The little blood-red purslane were the smallest, only the size of horsebeans, lining the paths and its banks, defying wind and rain, drought and sun. When the parched ground cracked into patterns like those on tortoises and the crops shrivelled up and died, the tiny, hardy purslane turned a brighter red and their leaves a more vivid green. Wang Ri Lian was like these little flowers. Despite incessant beatings, hunger and endless hard work, she grew up into a slender, lovely young woman. Her adopted parents loved her and made her one new dress each year, which made her look even prettier.

Since no word was ever heard of No. 2 Monk again after he was taken away by the soldiers, Great Learning and Aunt Yi Zhang Qing decided to look for another husband for Wang Ri Lian. As it was not fitting to broach this delicate matter directly with the young woman, they asked Liu Guandou, the ferryman, Ji Laocheng, the blacksmith, and Zheng Duanwu, the carpenter, to speak to the Dus for them. As soon as the subject was mentioned, Beangreen let out a long wail and began kicking up an awful row, hurling abuse at the visitors, and being altogether quite unreasonable. Her husband appeared to be more receptive to the idea. He did not want to see the girl waste her youth, he said. But they did not know whether their son was alive or dead and, moreover, a man and woman were joined in wedlock for ever, even though they were only betrothed and not really married. He asked the three men to consult a fortune-teller to read Wang Ri Lian's horoscope. Quite by accident, at precisely that moment, a wandering fortune-teller was heard advertising his presence outside.

Du Si rushed out and brought the fortune-teller in. He cast two horoscopes before them, one for Wang Ri Lian and one for the missing No. 2 Monk. After a long spiel of mumbo-jumbo he announced that No. 2 Monk was still alive and had become an official. He would return like the legendary Xue Pinggui after eighteen years, in all his official finery. Now, No. 2 Monk had already gone for eight years, so Wang Ri Lian must wait another ten summers and ten winters. There would be a happy reunion and all their adversities and sorrows would be turned to joy, the fortune-teller declared.

Actually, both Du Si and his wife, Beangreen, had their own evil designs. The lecherous Du Si saw Wang Ri Lian growing up into a lovely young woman and lusted for her. His wife, Beangreen the local slut, wanted Wang Ri Lian to serve her purposes. As her husband generally lived in his little shop by the ferry the year round and seldom came back, Beangreen usually shared her favours with other men. Now, she saw herself growing old and losing whatever attractions she did have and wanted Wang Ri Lian to act as a decoy to attract the lovers she was missing.

Beangreen arranged one night for one of her lovers to despoil the girl. The man was to come at midnight. It was mid-summer and the night was very sultry and hot. Beangreen complained loudly of the oppressive air and insisted on opening the windows and doors. About midnight, Beangreen sneaked outside through the back door and called to the man waiting under the fence. She said she would keep guard outside. The man slipped in silently like a weasel after chickens. At the same moment, the dark shadow of a man appeared at the front gate. There was no moon. It was pitch black. The two did not recognize each other and both made a rush for Wang Ri Lian's room in the west.

Wang Ri Lian was a big girl, well built, and had her wits about her. When she saw Beangreen's stealthy behaviour and looks and Du Si leering at her all the time, she began shutting her windows tightly and propping a stick against her door when she retired for the night. She also kept a sickle and a pair of sharp scissors by her side when she went to bed. She woke up when the two shadows broke into her room. She leapt to her feet. But before she could do anything, the two started to fight each other. Wang Ri Lian tossed her weapons through the window and scrambled out after them, shouting loudly to Aunt Yi Zhang Qing for help. Aunt Yi Zhang Qing ran out with a lamp and saw a flashing sickle hacking at a man's leg, two men locked together, rolling and fighting on the ground.

After this midnight incident Aunt Yi Zhang Qing insisted that Wang Ri Lian worked in the day for the Dus and slept in her house at night. Beangreen had to agree because she was clearly implicated.

When Learned went away herding, Wang Ri Lian slept with Aunt Yi Zhang Qing and her grandson on the same brick bed. When he returned, she shared the bed in the west room with Manzi, who was then only three. That was three years ago.

Although Wang Ri Lian was now safe beyond the evil designs of Du Si and Beangreen, she still worked every day for them from sunup to sundown. The failure of Beangreen's plot to have Wang Ri Lian raped by one of her own lovers was galling and she vented her frustration on Wang Ri Lian, making her work harder than ever, never giving the girl a moment's rest. Even at noon, she had to cut and collect reeds from the canal bed for fuel.

When young women in the village went out to work in the fields, they were always accompanied by a little boy, not so much to defend them as to guard against malicious tongues. Wang Ri Lian always took Manzi along with her.

4

Wang Ri Lian, carrying the boy in her basket on her back, headed out from the village for the canal.

This flat was about four square kilometres in area, criss-crossed by many small streams, with dunes rising up like so many islands. In spring the water came no higher than one's ankles, but when the rains came it reached as high as one's knees. None of the streams was wider than four or five feet so there was no need for bridges. A leap would take one across. The banks were covered with shady trees, in which birds built their nests. The rivulets were thick with rushes, reeds and shrubs and tangles of grass, where dragonflies hung delicately from the tips of the blades. Hiding in the depths of the thickets were red-necked water birds only a little larger than butterflies, which built nests just above the water and whistled songs of enchanting beauty. They were shy creatures and dived out of their nests into the water at the first sign of danger. They were very hard to catch. All over the dunes were scrub willows keeping the white sand under them cool in the hottest summer.

Manzi loved to play in this world of water and dunes. He went about capturing shrimps and crabs and tiddlers, darting into the thickets after the red-necked birds and sending swarms of dragonflies soaring into flight. He loved best to cunningly lay his snares under the trees, in the thickets, and on the ground, spreading finely woven nets to catch birds. He went about his work without a shred of clothing, running freely and happily, without a care in the world.

As soon as they reached the canal, Manzi asked Aunt Wang Ri Lian to set him down. He rushed with a yell towards the water, racing ahead of her, tearing through the grass, around clusters of shrubs to arrive panting, out of breath, on the summit of the highest dune, where he flung himself down on the cool white sand under the trees.

Wang Ri Lian climbed up to where he lay, also a little out of breath herself and began to break small willow wands to plait into a leafy crown to protect her head from the blazing sun. She had never owned even an old straw hat. She rolled her long thick black plait about her head and then put on the green willow crown, into which Manzi always wove flowers of many colours, fiery red, yellow, white and purple.

"It makes you look ever so nice," remarked the boy. She took off her tattered and much-mended blouse and tossed it to the boy, saying, "Look after it for me. Don't run wild like a kite with a broken string. And keep a sharp lookout for me. Shout if you see anyone coming."

Manzi, seeing the long tattered ribbon of cloth wound tightly about her, suggested, "Take that ragged thing off too. It'll be cooler."

"Stupid! How can a woman go about naked?" Wang Ri Lian rebuked him, blushing red.

Wang Ri Lian, wearing her crown of leaves and flowers, her basket in one hand and a sickle in the other, disappeared into the rushes. Manzi sat there holding her crumpled blouse, keeping watch from where he sat. It was not long before he felt bored, and the more bored he felt the sleepier he became and this made him even more annoyed with himself. He rubbed his eyes, shook his head and began to dig a hole in the sand furiously to bury the garment. He then picked up his snares and left to set his traps.

First he dug for worms in the clumps of grass and bushes, baited his snares and placed them with care in various places before cleverly covering them. After this he ducked into the bushes to keep watch, plucking a young leaf or two with which he imitated the cries of birds, to entice them to his traps. His heart always beat faster when he heard the flutter of wings above the traps. Quite often the snares were sprung without catching more than a feather or two, with the bird flying for dear life.

He tried to count the number of birds he caught by the snap of the snares. He knew he had to catch at least two or three dozen before he had enough to make a meal for Wang Ri Lian.

When he thought about his Aunt Wang Ri Lian not getting enough to eat, his little heart ached. He had seen her wan face sometimes turning paler than the fleshy part of the white cabbage leaf, perspiration beading her forehead and running past the corners of her eyes. He had seen her snatch and greedily swallow berries and sour wild pears to appease her hunger. It was this which had driven Manzi to steal the landlord's melons as they were ripening. The sweet doughy melons were soft and good to eat and could alleviate hunger pangs for a while. Moreover, it was fun to steal melons . There was an element of danger in it.

Thus he was a frequent visitor to the melon patch owned by Dong, a landlord living in the neighbouring village.

The melon patch was on the other side of the canal, just beyond the last dune ridge. It was about twenty *mu* all told, and there were temporary shelters on all sides for the guards, who kept watch day and night over the melons. In the centre of the field was a tall tower, where an armed guard stood overlooking the whole field. There were also two large dogs, which roamed about the field, and between the rows of melon were buried "ground guns", with their triggers tied to trip-strings. If anyone trying to steal melons inadvertently tripped over the string, the nearest gun would go off with a loud bang and wound the man with buckshot.

Manzi crept quietly through the grass and shrubs until he reached the edge of the melon patch. He saw the watchman on the raised platform clutching his gun, asleep, and the other guards in the sheds also asleep. The two dogs were also lying in the shade like their dozing masters.

Manzi was both bold and cautious. He first quietly examined the terrain with his sharp black eyes and then searched out the rows where there were signs of buried booby traps. These he picked out and marked in his memory. Then he moved, crawling and digging his elbows into the soil to propel him forward. When he got to the edge of the melon patch, he slid like a slippery eel and quickly lost himself in the melon vines.

Once inside the shelter of the tangle of vines, he was as safe as a fish in water, and the rustling of the leaves in the breeze was a great blessing and help.

He liked the musk-melons more than the doughy ones, for they quenched his thirst, were filling and left a fragrant taste in his mouth. But he liked best of all water-melons. However, they were too large to attack in the field. He had to break them open. So he first took them out of the field. It was tiring work, but Manzi knew how to accomplish that with skill. He would pick a fairly large one and then flop over on his back, legs apart, with the melon encircled in his legs, and then using his palms press down and bounce on his behind, moving himself and the melon slowly, very slowly, out of the patch. Once he reached the tall grass he was safe. But all this cost him a lot of effort and he would be soaked with sweat and covered with sand.

After he had heard about a dozen snares sprung, he set off for Landlord Dong's melon field. He first ate his fill and then picked three of the biggest and best doughy melons before searching for Wang Ri Lian.

In those tall clumps of rushes, even a six-foot man could easily lose himself. Manzi had no trouble disappearing among the rushes with his loot. As he made his way, he listened carefully for the sound of her sickle cutting the rushes. It was easy to find her, for Wang Ri Lian also liked to sing a little song as she worked. She had a low pleasing voice. The songs she sang were about love and the lyrics were considered quite daring. Manzi did not understand all the words, but he knew that such songs were never sung in the home.

Manzi made his way through the tall rushes, clutching the three doughy melons and straining his ears to catch the sound of her sickle or her singing. But he heard neither and he began to feel a little disturbed and also a little afraid. He stopped and tried to catch the sound of her singing, however faintly, but he heard only a sound like muffled sobbing. He moved softly towards it.

He saw her at last, lying stretched out face down on the heap of rushes she had cut, her hands clutching the earth sobbing, her body shaking with her crying. Manzi thought she was racked with hunger pains.

"You're hungry, Aunt!" he asked anxiously. "I've got some melons for you."

She turned to face him, her face gleaming with tears. "No ... no. I'm not hungry. You have them," she gasped.

"I'm full of melon!" He placed the three melons on the ground near her head and patted his drum-tight tummy to prove it.

"I . . . I can't. I don't want any."

"You're sick? I'll go and fetch Granny." He turned to run off.

"I'm not sick. Come back here." She stretched out a hand and caught hold of his ankle.

"Then why are you weeping?"

"No reason. I just wanted a good cry." She sat up and rubbed away her tears with the back of her hands.

Manzi stared fixedly at her and then broke out into a laugh. "I know why you're crying. You're thinking of Uncle Zhou Qin!"

"Who's thinking of him!" But even as she protested, tears were brimming in her eyes again. "What's he to me, anyway? And what am I to him?"

"You two ... you two. . . ." Manzi groped for words. "You are a couple."

"Not in this life, maybe the next," Wang Ri Lian said, her voice cold and edged with despair.

"How many years to go before the next life?" asked Manzi.

"If I die right now and get born again, it'll take another twenty years till I'm this age," she answered in a far-away voice.

"I don't want you to wait so long! I'll tell Uncle Zhou Qin to send the sedan-chair for you right away when he comes home," Manzi declared.

"He should have returned long ago," Wang Ri Lian said pensively. There was a note of peevishness in her voice. "When he finishes high school this year he's going to the capital to college. I can't expect him to remember a country girl, who cuts grass for fuel."

"I'll put a curse on him if he forgets you," said Manzi indignantly. "If I see him I'll harpoon him with Granny's fish spear and beat him with that stick behind the door too."

"No more! Hush!" She put a hand over his mouth. "I won't have you saying such things."

"I will put a curse on him. Just see if I don't!" Manzi was quite worked up and spat the words out.

"Please, please, don't. Be a good boy. If you curse him here and something happens to him, who will look after him?"

"All right. I won't for your sake."

"And you must ask Heaven to bless and protect him."

"Whatever for?"

"Because you've just cursed him. You must remove your curse."

"Old Man Heaven, won't you please bless and protect Uncle Zhou Qin." Manzi's voice quavered a little as he intoned his prayer. "And don't forget to let Aunt Wang Ri Lian and Uncle Zhou Qin get married."

She hugged him tightly to her and tears streamed down her cheeks.

Wang Ri Lian was really hungry. She demolished the three melons with several large bites and broke into a happy smile. Some colour returned to her cheeks and her eyes lit up and a smile appeared. Manzi observed the transformation with wonder.

"What are you staring at me like that for?" she asked.

"You're . . . you're beautiful, Aunt."

"Nonsense! You're growing up into a bad boy. I won't let you sleep with me any more."

"I'll sleep with Uncle Zhou Qin when he comes back."

Wang Ri Lian blushed. "Turn and turn about, how about it? One night with him and one night with me," she said softly.

"No," answered Manzi firmly. "I won't sleep with you ever again after Uncle Zhou Qin gets back."

"Why, you're an ungrateful little boy! Anyway, I was just joking. I'll miss you like anything."

"All right, then. The three of us will sleep together."

"Get away with you!" She lifted her hand as if to slap him, but merely patted his little bald head gently. "Get a move on and collect your snares, otherwise someone will make off with them."

Manzi leaped to his feet. He had forgotten all about his hunting. He scurried off.

5

Manzi worked his way along the canal bed collecting his snares and nets and found that he had caught more than twenty birds, two of them fat quails. One he would roast for his grandfather to go with his drink and the other he would give to Aunt Wang Ri Lian.

He returned to the highest dune and dug out the much-patched blue blouse from the sand. Wang Ri Lian had already gathered together all the bundles of reeds she had cut and had spread them out on the hot sand to dry.

The flowers in her hair were gone, and her hair was

in disarray, the big plait dangling loosely, bits of leaves and grass and sand clinging to it. It swung about her shoulders, neck and arms, which were covered with small bleeding cuts and scratches. The long, tattered ribbon of cloth swathing her breasts was wet through and splattered with mud.

"Aunt, come sit down and roast a bird," cried Manzi, dancing with impatience.

"I'm going to wash myself. You stand guard, will you?" Wang Ri Lian said in an exhausted voice.

They walked to a quiet, secluded spot by the canal where a sandbank curved about a pool and the willows grew thick right in the water. The limpid water was clear and clean at the bottom. Manzi sat on top of the dune as a sentinel.

"Shut your eyes, Manzi," she shouted. He closed them tight. Aunt Wang Ri Lian had told him that he would break out into boils as large as jujube dates if he watched a girl undress.

She slid into the water, the reddish willows hiding her from view, and then told Manzi to open his eyes as she had stripped. Manzi opened his eyes and kept watch for the approach of any males.

There was the sound of splashing and soon her clothes were clean and wet hanging from the boughs, and the long tattered strip of cloth too. She began to bathe and the splashing sounds were soothing to Manzi's ears, for he knew that she would not leave the water until her clothes were dry. He felt like a lone sentinel goose.

"Don't go out into the whirlpool, Aunt. I can't come to save you. I'm too small."

"I don't need you to save me," she laughed from the

other side of the willows. "I once pulled your Uncle Zhou Qin out of the whirlpool. I'm his saviour."

"I don't believe it. You're like my grandpa, always boasting," retorted the boy.

"I'm not kidding you."

"All right, tell me about it." Manzi slid down to the bank.

"Don't come any nearer, Manzi!"

"I will if you don't tell me, quick."

She told him the story. She was about ten when it had happened. She and Zhou Qin were digging for edible herbs in the flats and it was a roasting hot day. Zhou Qin was in the water swimming when he got cramp in his leg. He was swept into the whirlpool, his body contorted. He was dragged under and when he emerged shouting for help as he gulped water, she dived in and caught him by the neck and dragged him to shore. From then on, he always took her along as his swimming companion.

"Weren't you ashamed to swim with a boy?" asked Manzi.

"We were kids. We didn't know what shame was then. We played mother and father together and we even pledged our betrothal!"

"So you and Uncle Zhou Qin are married!" the boy exclaimed.

"Stop that," cried Wang Ri Lian. "I think I hear somebody coming. Go and have a look, will you?"

Manzi ran back to the top of the dune, peering about him with his hands shading his eyes. Suddenly he caught sight of someone walking along the path holding an open umbrella.

"Duck!" he shouted. "Someone's coming!"

He heard her swimming into the reeds growing out of the water. Manzi, on tiptoe, saw that it was a young man dressed like a student coming along the path with a little bundle on his back.

"It's Uncle Zhou Qin!" he yelled.

"Stop that nonsense!" she said, but the boy was already yelling at the top of his voice to his uncle and running to greet him.

"Manzi!" the young man exclaimed, folding the umbrella.

Zhou Qin was in his early twenties, a tall, slender young man, with black bushy brows and a pair of laughing eyes. His face was radiant. One could see at first glance that he was a quiet, thoughtful man.

He raced up to meet the running Manzi, arms outstretched to embrace the boy.

The boy skipped out of his reach. "Can't dirty your gown!" he cried.

"What are you doing here?" he asked Manzi.

"Guess," answered the boy.

Zhou Qin pretended to think hard, frowning, and then said, "I give up."

"Follow me," said Manzi, taking him by the hand.

Wang Ri Lian had swum up close to the willows by the bank and was peeking through the reeds at the man she thought of constantly. Her heart pounded and her face burnt bright red.

"Don't bring him any closer, Manzi!" she screamed, letting Zhou Qin know where she was.

"Why are you so shy all of a sudden?" Manzi teased. "Aren't you old swimming partners? And aren't you two betrothed?"

"Quit it, Manzi! And you, Zhou Qin, please go further away."

"Come, let's do as she says," said Zhou Qin, pointing to a clump of trees some yards away.

When they were seated on the white sand in the shade of the trees, the boy asked, "Did you and Aunt Wang Ri Lian really have a betrothal?"

"That was when we were kids," Zhou Qin replied, stroking the boy's bald head. "It was all a game."

"Where did you hold the ceremony?"

"Oh, right here by this clump of trees."

"Did you have on your best clothes?" the boy persisted.

"I was dressed exactly the way you are now. But she had on an apron-diaper."

"Did you wear a red pompon hat?"

"I had a wreath of willow wands."

"And Aunt had a red veil over her?"

"She had a large lotus leaf over her."

"Did you wear a red sash?"

"We had two willow wands with flowers."

"And built a Heaven and Earth altar?"

"We heaped up a pile of sand."

"Did you burn incense?"

"We had three sticks of mugwort."

"Where was the bridal suite?"

"We drew a square on the ground about us."

"Did you eat sons-and-grandsons cakes?"

"We picked some wild pears and put them on two large leaves."

"And did you have longevity noodles?"

"Two sweet reed roots."

"What are you telling him?" asked Wang Ri Lian, bursting out of the patch of bushes.

Manzi looked up and saw that her face was radiant and shining like a lotus flower after rain. She had forgotten to wind the long strip of tattered cloth about her body and had hastily thrown on her newly washed and just dried blue and white blouse tightly about her, which showed the full roundness of her young breasts.

"I like thinking about the days when I was a boy," said Zhou Qin, partly evading her question.

"Why didn't you get off at the village stop?" Wang Ri Lian asked.

"I thought I'd find you here so I got off a stop earlier to see if I'd run into you."

"Why are you half a month late?" It sounded like an accusation.

"I took the college exams in Beijing."

"Did you pass?"

"The results aren't out yet."

She lowered her eyes, bit her lips and a red flush rose up her neck. She jerked her head up and eyes fixed on him, asked, "Do you know what's today's date?"

"July seventh." His voice shook a little. "That's why I picked today to come home."

"The seventh day of the seventh month is when the Weaving Maid and the Cowherd meet!" exclaimed Manzi. "You're the Cowherd and Aunt Wang Ri Lian is the Weaving Maid."

"Don't be silly. Go and see if anyone is coming," she said to the boy.

Manzi broke off a willow twig and drew a rectangle on the sand about them. "You two are to stay inside and talk at home." Then he left them and climbed up a wild pear tree to scan the countryside. The day was still scalding hot and there was not a soul in sight.

To the boy, Zhou Qin was a great man, a learned man, a star from some heavenly firmament.

Manzi loved to listen to the stories the old people told. From his grandfather, grandmother, the ferryman, the carpenter and the blacksmith and even from the little shopkeeper, Du Si, he had heard snatches about the past, about Zhou Fangzhou, Zhou Qin's father, who had been a schoolteacher in Yutian Primary School. Nine years earlier he had led the peasant uprising east of Beijing. He was beheaded after the uprising, which was crushed by government troops. His wife had then gone to live with her mother and brother, Liu Guandou, the ferryman, taking her son with her. She had died not long after and the boy grew up with his maternal grandmother and uncle. The boy came first in an exam and was admitted into the Luhe Middle School in Tongzhou run by American missionaries. He was always first or second in his class throughout his years at school.

Tongzhou was about twenty kilometres from the village where Zhou Qin lived and the boy returned home every Saturday to spend the weekend, leaving again for school the following afternoon. He was a filial boy. He was poor and couldn't afford to hire a cart or donkey, so he always walked, breaking his journey to swim in the river in summer. In winter he would ride a sled home. The sled shot along like a meteor over the ice. The year before last his maternal grandmother had died, but the boy treated his uncle as filially as he had looked after his grandmother, dutifully returning home every weekend. Liu Guandou did not want the lad to be away from his studies so often and told him to come home once a month. He spent his one and a half month summer holiday and the fortnight winter holiday at home, helping his uncle on the ferry and collecting firewood. The two got along well, without ever a cross word coming between them.

Manzi liked Zhou Qin's company not only because he could tell him engrossing stories and teach him more characters than the old scholar could have in an age, but also because Zhou Qin loved the boy like Wang Ri Lian.

Liu Guandou's house near Manzi's home was also a three-roomed adobe hut surrounded on four sides by a willow fence. Liu Guandou spent most of his time on the ferry, which left Zhou Qin alone in the house, so when Manzi visited his uncle to listen to his stories and grew too sleepy to go home, he slept with him. Sometimes, after a specially tiring day, Manzi would wet the brick bed, but Zhou Qin never said anything, neither to the boy himself nor to anyone else, knowing that it would hurt Manzi's feelings.

Another reason why Manzi liked being with Zhou Qin was because Wang Ri Lian would come to carry him home after he fell asleep. He liked the soft feel of her body and her fragrance, which was like summer lilac. On one occasion when he was woken up, he had opened his eyes a tiny slit after she had picked him up in her arms. He had seen her sitting side by side on the edge of the brick bed with Zhou Qin, reluctant to leave. She had thrown her long braid about Zhou Qin's neck. Manzi had wanted to laugh, but something warned him to keep quiet and he had closed his eyes and gone back to sleep.

Recalling this as he stood perched on the tree high above the ground, Manzi looked down and stole a glance at the two below. It was as he expected. Wang Ri Lian had thrown her big black braid again about Zhou Qin like that night, probably to tie him up like he had been tied up by his grandfather, Manzi thought to himself. He stuffed a hand in his mouth to keep from laughing aloud. He did not want to disturb this pair of mandarin ducks. Neither did he dare look again. If he peeked again at the pair he would probably break out into boils too, he thought.

6

On the night of the seventh of the seventh month, Manzi did not sleep.

His grandmother had told him that on that night, about midnight, a flock of magpies would build a bridge across the Milky Way for the Cowherd to cross with his shoulder pole and baskets to visit this Weaving Maid, the son in the front basket and the daughter in the other one. The Cowherd and the Weaving Maid on their annual meeting would weep. A sharp-eyed boy, she had told him, could see the magpies building the bridge and hear the two weeping at their annual meeting. Last year, Manzi had sneaked out to try and hear the weeping, but he had heard nothing, for it was raining and all he had succeeded in was catching a bad cold. He saw neither the Weaving Maid nor the Cowherd.

This year, the stars were bright and the Milky Way shone brilliantly in the sky. There would be no rain tonight and he would be sure to see and hear them meeting and weeping. He was determined not to go to sleep and miss it.

After supper, the sickle moon rose like a small vessel and sailed up from the southeast. Only when Wang Ri Lian had finished weaving a mat and completed a basket, did Beangreen tell her to go to bed and not to "stick to her bed like glue tomorrow".

Wang Ri Lian left and went over to sleep at Aunt Yi Zhang Qing's house next door.

Aunt Yi Zhang Qing had already woken from her first sleep when she heard Wang Ri Lian come in.

"Don't be too long, daughter. Go and burn some incense at the back. I've left a needle and thread and incense for you by the Kitchen God."

"Thank you. I'll do all that."

Wang Ri Lian pushed open the door, which squeaked a little, and Manzi firmly shut his eyes, pretending to sleep. He would slip out as soon as she left to burn the incense offering to the moon.

Praying to the moon was a superstitious practice, but it was a pretty and innocent thing. On that night, by the light of the moon, a girl was supposed to thread a needle with a red thread. If she succeeded at the first attempt then she would marry the man she loved within the year.

Wang Ri Lian did not leave. She picked up a fan and began driving the mosquitoes from the sleeping form of the boy and then sat down on the edge of the brick bed. Manzi peeked at her and saw her sitting there lost in thought. She then let out a long sigh, her face in her hands. She remained like this for a seemingly unending length of time and Manzi wondered what was troubling her. He dared not say anything lest she forbade him to leave the house to hear the Cowherd and the Weaving Maid weep.

After a long, long silence, Wang Ri Lian stood up, as if she had at last made up her mind and went to the room outside where the Kitchen God was. Manzi guessed she was lighting the incense and then going out to the back courtyard.

This was the moment. Manzi slid off the brick bed and tiptoed in his bare feet out into the yard.

He peered up at the night sky and the hazy Milky Way. He seemed to be able to make out a bridge and the forms of two persons. That would be the Cowherd and the Weaving Maid meeting, he figured. He went quietly over to the grape trellis and putting a hand behind his ear, tried to catch the sound of weeping.

The grape bower was about three or four paces from the house where his grandfather and grandmother were sleeping soundly. Earlier that evening, Liu Guandou, the ferryman, had caught several large fish and bought himself some meat and a big flask of wine to treat his cronies to mark his nephew's return. They had had a grand time and Learned had staggered home, plonked himself down on the brick bed in the east room and had fallen asleep at once. His snoring was almost deafening. It interfered with Manzi's trying to catch the sound of the sobbing of the lovers by the Milky Way. Manzi was vexed and wanted to shout at his grandfather to tell him to stop, but he was afraid of waking him for he was sure to be sent back inside to bed.

He decided to steal over to the backyard of Zhou Qin, who was sure not to snore, being a scholar. He might be able to hear better there.

He crept out quietly, hugging the wall until he came to a gaping hole in the fence, through which he crawled on all fours until he reached Zhou Qin's trellis of vines. Then he stood erect again.

After his thumping heart had calmed down, he discerned above the rustle of the breeze the sound of someone sobbing softly. He was thrilled until he suddenly realized that the sobbing was not coming down from the sky, nor from out of the ground, but from the room where his Uncle Zhou Qin slept.

He gave an involuntary start. Who could that be? He wanted to run away, but on second thoughts he wanted to find out who was sobbing at this time of the night. He crawled over to the window.

"I'll spend the rest of my life with you . . . but it won't be this life." It was Wang Ri Lian's voice. She was speaking through her tears. "I burnt three joss-sticks and two red candles and made obeisances but . . . but I couldn't get the red thread to go through the eyelet of my needle. . . ."

"But that's all superstition!" Zhou Qin said quietly with a chuckle. "How can a needle and thread decide a person's destiny? It's not often anyone can thread a needle in that light, so don't upset yourself."

"You're wrong!" cried Wang Ri Lian in a pained voice. "I'm fated to be poor and to suffer. It's fated that I'll never marry you."

"I don't believe in fate. I believe in human beings!" Zhou Qin said firmly. "I'll rescue you from this awful situation. We'll share whatever we have together as equals for the rest of our lives."

"Everything is fated. Man can decide nothing." Wang Ri Lian continued to protest and to sigh. "I've given you my heart, let me give you my body tonight. Let's have one night, just one night of happiness together."

"All the more reason why I must marry you."

"I don't want to hold you back in any way," Wang Ri Lian said in almost a whimper. "I'm just afraid that I may never see this year out. Once you leave for Beijing, that'll be the end of all that is between us. If they try to do anything to me, I'll pit my life against them."

"Are Du Si and that pimp of Beangreen's still molesting you?" Zhou Qin asked her fiercely.

"No. They've given up, but they've got together and are trying to sell me as a concubine to Landlord Dong. I overheard snatches of their talk one day when they were drinking together."

"That son of a bitch!" Zhou Qin swore. "Yin Rugeng has made himself a king and that Landlord Dong is in cahoots with him. He's a traitor. We've got to crush them."

"But they've got guns, and you've only a few books. How can you crush them?" Wang Ri Lian asked anxiously.

"Are you really willing to live and die with me?" Zhou Qin suddenly asked earnestly, soberly.

"We've known each other since we were children, and yet you've never trusted me?" Wang Ri Lian began to cry again. "I want to be with you. I'll do anything for you, go through anything for you. Die for you."

"I believe you would," said Zhou Qin huskily. "I was a fortnight late in coming home not just because of the exam. . . ."

"What have you been doing?"

"We set up the Tongzhou branch of the Anti-Japanese National Salvation Association. We're going to organize an armed force later."

"What do you want me to do?"

"Join us. Fight the Japs, save the nation, wipe out the traitors."

"I'm only a woman. What can I do?"

"The nation is in danger and everyone, man, woman and child can and must do their bit."

Manzi almost wanted to leap up and shout, "Let me join too," but he didn't. He heard Wang Ri Lian say, "If it comes to fighting, I'm better at it than you." Manzi did not hear anything more, only whispers and sighs. He was also very tired and wanted to go home. His legs gave way under him and he fell asleep by the window.

He didn't know how long he slept before he felt himself being picked up and shaken. He was too weary to open his eyes.

"Wake up, Manzi." Wang Ri Lian shook him.

He finally woke up to find himself lying on Zhou Qin's brick bed. The room was filled with mugwort smoke to keep the mosquitoes away. Aunt Wang Ri Lian's hair was in disorder and she looked a little anxious. "Have you been sleep-walking, Manzi? How did you come to be outside there?"

"I wanted to hear them sobbing and found it was only you."

"Did you hear what we said?" she asked anxiously.

Manzi nodded. "Uncle Zhou Qin wants to marry you and you agreed."

"Please, please don't tell a soul what you heard tonight, Manzi," Wang Ri Lian pleaded. "If you so much as utter a word then your Uncle Zhou Qin and I will die."

"So you can't trust me either!" Manzi said with a surly pout. "Did I ever tell anyone about you two at the canal, and that you put your plait around him?"

"Manzi, you little darling," cried Wang Ri Lian, clasping him to her breast.

7

Manzi walked with his Uncle Zhou Qin to the blacksmith's. It was about a mile away. Zhou Qin went to see Ji the blacksmith and Manzi the little groom, Qian Niu Er, who was only a few years older than him. The two had struck up a friendship as boys will do, while they playing at the canal banks.

The Beijing-Tianjin gravel road cut across the North Canal at this point and it was there that Ji had set up his forge. His house consisted of only one room with a shed attached to it. In front and behind were sunflowers, and to one side was a vegetable garden.

Ji Laocheng was over fifty and as solid as a stone pillar. He was a good blacksmith and his skill was widely known, but he could seldom earn enough to eat his fill. He had no dependants and had the reputation of having a fiery temper. A believer in neither ghosts nor gods, his only loves were spirits and snuff.

One noon, after he had swept the yard and sprinkled water everywhere to keep down the dust and to make the place a little cooler, he sat down to have his lunch: two cold steamed corn buns and some water. After he had finished his simple meal, he sat naked to the waist, his hairy navel protruding above his loose, knee-length trousers. Picking up a battered fan, he began chasing away the botflies. Then he stuffed a little pinch of snuff in his nostrils, which produced a succession of loud and satisfying sneezes. His simple desires thus fulfilled, he began to doze in the mid-day heat, still sitting upright, legs crossed, on his tattered straw mat. Suddenly, he was awakened by a tremendous explosion. Looking about he saw a thin boy grinning and standing half-hidden in the sunflowers.

"Come here, you little bastard!" Ji roared, then realized that he had woken himself up. Qian Niu Er had stolen a big pinch of snuff and had stuck it in his nostrils. The man was not angry but was, in fact, laughing at the trick the boy had played on him.

No one could explain why the big blacksmith and the thin boy got on so well together. Ji had an explosive temper and no one dared bully him physically. Qian Niu Er was quiet and sweet-natured and was for ever being beaten and bullied by his employers, the landlord Dong and his son. The boy did odd jobs for the landlord and ate whatever was given him, when they remembered to feed him. His chief task was to look after the landlord's horses, taking them to the canal to graze and cutting enough grass to fill the big basket to bring back to the stables. He seldom spoke, for there was no one to talk to. His companions were his charges, and when they were grazing, Qian Niu Er in his loneliness would often creep up to Ji's forge and watch him at work. As he just stood and watched from a distance and did not make a nuisance of himself, no one took much notice of him. But the boy noted everything he saw. He watched closely what the blacksmith did and later went over and over in his mind every move he had seen Ji make.

One day a big stallion the blacksmith was shoeing proved more troublesome than other horses. It reared and kicked and turned to bite the man. Ji lost his temper and was about to do something drastic when Qian Niu Er suddenly ran up to him, shouting, "Don't do that! You'll hurt him!" He butted the surprised blacksmith aside and seizing the reins, led the stallion around in a circle, whistling softly. The animal quietly allowed Qian Niu Er to lead him and then licked his shoulder as if returning the strange boy's affection. It seemed to know the boy and understand his intention. Qian Niu Er led the stallion back to the post and, when Ji came over to resume his work, Qian Niu Er suggested, "Please let me shoe him."

Ji was even more astonished. "You?" he asked. Flinging the tools on the ground, he walked away, saying, "Go ahead, but if you make a mess of it, I'll sell you to pay for the horse!"

Qian Niu Er said nothing. He picked up the hammer and shoe and began to work.

He did a very neat job, although it was his first time. In the end, Ji cuffed him and laughed. "You cheeky little brat! Taking over my job, eh?" he cried in mock anger.

But from that day on the boy and the man became close friends.

Ji, who was also something of a vet, had cured the hoof of a favourite horse of a man in a neighbouring village that day. In gratitude the man had presented Ji with wine and meat. Ji went and bought himself five *jin* of flat-bread from a small stall and invited Qian Niu Er to stay for the meal. But the boy hung back. Ji bellowed at him and threatened to beat him if he refused his invitation, so Qian Niu Er bolted down the food like the hungry boy he indeed was. Ji stood there watching immensely pleased, his big belly heaving as he chuckled loudly.

After the huge meal, Qian Niu Er found himself a corner in the shed and fell asleep, dead to the world. Suddenly the landlord's son walked in and began to strike the sleeping boy with his whip. Qian Niu Er woke and ran to the canal in a daze, pursued by the man lashing at him.

Ji snatched away the whip with a loud roar and dragged the young master to his shed, shouting, "You dare to whip my guest, do you? Striking him is the same as spitting in my face. You know that? You'll get as good as you gave from me! I'll shoe you like I shoe a horse. You're not human. You're an animal!" He tied the young master to a post, took off the shrieking man's shoes and socks and went to fetch his tools. The stream of invective and threats turned to piteous pleading. The man knew the blacksmith had the reputation of being an eccentric who was never cowed by threats. He began to shout to his groom whom he had just whipped. "Help! Qian Niu Er, help!"

Qian Niu Er came running back at his master's cries.

He seized Ji by the arm and begged him not to carry out his threat. "You can't do that. Stop it!"

"Oh, can't I just? I believe in an eye for an eye. If I start to beat him, I'll probably break him in two. How about you giving him a good thrashing?"

"Me? Oh, no, no!" cried the boy, alarmed.

"You sniffling coward! If you won't, I will."

"Qian Niu Er please, you beat me. Don't let him beat me," pleaded the young master.

"I won't beat you and I won't let him beat you. And you mustn't ever beat me again," said the boy, as he began to untie his master.

"You afraid of him?" Ji jeered at Qian Niu Er, but made no move to stop him.

"If I beat him, he'd beat me ten times worse in return."

"If he beats you again, kill him," advised the blacksmith.

"Then the authorities would cut off my head."

"You nitwit, haven't you a pair of legs to flee with?"

"But where could I run to? There are authorities everywhere. They work for the rich, so I'd be caught sooner or later."

"You're right there, my boy," sighed the blacksmith. "They do work for the rich. I guess the only way out for us is to rise up and rebel."

After that incident the boy and man were firmer friends than ever. From then on, Qian Niu Er would call on Ji whenever he was free. In summer they would sit out late under the moon. In winter they went to sleep early, on the heated brick bed. They seldom spoke, enjoying each other's presence. Their companionship needed no words, it was evident. There was a deep tacit understanding between the two lonely human beings.

When Manzi and Zhou Qin arrived at the forge, Ji was in the middle of shaving Qian Niu Er's head.

"Qian Niu Er!" Manzi gave a shout of delight and rushed over to the boy.

"Uncle Ji, how are you?" Zhou Qin greeted the older man, strode up to him and then bowed respectfully.

"My student nephew!" Ji's eyes became slits when he smiled. He folded the big open razor and turned to have a good look at his nephew.

"Finish shaving me first! Please!" Qian Niu Er begged.

The big blacksmith twitched one of the boy's ears and pulled him off the stool. "Don't feel like shaving right now," he said, and, turning to Zhou Qin, invited the young man inside his room.

"But you must finish shaving him," protested Zhou Qin with a laugh.

"Oh, he can wait. I haven't seen you for over a month. Come inside and we'll have a real good chat."

"It's all your fault! Why did you come right in the middle of his shaving me?" Qian Niu Er glared at Manzi, one hand on his half-shaven head.

Manzi pushed the older boy out of the shed without a word. Qian Niu Er was stronger, but he did not protest. He just stood there by the roadside under the hot sun.

Manzi stood just outside the shed, ignoring his companion, pretending not to see him, acting as a lookout while Zhou Qin talked to Ji.

From inside the house came the sound of Ji's booming voice. His fist sometimes pounded on the adobe wall, showering down bits of earth from the roof.

"When I was with your father during the uprising. . . ."

"Ssh! Not so loud, please!"

"These old bones are still sturdy and they'll fight the Japs with you!" Ji's voice was a little lower, but still it could be heard outside.

Manzi did not know Ji had taken part in the peasant uprising east of Beijing. He had learned that Ji had been in prison when he had overheard Du Si, the shopkeeper, yell during a quarrel with Ji, "You jailbird! You were locked up for five years!" That made Ji so mad that he went for Du Si, who fled and hid himself in the women's lavatory, with his wife standing guard outside. Ji stalked off, muttering and cursing. He did not know how to handle women, let alone fight with them.

Manzi remembered another time when Ji had broken down when he caught sight of a photo of Zhou Qin's father. Zhou Qin had returned home during the Qing Ming Festival with three wreaths. Two had his grandmother's and mother's names and the third, his father's. He had also brought a photo of his dead father, whose body the authorities had not allowed the family to reclaim after his execution at Yutian. There was only a name carved on his mother's tombstone.

"Our Party representative! . . ." Ji the blacksmith had cried out in anguish when he saw the photo Zhou Qin had brought home. Manzi, too, had burst into tears, without quite knowing why. Ji and Zhou Qin went on talking inside and Manzi could hear the blacksmith's clear affirmative to whatever Zhou Qin was telling him. Manzi sensed the strong bond which held the two men together.

"Come and play," cried Qian Niu Er from the other side of road. "Don't be mad at me."

"I won't," replied Manzi, looking even more important than ever.

"I'll catch you a little bird with coloured feathers," Qian Niu Er offered, sweat glistening on his half-shaven head.

"Go away. I'm not going to play with you."

"I'll make you a bird cage of willow wands, too."

Manzi felt tempted. For the first time he looked directly at the other boy. "A bird cage of willow wands," he repeated slowly.

"I'll catch you a big-bellied grasshopper and make an eight-sided cage for it. How's that?"

Manzi was sorely tempted now. His eyes lit up and he began to fidget.

"I've got a gun buried. . . ." Ji's words were cut short by Zhou's warning, "Ssh!"

"You run along. I'm not going," said Manzi firmly.

"I'll carry you on my back," Qian Niu Er persisted.

"I'm not coming." Manzi shook his head.

Qian Niu Er, almost in tears, sidled over the road towards Manzi, "Let me sit down with you, eh?"

"Stay where you are!" cried Manzi. "Get back to the other side."

Qian Niu Er did as he was ordered, mumbling, "Why are you so hard on me today? Aren't we pals any more?"

"We are, but you can't come over. Uncle Zhou Qin and Uncle Ji are talking inside. I've got to stand guard."

"It's settled then!" And the two boys heard the blacksmith's hearty laugh. He seemed elated.

Zhou Qin reappeared and, giving Manzi a friendly pat on the shoulder, said, "Come on, let's go call on Zheng the carpenter."

"And I'll see my god-mother, too," answered Manzi, falling into step with Zhou.

Ji called to Qian Niu Er, "Come here, boy. I'll finish shaving you. Sorry to have kept you waiting."

Qian Niu Er just stood there glowering. The blacksmith ran over and caught him under the arms and dragged him back inside the shed. The boy howled and kicked so Ji tied him gently to a post and began where he had left off.

8

Yin Rugeng set up an anti-Communist autonomous government at the behest of the Japanese invaders in eastern Hebei Province. He began to renovate an old imperial residence in Tongzhou and made it his home, turning the nearby lake and land into his private park. In front of his palace the Tonghui Canal divided the city north and south. Zheng Duanwu, being the best carpenter in the district, was commissioned to do the job. He was made to work day and night, carving doors and door-frames and windows, putting up decorated corridors. His skill was in great demand. Yin drove the artisans mercilessly, eager to move into his palace. Zheng grew thinner and thinner. Before the palace was completed, Yin ordered a family temple to be erected in the grounds as he was a self-styled pious

Buddhist. One day, when the carpenters were fixing the central beam for the temple, Yin ordered Zheng to climb up and check its alignment. Though dizzy and exhausted, Zheng did as he was ordered. When he got to the top, a sudden spell of vertigo seized him. He blacked out and fell. The others picked him up and carried him home on a door. He had broken his right leg and lost a lot of blood. For six months he lay on his bed and never fully recovered. He could not saw or use a hammer and never again held a chisel or drew a line with the ink-boat. He turned to growing melons for a living and moved out of his house to live in a hut near his little plot. But that was not the only reason why he went to live by himself. He could not bear to see his son and daughter-in-law use the tools so clumsily that he had wielded so skilfully. As the saying goes: out of sight, out of mind.

His son Zheng Er and daughter-in-law He Niu were both a year older than Zhou Qin and the three had been good friends since childhood.

Zheng Er and his wife made an interesting couple.

When Zheng Er had been Manzi's age, his father had come home from work in another village with two baskets on either end of his shoulder pole. Zheng Er was romping outside with his dog, his bottom bare. When he heard sobbing from one of the baskets he tumbled off his dog in surprise. He went up and peered into the basket where the noise was coming from and saw a big-eyed girl with a round wet face about his age inside. She was a roly-poly thing, as naked as the day she was born.

"Where did you find this fat thing, dad?" he asked.

"She's going to be your wife one day, son," answered

his father, who was apparently very pleased with himself. "She's called He Niu."

Zheng Er stuck out his tongue and made a face. The girl, who had stopped crying, suddenly giggled.

At her first meal in the house of her future husband, the little girl gulped down three maize cakes and a huge half bowl of maize mush mixed with vegetables. She licked the bowl so clean that it needed no washing.

The good carpenter's wife was astounded and began to scold her husband, "How are we going to feed her? We haven't enough even for ourselves."

"Ah, woman, you can't see further than your own nose! When she grows up she'll bear you a strong grandson, who'll be a better carpenter than me. Look at her. She's healthy and strong."

He was right in one respect. The girl was certainly strong and healthy. At the age of ten, she was helping the carpenter like a sturdy boy. She seemed to have an inexhaustible supply of energy. She could handle tools like a boy, but at sewing she seemed all thumbs. Zheng's wife gave up trying to teach her to sew and cook and let her grow up as she pleased. She was a great help to the carpenter. He never ceased to point out his future daughter-in-law with pride to others. "She's as good as two sons," he would say. "She's a godsend."

The girl grew taller and stronger than her future husband and ate more too. The two often squabbled and fought and at first were fairly evenly matched, but in time she got the better of Zheng Er. Her future husband learned to fear and respect her at an early age until they fought no more.

Love stole in amidst tears and laughter, sweat and hard toil. He Niu always let Zheng Er eat his fill before she polished off the remainder, and, when food grew scarce because Zheng Duanwu was out of work, she gave her portion to Zheng Er although her adopted father had divided the food fairly into four portions. Though Zheng Er protested, she made him eat it. She had the stronger will, so generally Zheng Er did as he was told.

When the two reached their eighteenth year, He Niu was a well-built young woman. They had long ceased to tease and push each other about in front of their parents. The adults noticed this and understood. Wanting a grandson badly, they decided it was time they were married.

On their wedding night, after putting out the light, He Niu laid down three conditions, and eavesdroppers outside the nuptial room overheard them clearly and could hardly choke back their laughter.

"I want you to promise three things, otherwise I won't let you come near me."

"I'll promise you three hundred things! Tell me the first."

"There's a saying, a wife brought home is to be ridden or beaten as the master pleases. Well, I want you to promise you'll do neither."

"Whoever said that was a scoundrel. I promise. Now what is the second condition?"

"Ma is getting on and can't sew and cook, so you'll have to learn to do both. Not me."

"What? That's too much. I'm a man," protested the bridegroom.

"Then keep away from me!" snapped He Niu.

Zheng Er hurriedly consented and asked her third condition.

"As of tomorrow, you're not to joke with or tease other women."

Now, Zheng Er was a happy-go-lucky sort who liked doing this. He meant nothing by it and it was just his character. He hesitated. Suddenly there was a loud slap and a yelp from Zheng Er. He had been a fraction too long in giving his reply.

"I promise, I promise," he yelled for all to hear.

When the two had been children they had gone along with all the other village kids to gather firewood and cut grass for fuel along the canal and in the flats. There, they made friends with others but Zhou Qin was their closest companion. Zhou Qin was quiet, whereas Zheng Er was boisterous and played pranks. He Niu was rough and rather impatient, so she and her future husband often clashed. She then sided with Zhou Qin when Zheng Er drove him almost to tears. She would shake a fist at Zheng Er and he would back off. She was stronger and worked faster, so it was she who often helped Zhou Qin with his work.

One of the games they played as children was to hold mock weddings. Zheng Er always played the part of the local trumpeter, the master of ceremonies, or the fortune-bringer, who led the young couple to their bridal bed. Zhou Qin was always given the part of the shy groom and He Niu the bride.

Zhou Qin always protested, his face scarlet. "You're supposed to be her husband. You be the groom!"

"This is only a game," Zheng Er yelled back. He was keen to play the parts he liked. "Anyway, you can really marry her if you like when we are grown up."

"I will not marry him!" protested He Niu. She did not like being pushed around either. "Zhou Qin's much prettier than me and he's not nearly as strong as me, either! Let him be my wife!"

"That's right! He should be the bride!" Zheng Er rolled on the ground laughing. He could see nothing funnier.

"No. I'm not going to play with you any more!" cried Zhou Qin, when he realized that the two had ganged up on him. "Wives are all women. Whoever heard of a man being a wife?"

"The stronger one is the husband and the prettier one is the wife," announced He Niu authoritatively.

Zhou Qin wanted to flee but Zheng Er seized him and twisted his arms. He Niu threatened him with her fists, so Zhou Qin was forced to submit.

He allowed He Niu to deck him out as the bride. She took off her floral blouse and put it on him and made him give her his white shirt. Then she made him a garland of willow wands and stuck two flowers behind his ears. A reddish juice from some crushed flowers was applied as rouge to make his cheeks redder and a lotus leaf was put on his head to serve as the bridal head-dress. Zhou Qin put up a struggle, but to no avail. He made a very miserable bride.

Zheng Er blew his whistle in lieu of a trumpet and commanded the "bride" to walk round and round in the sand pretending she was being carried to her "husband's" house in a sedan-chair. After much exhortation and laughter on the part of his playmates, the "bride" arrived and He Niu walked up to him and made him fall on his knees before a mound of sand with three mugwort stems fixed in it as candles.

"Kowtow to heaven and earth!" Zheng Er shouted in delight.

"Kowtow to your parents!"

"Kowtow to each other and enter the bridal chamber!"

Zhou was forced to make his deep kowtows and then He Niu literally dragged him over to a square they had marked on the ground. Zheng Er then proffered two wild pears on a leaf to the "bride" and "groom". He raised his voice and, imitating the fortune-bringer, asked in a high falsetto, "Will you produce?"

"Produce!" He Niu answered loud and clear. "Come on, you must say the same, too."

"Produce," muttered Zhou Qin almost under his breath.

The fortune-bringer then gave the two a stem of grass each to chew, representing "longevity noodles".

Here the ceremonies came to an end, but Zheng Er was enjoying himself. He made them pretend to be man and wife talking to each other on their first night together while he was the traditional eavesdropper. He Niu readily fell in with his game.

"Do you want to be my wife?" asked He Niu in a loud whisper.

"I . . . yes . . . no!" Zhou Qin roared out the last word. Enough was enough!

"Why not?" demanded He Niu to her enraged "bride".

"You can't make a horse drink if it doesn't want to," sobbed Zhou Qin. "Things can't be forced."

"Too late, my pet. We're already married," He Niu answered gleefully.

Thereafter, Zhou Qin deliberately avoided them. He went to play with Wang Ri Lian instead. And when they played the wedding game, He Niu marched up to them demanding angrily what Wang Ri Lian meant by stealing her "bride". Zheng Er joined in too, threatening Zhou Qin with dire consequences if he "married" Wang Ri Lian, because No. 2 Monk would come and break his legs if he heard about it. "I think you should be He Niu's wife. I don't mind in the least."

When they grew older, they stopped playing these childish games and Zheng Er never again acted so magnanimously. Zhou Qin left to study at Luhe Middle School and seldom returned except during the holidays. When He Niu showed any signs of friendship to him, Zheng Er became extremely jealous.

For He Niu's and Zheng Er's wedding, Zhou Qin arrived a day late because of his exams.

"Wife, you're late! I've found another," He Niu teased him.

"Zheng Er has broken his promise. He said he'd marry us!" retorted Zhou Qin.

"Ah, but remember what you said? Things can't be forced. So, I'm not making you do anything against your own will."

They laughed over their childhood games.

Three years after their marriage, He Niu was still childless. Her mother-in-law almost went crazy longing for a grandson. She went to the various temples to burn incense and pray. Each month she waited to see her prayers answered, but in vain. He Niu, too, was very upset. She felt she owed it to her parents-in-law. She wept silently. Her husband, Zheng Er, was very considerate. Instead of blaming her, he consoled her with gentle words.

One night, he suggested that they fake a pregnancy.

He Niu would pretend to be with child. She would show all the symptoms of a pregnant woman just to make her mother-in-law happy. The old lady was taken in and she went and spread the good news to all her friends and relatives. She promised she would invite them all to a huge feast if her daughter-in-law produced a grandson, even if it meant putting the family into debt. She was very happy, but unfortunately died before she saw through the well-meaning hoax of her son.

On her deathbed she took He Niu's calloused hands in hers and smiled in contentment. "Daughter, don't work so hard. Take good care of my grandson." Those were her last words to He Niu, and the younger woman wept her heart out.

One day, He Niu learned of a sure remedy for barrenness from goodness knows where. She and her husband dressed up and together went to pay Aunt Yi Zhang Qing a visit. They explained that they had come "to borrow" Manzi to "warm their bed". A little boy sleeping in their bed was sure to bring them a baby boy, He Niu told her.

Aunt Yi Zhang Qing wanted to laugh and tell them they were a couple of fools, but she refrained. Her husband was related to Zheng, the carpenter, so she lent them her grandson.

Now, this had been a couple of years earlier, when Manzi was almost five. The boy ate his meals with the Zhengs and at night slept under He Niu's quilt, sucking her hard nipples until he fell asleep. But this remedy proved to be useless and He Niu still did not conceive.

He Niu's mother-in-law had died and her father-in-law was now a cripple, living by himself in a hut beside his little melon patch by the river. He Niu and Zheng

Er earned barely enough to live on, yet they were a happy and carefree couple, not weighed down by their poverty. They gave up having a child of their own and adopted Manzi as their god-child. The boy was coming with Zhou Qin to visit them.

9

The sun was sinking beyond the river.

Manzi and his Uncle Zhou had supper with the Zhengs and then set off for home along the narrow lane as dusk fell. The summer evening was as lovely as a painting. The fiery sunset coloured the fields and villages, canal and woods in radiant hues. People hurried home through the twilight: peasants with their hoes and spades, shepherd boys with their flocks and whips. Smoke rose over the villages to mix with the mist rising from the water. Birds flew silently to their nesting places and poultry, cattle and sheep to their coops, sheds and folds. Crickets started chirping as the moon rose from behind the willows.

Manzi carried a basket containing Zheng's supper, because on their way home they would pass by his melon plot.

Zheng's melon plot stretched from the bank down to the water. It had been less than a sixth of an acre but his son and He Niu had reclaimed a little more land for him after a winter and spring of hard work. The old carpenter proved equally good at growing melons as he had been working with wood. His melons grew prolifically and, moreover, were fine, juicy and sweet. Strange to say, no one ever stole them. Maybe it was not so strange, for the old carpenter never hurt a soul by either word or deed. He led a strict and sober life and his work was respected by all his fellow carpenters. He was liked by the people in the neighbourhood. Even a thief would have thought twice before stealing a melon from Zheng and earning the wrath of the community. Zheng did not move to the hut to guard his melons from men, but from animals which devoured them at night. During the day, he often left his field to have a chat with Liu, the ferryman, or stroll along to the forge to speak with Ji. He might be away half a day, yet he never worried about his melons. If a melon went missing, he was sure that somewhere under the profusion of leaves he would find some coins.

When Manzi and Zhou Qin came to the melon patch, the boy hesitated and said, "You give him his supper."

"What's the matter?" asked Zhou Qin puzzled.

"I don't want to go. Every time I go he makes me eat a lot of his melons."

"Well, what's wrong with that? Just eat what you want to. Water-melons can't harm you. When you've had enough just pee and that's that."

Manzi shook his head. "Grandpa Zheng needs the melons."

"I see," said Zhou Qin. He understood and appreciated the boy's hesitation. He went towards the hut by himself, shouting, "Uncle Zheng!"

There was no answer, but he heard a woman's voice replying, "Put the basket on the hook hanging from the beam. Your Uncle Zheng is with your uncle on the ferry. They're having a get-together there. He wants you to hurry over."

The woman's voice was husky and sweet, and Zhou

Qin realized that it belonged to his Uncle Liu's mistress Yun Zhe Yue, a ballad singer who visited the villages along the river every summer.

"Are you afraid to go home by yourself, Manzi?" he called back to the boy waiting across the field.

"No. But I want you to carry me home to sleep with you. I'll wait for you with Granny here," Manzi answered and ran up to where Yun Zhe Yue stood waiting.

Liu, the ferryman, was well-built, tall and sturdy and narrow hipped. He was extremely handsome for a man of thirty-nine, quiet, well-spoken and was one of the few people whom Learned admired.

In his younger days Liu had worked as a hired hand for Landlord Dong, whose daughter had fallen in love with him and become pregnant by him. Naturally the landlord was outraged. He had his daughter quietly strangled and her body hung up in the back pavilion, announcing that she had committed suicide because someone had attempted to violate her.

Dong declared that he would catch Liu and skin him alive. Liu fled, carrying with him a letter of introduction from his brother-in-law, and went to join the Northern Expeditionary Army in Henan Province. Two years later he returned, a feared marksman. Dong was after his blood still. He sent his men to capture Liu alive. Just as the thugs were tying up Liu, his sworn brother, a deputy company commander, happened to arrive with his troops in the village to visit him. Liu's assailants were driven off leaving behind two dead.

Instead of thanking his rescuers, Liu angrily reviled his sworn brother officer. "Get out of my sight! You've allied yourself with the Kuomintang reactionaries. You're a disgrace to the memory of our dead commander! I want nothing to do with you!"

His friend went down on his knees. "Brother, you saved my life three times. There's nothing I won't do for you."

"Then give me a gun and two hundred rounds of ammunition."

The officer quickly handed his revolver to Liu along with the bullets. Liu told him to take off his officer's cap and hang it on a branch. Then he fired at and destroyed the KMT insignia.

"Now, get out of my sight! We're quits!"

The officer dared not disobey. He kowtowed and left with his men. Before returning to his quarters in the nearby town, he first paid Dong a visit. He warned the landlord that if any harm came to Liu, he would return and deal with him and wipe out the Dong family to the last member. Dong left Liu alone, although Liu refused to have anything more to do with the officer, who was now the chief of security in the nearby town of Tongzhou.

Liu and his friend had once served under Jiang Xianyun, a Communist and a commander of a regiment of the Northern Expeditionary Army and one of the first graduates of the Huangpu Military College. He was known and respected for his courage, integrity and wisdom. Under his command the regiment had routed all the armies of the reactionary warlords from the south to Henan Province. After he was killed in action, he was replaced by a KMT officer, who immediately began to get rid of those who remained faithful to the dead commander and his ideals. Liu was at that time a platoon leader, and his sworn brother officer his deputy.

He tore off his insignia and left for home. His friend took over from him.

When Liu reached home, the peasant uprising to the east of Beijing had already been crushed. His sister had been left a widow, so she and her only child, a son, came to live with him and their mother. Liu had bought a large boat with what little money he had left and also the proceeds from selling his horse. Thus, with the boat, he earned enough to provide for his mother, sister and nephew.

Liu was much sought after by the local match-makers, but for all their persuasive tongues, Liu refused to marry any of their clients. Once, Learned himself broached the subject with Liu. But he, too, was unsuccessful. This aroused the wrath of Aunt Yi Zhang Qing, who went off to speak to Liu.

"Men and women must marry. You're already over thirty and your brother and I are both worried. Why don't you listen to us?"

"Sister, I do appreciate your concern, but you must listen to me. My sister has had a hard life and as we are of the same mother and father, I must look after her. If I marry, and even if I marry a virtuous wife, with two women living under the same roof there are bound to be quarrels. I cannot bear to make my sister suffer more."

Aunt Yi Zhang Qing agreed he had a point and did not press the matter. It was not until after Zhou Qin's mother's death some two years later that Aunt Yi Zhang Qing revived the topic.

"I can't marry," Liu said to Aunt Yi Zhang Qing with a long sigh. "The boy's an orphan. If I marry, who knows how my wife will treat him? Even if she turns out to be a fine woman, she might treat him badly once she has children of her own. I think I must remain single and look after my nephew."

Aunt Yi Zhang Qing was moved to tears and after that left him in peace.

At dawn each morning, Liu would untie his boat and ferry people across the canal, not returning home until well after sunset. In those days there was a saying: "Drivers, boatmen, innkeepers, porters and brokers, all ought to be killed even if they don't deserve it." Of course, this was an infamous generalization, but such men on the whole were uncivil and unruly. Boatmen were usually crude and vulgar. In summer, they wore only a pair of short pants, naked to the waist, swearing and fighting on the flimsiest pretext. However, Liu was different. On the hottest days he wore his shirt buttoned up to the neck and a pair of dark-coloured trousers rolled up to the knee. He was invariably patient and polite, and no one had ever heard him swear or utter a rude word. Moreover, there was always a smile on his face. He could take three carts and a lot of passengers over on his ferry without help, handling the long pole with great skill. He could send his boat gliding smoothly far out from the bank with one shove from his pole and with a few deft plunges. Then he transported his passengers safely to the other side a hundred metres away without once rocking his boat.

He manoeuvred his boat with great dexterity and the minimum of exertion. On reaching the other bank he sent his rope coiling around a willow at one go and considerately put a plank down to help his passengers and carts disembark, never hurrying them.

Then one day, on the Dragon Boat Festival, several

years ago, a woman ballad singer turned up from Tongzhou. Yun Zhe Yue was her name. She put up at the little inn kept by Du Si. As soon as she stepped into Liu's boat, she noticed Liu's fine physique and carriage and immediately fell head over heels in love with him. Though only in her twenties and unmarried, her loose living and heavy opium-smoking had left their mark on her. She looked worn. The bloom of youth had left her. In the middle of the night, she suddenly was seized by an irresistible longing to see Liu. She climbed over the wall of the inn and made her way to Liu's boat and offered herself to him. Liu was a decent sort, who never fooled around with women or touched opium. Yun Zhe Yue was as wanton as a woman could be and very experienced. Despite all her efforts, she met with a blank, polite refusal. Finally, Liu had to drag her out, throw her bodily off the boat and punt across to the other bank to escape her.

But Yun Zhe Yue was not one to give up so easily. She decided to stay. She gave ballad recitals every day at the ferry and in the evenings after the last stragglers had left, she would stand alone in the night and sing, her voice floating across the canal to Liu.

She had a good voice and she now sang with feeling, even if only for one unwilling listener. Liu, in his boat tied up on the opposite bank, could not sleep. Her voice disturbed him.

One evening, he came out of his cabin and standing on deck in the moonlight, shouted to the solitary singer on the other side of the canal, "Why don't you save your voice? You have to earn your living with it. If you stop, you'll get some sleep and so will I. I need sleep as I also have to work for a living."

"If you're not going to let me share your cabin, I'll stand here and sing. Neither of us will get any sleep and neither of us will be able to earn a living, so we'll both starve to death together."

Liu saw it was pointless to argue with her, so before turning in again, he flung at her, "The cabin door's open! Come if you can swim!"

He heard a splash and he turned round. She had jumped into the water. He did not see her surface so he plunged in after her, found her and helped her on to his boat.

He was so moved that he allowed her to stay with him.

From that night on, Yun Zhe Yue never again touched an opium pipe and stopped painting her face. Gradually, she resumed her good looks. The withering flower revived. But she was no good as a housewife. She did not know how to cook or sew as she had never been taught. She had been made to sing ballads for a living ever since her childhood. The two met every night. Yun Zhe Yue taught herself how to cook and sew. As a couple they got on famously together.

When Aunt Yi Zhang Qing heard about the affair, she hurried over to Liu. "What's this about you carrying on with a slut? Don't you know it's ruining your reputation?" she spoke her mind.

"She's a simple person, but she has a good character."

"Then marry her and silence all those gossipmongers."

"She's used to her freedom. I haven't the heart to cage her."

Aunt Yi Zhang Qing invited Yun Zhe Yue to visit

her. She bluntly told the woman to marry Liu if she really had his interests at heart.

"I can't. I'm not fit to be his wife. He should marry a good girl from a good family. Whenever he finds such a girl, I promise to leave him and never see him again."

But Liu refused to look at another woman. The two lived together like this for several years, always loving and considerate to each other. To avoid gossip after work Liu took his boat down the canal to a secluded spot and waited for Yun Zhe Yue.

Manzi liked her voice and the stories she sang. He called her his "Granny Yun" and tonight he was cuddled up against her, while Zhou Qin went off to the meeting on the ferryman's boat.

"Sing something, Granny," he begged.

Yun Zhe Yue crooned a lullaby in a soft nasal tone, a far-away look in her eyes.

> The breeze blows through the trees,
> The moon shines brightly
> Through the foliage.
> Crickets chirrup
> Babies slumber in their cradles. . . .

Manzi soon fell asleep beside her.

When he woke, it was broad daylight and he found himself lying on Zhou Qin's brick bed. Zhou Qin was writing at his desk.

10

In the last few days, Zhou Qin had been writing new lyrics for Yun Zhe Yue and holding meetings with his

Uncle Liu, Learned, Ji and Zheng. Sometimes they assembled in the hut by the melon patch, and sometimes on his uncle's boat. Zheng Er and his wife He Niu would stand watch over the melons, or Yun Zhe Yue acted as lookout. Manzi was excluded because, as his grandfather said, the boy was still "only knee-high to a grasshopper" and could not be entrusted with such an important task.

For some days Wang Ri Lian had been confined to work about the house by Beangreen, who refused to let her out of sight. She wasn't even allowed to go out to the flats to gather firewood. This deprived Manzi of the company of his aunt and the boy was at a loose end. His friend Qian Niu Er was useless too, like some waterlogged *muyu* (a musical instrument), which gave no response no matter how hard it was struck. Manzi left him and flitted off to find some other amusement.

When he got to the wall surrounding Du Si's inn near the ferry, he saw Captain Ma Leizi riding along on a shining new bicycle. Manzi's interest quickly fixed on this, because in that area in those days a bicycle was a great rarity. He hurried after him and saw the policeman ride into Du Si's courtyard.

Du Si's inn was about a hundred yards from the ferry, surrounded by a three-foot high wall of tamped earth. Inside the wicker gate on the east and west were stables for the carts and mules. Chickens and sparrows scratched the dung and straw littering the yard. Facing the gate was a long low building where carters, coolies and itinerant workmen stopped for the night. Inside the building running down the length of the long building was a passageway, on either side of which were two brick beds lining both sides, each accommodating about thirty men. Each night, travellers putting up at the inn would crowd around a flickering oil lamp noisily playing dice and gambling. Through the door at the end of the passageway was the room where Du Si and three of his assistants slept. Off this ran another corridor leading to separate white-washed rooms. Here, for ten times the price of a night in the other rooms, merchants, wealthier travellers and rich young ne'er-do-wells would give parties, play mahjong and smoke opium. Du Si also brought prostitutes for these clients from Tongzhou by boat.

Manzi had once seen one of these boats pull in the shore and discharge its living merchandise, watched by a one-eyed ruffian, constantly clicking two metal balls in his left hand and wielding a whip in his right. Manzi had seen the women, haggard with lifeless eyes, their faces gaudily painted and their mouths scarlet smeared. They were what Manzi imagined witches looked like. Manzi would never forget the sight, nor what had happened after the women reached the courtyard on to which the separate rooms opened. He did not understand all the lewd remarks and the lascivious looks, but he was disgusted, angry and bewildered. He saw two of the women being grabbed and pushed inside a room and two men seizing one girl, tugging and pushing her. One younger girl, who probably was no more than fifteen, shrieked, "Leave me alone! I'm not well." Her screams were cut short as the whip slashed on her again and again. She fell on her knees. Manzi picked up a piece of broken tile and sent it hurtling towards the one-eyed man. It struck him on the head and he fell, blood streaming from the cut on the side of his head. Manzi dashed home without looking round once.

Du Si was a pale, hollow-eyed man with a bad reputation. Opium and dissipation had turned him into something repulsive and inhuman. No local man nor woman wanted to have anything to do with him. They simply avoided him. Two years ago, Du Si had joined a secret society and become a vegetarian. He wore a string of beads around his neck and was continually muttering, "Amitabha!"

Du Si and Captain Ma Leizi were old cronies. They had worked together on many a shady deal, with Du Si the brains behind the schemes, for the police captain had power over an area of about fifteen square kilometres but very little intelligence.

"Du Si," the captain called in a loud voice, "we're in luck. We've got a big deal right here on our doorsteps!"

Du Si came out, grinning horribly. "Amitabha, you're back. Come right on in, I'll have a pipe lit for you."

Ma Leizi slipped into the west wing where Du Si had his private quarters.

"A big deal?" Suddenly Manzi recalled what his Aunt Wang Ri Lian had said that night he was standing outside Zhou Qin's room. He had heard her say, "Landlord Dong wants me as his concubine. They're trying to arrange it now." Manzi crept stealthily round the low wall until he stood right under the window of Du Si's room.

"Now, what's this big deal? Will it bring in much money?" the boy heard Du Si ask.

"The police are after Zhou Wenbin. He's the top Commie east of Beijing. There's a five-hundred-yuan reward for him. How about that, eh?"

Du Si gave a low whistle. "So much! But where can we find him?"

"Zhou Qin! Get Zhou Qin!" Ma Leizi gave a loud laugh and thumped a fist on the low table beside him.

"What do you mean? What has Zhou Qin got to do with us catching Zhou Wenbin?"

Manzi had to put his ear closer to the window to hear the police captain clearly.

"This Commie went to the same middle school as Zhou Qin. Zhou Qin took part in the student demonstration last winter. Zhou Wenbin organized that. Now, do you get me?"

"I'm beginning to."

"The Red has no permanent residence. He's here one moment, gone the next. What they call 'underground activities'. Now, listen to me. Zhou Wenbin is sure to come and call on Zhou Qin one day. I want you to keep your eyes and ears open and if you find any stranger coming to see Zhou Qin, let me know, or grab him first and then let me know."

"Amitabha!" Du Si exclaimed, clicking his tongue. "You want me to arrest Zhou Qin? How am I to handle his uncle Liu?"

"If Liu gives you any trouble, I'll have him arrested too," snarled the police captain. "He's under my jurisdiction. Besides, he's been a thorn in my flesh for a long time."

"Amitabha! If you lock up Liu that's one problem less for me too!"

Manzi heard Ma Leizi draw noisily on his long pipe and then the police captain continued, "What about that girl up at your place? Why don't you get rid of her now for a good price? Sell her while she's still young.

In another few years, she won't fetch much. She's ripe for the plucking now."

"Well, for one thing, Master Dong isn't too keen. He won't give me what I'm asking," sighed Du Si. "And another thing, she's not so manageable, ever since Learned and his wife adopted her. You'll have to give me a hand with her."

"I'll throw Learned into the clink, too!"

"On what charge?"

"Conspiring with Zhou Qin and Liu!"

Manzi had heard enough to frighten him. He ran off home as fast as his legs could carry him.

When he got there, it was already quite dark. He saw Zhou Qin walking about the yard humming some lines he had composed for Yun Zhe Yue.

"Uncle Zhou Qin!" The boy tugged and dragged him into the house. "Do . . . do you know Zhou Wenbin?"

Zhou Qin looked at the boy and slowly asked, "Where did you hear that name?"

He listened as the boy gasped out his story and then said softly, "Those two curs want to try to catch a leopard, eh!"

"They want to get you and Grandpa Liu. And . . . and they want to sell Aunt Wang Ri Lian to that Dong and put my grandpa in jail too!"

"Don't worry, Manzi. Those two make a lot of noise but they can't hurt any of us. Now, don't tell anyone what you've just told me. Not even Aunt Wang Ri Lian."

Manzi nodded.

But that night the boy tossed and turned on the brick bed, unable to sleep. It was well after midnight when he heard the creak of the door and his Aunt Wang Ri Lian entered.

For the last few days, Wang Ri Lian had been forced to stay home. Beangreen had even made her a new smock of coloured cotton cloth and a pair of black trousers. Her two thick black plaits were tied with red ribbon. She had never looked lovelier. Of course, Beangreen had given her new clothes so as to demand a better price for the girl.

When she entered the room and saw Manzi tossing restlessly on the brick bed, she picked up a fan to drive away what she thought were mosquitoes troubling the boy.

Suddenly, she heard Manzi break out sobbing.

"A nightmare?" she asked gently.

"No . . . oo."

"Then what's the matter?"

"Uncle Zhou Qin said I wasn't to tell you."

"Your uncle wants you to keep a secret from me?" She took the boy into her lap. "Is he going away to study in Beijing?"

"No."

"Is someone . . . is someone match-making for him?" Her voice trembled a little.

"No. Not that."

"Then, what is it?"

"I . . . I can't tell you."

"Manzi," Wang Ri Lian said sternly, "why can't you tell me? Has he thrown me over?"

"No!" Manzi almost shouted. "It's not that at all. Du Si and Ma Leizi are plotting to sell you to Dong. Uncle said I wasn't to tell you."

"And he's not going to lift a finger to help me?"

cried Wang Ri Lian, her voice trembling with anger now. "I'll have this out with him! Where is he?"

"He's on the ferry boat with Grandpa Liu."

Wang Ri Lian jumped off the edge of the brick bed and made for the door, followed by Manzi, who was thoroughly awake and frightened. Aunt Yi Zhang Qing had heard the commotion and shouted after them, but they ran off without stopping to answer.

A cock-crow was heard. The stars were beginning to fade. The grass was wet beneath their hurrying feet. Manzi caught up with Wang Ri Lian, who took him by the hand. The boat was tied up near the melon patch. Before Wang Ri Lian and Manzi got up close enough to hear the voices distinctly, they were stopped by Zheng. He was joined by Yun Zhe Yue. They asked why she had come, but Wang Ri Lian did not answer. She ran towards the boat tied up by the bank.

"Foster-father, help your daughter!" she cried and fell on her knees by the water's edge. "If you don't help me, I'll throw myself into the canal with a stone tied around my neck."

"That's a fate for old Ma Leizi," Learned said, his voice sounding loud in the night air.

"Wang Ri Lian, don't upset yourself," said Ji. "I promise you that Zhou Qin and you will be married within the week."

Wang Ri Lian's tearful eyes looked up, puzzled. Her gaze fell on Ji and then on Learned's face and then on Liu before finally resting on Zhou Qin, who came off the boat and helped her to her feet.

"The old people are behind us, so don't you worry. Now go home and get some sleep," he said this in a low voice, close to her ear.

Liu standing on the bow of the boat said nothing. In the moonlight he looked like some statue of a hero of old.

II

Never once in her life could she remember ever staying in bed after the sun had already risen. Beangreen was screaming at her from over the fence to get up.

"Wang Ri Lian is not well," said Aunt Yi Zhang Qing with a smile. "If you like, I'll come over and give you a hand."

"What do you mean? She was all right last night," Beangreen replied truculently. "Anyway, I can't let you help me. What's wrong with her?"

"I don't quite know," answered Aunt Yi Zhang Qing, looking grave and worried. "She's probably overworked. The girl hasn't had a day's rest, you know."

Beangreen saw she would get nothing more from the older woman and went back into her house. Beangreen was already fifty, but she still painted her face and plucked her eyebrows, fighting vainly to maintain the illusion that she was an attractive woman. She wore light-coloured clothing, dangling ear-rings and walked swaying her hips.

Once upon a time her hands had been quite nimble but now they were plump and clumsy. For years she had never done much work and now she was older and much lazier, not even setting upright a bottle of oil if it tipped over. She left all the work for Wang Ri Lian to do. If Wang Ri Lian did not come, there would be no fire or a hot meal, but in the larder there was always something sent by one of her lovers. She went and opened it, took out a package and began to untie the string. Then she ate, ignoring the hungry chickens and the pigs protesting outside.

Suddenly the gate latch was lifted and Learned and Aunt Yi Zhang Qing stepped into the courtyard. Learned was in a long robe and his wife had her hair neatly combed and was dressed in a royal blue garment. Her two large copper bracelets were shining brightly. They looked very serious.

Beangreen hurriedly swallowed down the mouthful of cake, almost choking but managing to stutter a greeting. "Come in, come in," she said, pulling back the door curtain and admitting her unexpected visitors.

The room was not very large, and a stranger would have thought he had stepped into that of a newly-wed couple. The ceiling was papered a light mauve and the white-washed walls showed up the lurid New Year paintings of love birds and ancient beauties. A bright red paper character meaning happiness was pasted over the paper window. On the brick bed was a new mat and several bright red quilts were folded and stacked in a corner.

Beangreen handed Learned a shallow basket of shredded tobacco and a long-stemmed pipe with a small bowl. Learned, sitting very upright and looking straight ahead of him, fished out his own pipe and tobacco. He filled it and lit it.

"Sister," said Aunt Yi Zhang Qing, clearing her throat and speaking with some difficulty, "the autumn harvest will soon be over and it is our custom, as you know, for parents to fetch their daughters home for a few days. We have come to tell you that we would like

Wang Ri Lian to stay with us for a few days. You will allow her, won't you?"

Beangreen was a mean and vicious woman and would have screamed abuse and refusal, but she remembered the beating she had taken at the hands of Aunt Yi Zhang Qing, and decided to try delaying tactics.

"I know how much you love her, but don't forget that I love her too. I'll let her stay with you for two days. How's that? But she must come back three times a day to feed the pigs."

"Is Du Si at home?" A man's voice was heard out in the courtyard. It was Ji, the blacksmith.

Beangreen got up and hurried out to greet the caller, her heart beating fearfully. Ji was dressed neater than usual and he wore a red cap.

"Ah, it's you, younger brother! What welcome wind has blown you here today? You come so rarely." Beangreen was younger than the blacksmith, but as her husband was older than Ji, she called him "younger brother".

"I wouldn't have come if it wasn't important," replied Ji, pushing his way into the house. He saw Learned and Aunt Yi Zhang Qing seated there and appeared pleasantly surprised. "What luck to find you two here! I was going to visit you later but now I'll save myself some time."

Beangreen again proffered her basket of tobacco and a pipe. Ji ignored it and took out his snuff box and proceeded to take a pinch. He immediately gave a violent sneeze, followed in quick succession by other sneezes. Beangreen's little boudoir seemed to shake under the impact.

"Stop! You'll bring the roof down on us!" yelped Beangreen, clapping her hands to her ears.

"What brings you here, Ji?" asked Learned, speaking for the first time.

Ji stopped sneezing and, drawing himself up, said solemnly, "I've come to act as a match-maker for Wang Ri Lian."

"But I'm her mother-in-law!" cried Beangreen.

"We all know that and we all know how well you've treated her after your son was taken away." Ji's voice was heavy with sarcasm. And then with a mischievous grin, he went on, "But now, there's a really heaven-sent match at hand. They're made for each other and I must do a good deed to earn some merit. I want to help bring this match about."

"But you can't do that!" protested Learned. "After all, Wang Ri Lian is our foster-daughter. If we don't agree, it's useless for you to interfere."

"Now, will you please let me finish," said Ji, making a polite gesture.

"Shut up. I don't want to hear!" shouted Beangreen, livid.

"But listen anyway," bellowed Ji. "When you hear what I have to say, you'll nod like a chicken pecking at grain. The man I have in mind is very talented and right here in our locality."

"Who is he?" Aunt Yi Zhang Qing asked impatiently.

"Zhou Qin. You agree, don't you? Come, you must be frank!"

"I couldn't have found a better man!" Learned answered with a big smile. "That's wonderful!"

"I'm all for it, too," said Aunt Yi Zhang Qing.

"And how about you," Ji asked, turning to Beangreen.

"Get out of my house!" shouted Beangreen.

"What! You dare refuse my offer? You want to insult me!" Ji banged a fist on the brick bed and broke off a piece of mud.

Beangreen was alarmed. She quickly slid off the bed, mumbling, "I can't decide. I'm only a woman. It's for my husband to decide."

"I want to hear what you have to say!" roared Ji.

"OK, I agree," said Beangreen, rolling her eyes and making for the door.

But Ji barred the way. He wasn't going to let her get away so easily. "You can't leave your guests. Especially a guest who comes so rarely. Anyway, someone has gone to fetch Du Si."

Zheng, the carpenter, had gone to fetch the scrawny innkeeper.

The day happened to be the fifteenth of July by the lunar calendar which was called "Spirits Day", and on this day no one crossed water, so the ferry was not used and the inn was almost empty of horses and carts. Liu's boat was tied up on the opposite bank.

Du Si and Ma Leizi, squatting under the willows, were eating and drinking.

"Brother, I've a favour to ask you," announced Zheng, walking up to them. "Could we talk about it over at your place?"

"Sure, go ahead. I'll wait for you here," Ma Leizi answered for Du Si. He wanted Du Si out of the way so that he could have all the food and drink.

Du Si saw it was useless to protest, so he followed Zheng to his house.

Once Du Si was out of sight, the captain began to wolf down the food. He stripped off his tunic and took another long drink. He was enjoying himself when he caught sight of Yun Zhe Yue stepping off Liu's boat wearing only a green vest. He saw her going towards the canal, a bundle of washing and a basin in her hands.

Ma Leizi gave a low whistle and cried out in a hoarse, eager voice, "Hey, Yun Zhe Yue! Come on over here. I'll give you a hand with your washing."

"Captain, you know I can't swim," she answered gaily and waved a plump white arm at him.

"I'd swim over and help you, only Liu might not like it."

"He's not on the boat." Yun Zhe Yue threw him an inviting look.

"Where is he?"

"Gone to buy paper money to offer to the water spirits tonight."

"Then I'll come over. Can't see you there all alone by your little self." Ma Leizi dived into the water.

"It's Spirits Day today, Captain. The water spirits will drag you away!" Yun Zhe Yue cried out in alarm.

"They're afraid of evil-minded people and I'm very wicked. They can't hurt me," the policeman in the water shouted back.

He had hardly finished when he felt hands grip his legs and drag him under.

For a moment Ma Leizi was seized by panic. Then he recovered quickly. He was a good swimmer. He saw it was Liu who had him in his grasp. He realized that he had fallen into a trap and struggled to get free. But Liu had him in a vice-like grip and was trying to drown him. The two men were swept swiftly along, fighting and clawing at each other. Ma Leizi was losing, for he was not as strong. Liu floated with the current for about another kilometre with the lifeless body of Ma Leizi before dragging the corpse into a thick patch of reeds. Liu made sure he was unobserved and then hurriedly covered the body and left, making his way home through the cover provided by the tall fields of maize.

Du Si followed Zheng. As soon as he stepped inside his door and saw Learned, Aunt Yi Zhang Qing and Ji waiting for him, he sensed that something was up.

"What an honour you all do me paying me a visit," he beamed.

"We've come to fetch Wang Ri Lian home. Your wife has agreed," Learned and Aunt Yi Zhang Qing said in unison.

"Your wife has agreed. I've come as a match-maker. We want to hear what you have to say." Ji did not mince words.

"You can't break up my family! My son is an officer and is going to come back full of honour after eighteen years. My daughter-in-law is waiting for him to return," protested Du Si.

"Who said your son has become an officer?" Ji demanded.

"Don't you remember? Tiezui, the fortune-teller, said so."

"Crap! I don't remember a thing," replied the blacksmith.

Suddenly they all heard the sound of a flute. Du Si let out an audible sigh as if his saviour had come to his rescue.

"There he is now!" exclaimed Du Si. "I'll bring him in and let you all hear for yourselves."

"Stay where you are. I'll bring him," said Ji.

A few moments later Ji reappeared with the fortune-teller. The man asked the hours and dates of No. 2 Monk's and Wang Ri Lian's births and counted on his fingers mumbling incoherently to himself.

"This is most auspicious!" the fortune-teller cried, slapping his thighs.

"Has No. 2 Monk been promoted?" inquired Du Si anxiously.

"Yes. He is now a brigadier."

"When is he coming home?"

"He comes back eighteen years after he left."

"There, what did I tell you!" crowed Du Si. Turning to the fortune-teller, he asked, "My daughter-in-law will have to wait a few more years before she welcomes him back, won't she?"

"Oh, no need to wait," The fortune-teller shook his head. "Your son has married the daughter of his commanding officer. Wang Ri Lian was not destined to share his good fortune."

"You're lying!" cried the little innkeeper in a rage. "Why have you changed? That wasn't what you said two years ago."

"Who says I've changed?"

"You said No. 2 Monk had become a battalion commander and Wang Ri Lian was to wait for him."

"That was when he had been a battalion commander two years ago. Wang Ri Lian would have made a good match then. But your son has been promoted, so Wang Ri Lian is not good enough now!"

"Shit! You're making all this up!" shouted the innkeeper. "You're just saying that because you've been paid to say it!"

"How dare you!" cried the outraged fortune-teller. "Let me tell you something else for free. Wang Ri Lian was born under an unlucky star. She'll bring misfortune to her father-in-law and mother-in-law. If you don't send her away, you'll meet with misfortune after misfortune."

Learned had a present ready, which he thrust into the fortune-teller's hands.

Tiezui made his way out and ran into one of Du Si's young assistants. Both fell. The younger man quickly helped the other to his feet, then ran inside to Du Si, crying, "Master, something terrible's happened. Captain Ma Leizi has been dragged off by water spirits!"

"Someone go and help him," cried Du Si, stamping his feet helplessly.

"He shouldn't have gone into the canal today," said Du Si.

"Don't go!" implored Beangreen, throwing herself on her husband. "Forget about him and the ten dollars. I don't want you to be taken away by the spirits, too."

"Yes. Remember what the fortune-teller just said, Du Si," reminded Learned.

Du Si stamped helplessly, hands clasping his head and intoning a prayer, "Amitabha, Amitabha!"

"Stop it," commanded Ji, taking Du Si by the scruff of his neck. "You haven't even the little sense your wife has. And you call yourself a man. Now, how much do you want?"

"We bought her. Paid good money for her," said Du Si, grinding his teeth. "We've fed and clothed her these twelve long years. I can't give her away for nothing."

"Shut up and say how much you want," ordered Ji.

"Thirty silver dollars," said Beangreen.

"You shut your mouth, woman! I won't take less than fifty dollars." Du Si suddenly was the master again.

"Du Si, you're worse than a greedy, ravenous wolf!" Ji spat. "But I'll give you fifty if you throw in your wife as well."

"Fifty is what I'm asking and I won't bargain," said Du Si through clenched teeth.

"I'll slit you open and see what guts you have!" roared the blacksmith, seizing Du Si by the chest and picking up the pair of scissors from the brick bed with the other hand.

"Help . . . help. . . !" Ji's strong hand choked off Du Si's cries. Du Si's eyes were bulging out of their sockets.

"Please let him go this time. I'll ask him to do as you say," pleaded Beangreen.

"Why are you interceding for him? If I strangle him, you can get yourself a new husband. With luck you might even conceive."

"Stop it, Ji. Don't go too far," Learned interposed. And, turning to the hapless innkeeper he said, "You're asking too much. Wang Ri Lian has slaved for you all these years. Who supported whom these twelve years? Be reasonable. Bring me an abacus and I'll tot things up for you."

"Never mind that. I'll. . . . I'll settle for thirty," croaked Du Si.

"Bring me paper and a brush I'll write down the terms clearly," said Learned in a loud voice.

"I'll get them for you, Grandpa!" cried Manzi, who had been a silent witness to all that was happening from across the fence. The boy hurried away.

"Who's going to pay me?" shrilled Du Si pathetically.

"I'll pay you!" retorted Learned, slapping his chest.

"I want cash. None of your credit business," Du Si pressed.

"I'll let you have two *mu* of our land," replied Learned.

"Done! No going back on your word," cried Du Si, his eyes sparkling.

"I've never gone back on my word, as you should know," said Learned, a little incensed. "I'll give two *mu* to buy back my daughter's freedom and another two *mu* as her dowry. That's only half of what I own."

Manzi returned breathless with paper and brush and ink from Zhou Qin's study.

Du Si, an innkeeper, knew how to write and count. It was he who wrote down the terms. Then he and his wife both inked their thumbs and signed the deed with their fingerprints. Learned went home and came back with the title-deed, which he threw at Du Si.

When the transaction was over, Zheng, who had remained silent throughout the proceedings, suddenly spoke up, "Ji is acting for Zhou Qin, so let me be the match-maker for Wang Ri Lian."

"Many thanks for your offer, Brother," replied Learned and roared with pleasure. "We'll have to trouble your children to help with the wedding."

12

Learned's courtyard was filled with jubilation. Magpies, harbingers of happiness, called from morning to night on the branches, and, although Learned and Aunt Yi Zhang Qing had given away half their property, they had gained the goodwill of all in the village, young and old. They were radiant with happiness.

What moved them most was when Liu came to call on them that evening right after they had settled the affair with Du Si and Beangreen. This fearless man had walked into the house and immediately dropped to his knees and said, his voice choked with tears, "Whatever I do, I shall never be able to repay you two for what you have done."

Liu had brooded often over this matter. It had weighed heavily on him for a long time. He had only a mud hut of three rooms and did not own an inch of land. He felt he owed it to his dead sister and brother-in-law to do something for their son, Zhou Qin.

Aunt Yi Zhang Qing, some twenty years older than Liu, felt her heart turn over at the sight of the man who had so loyally stood by his sister and brother-in-law. She made him get up and said brusquely to keep herself from crying, "Why thank me? I didn't do it for you. I did it for that poor girl Wang Ri Lian."

"Yes, yes. We did it for Wang Ri Lian and for Zhou Qin," Learned hurriedly added. "And you know the old saying, 'A father-in-law owns half the son-in-law.' From now on Zhou Qin is my son too. You see, I've got the best part of the bargain, so why should you thank me?"

Liu said nothing. He could not find the words to express himself. He turned and left, his eyes brimming with tears.

Earlier, when Learned and Aunt Yi Zhang Qing had returned home from Du Si's house on the other side of the fence, Wang Ri Lian had fallen down on her knees before them.

"Father, Mother, I can't take what is yours. The land is your livelihood! I don't want it as a dowry."

"Come here, daughter," cried Aunt Yi Zhang Qing, folding the girl into her bosom. "Don't hold it against me for not being able to give you something better. I'd have given you a big three-roomed house and ten hectares if I could. But I have nothing!"

"We'll give her another two *mu*," said Learned, moved by the sight of the two weeping women. "That'll leave us two *mu*. That's all we need for our burial ground."

"Oh, stop, please," begged Wang Ri Lian. "How will I ever look brother and sister-in-law in the eye again?"

"Your brother has inherited the shop from his father-in-law. He won't need the land."

"No, no! I won't hear of it," cried Wang Ri Lian. "And there is little Manzi, too."

"Ho, ho!" Learned let out a bellow of laughter. "He won't miss two *mu* of land. He's destined to become a great man. Poor families breed generals and from thatched huts emerge great scholars."

"I shall refuse to marry, if you force the land on me," protested Wang Ri Lian.

The old couple decided not to pursue the matter

further, but they insisted that they make the wedding a big event.

So Zhou Qin came over to try and dissuade them.

"Uncle, Aunt," he began, "your kindness is already boundless. You mustn't go in for such extravagances."

Now, the local custom in the village was that the prospective son-in-law should not call on his future parents-in-law. If a man did that, it was sure to set tongues wagging. So when Zhou Qin arrived and pleaded with them Learned and Aunt Yi Zhang Qing were not too pleased.

"Zhou Qin, this is none of your business. You're not married to Wang Ri Lian yet," Aunt Yi Zhang Qing said curtly.

"That's right," chimed in Learned. "Wang Ri Lian may not be my own daughter, but she is dearer to me than if she were. Marriage is one of the major events in one's life. I must do right by her. She must not be mocked and shamed behind our backs."

But Zhou Qin continued to argue, "Uncle, Aunt, you are both sensible people. Listen to me, please. With our country in such dire straits, we'll really be mocked if we spend lavishly on a wedding. The enemy is trying to take over our country."

"You have a point there," said Learned, and repeated it, as if he had suddenly seen the profundity of Zhou Qin's argument.

But Aunt Yi Zhang Qing was not so easily put off. When Wang Ri Lian threw herself into her lap and pleaded in a teasing way, she relented. "But it's not doing right by you, child," she said resignedly. "I still think it's being unfair to you."

Wang Ri Lian tugged Zhou Qin by the sleeve and whispered, "Say thank you to Father and Mother."

"Uncle, Aunt, I. . . ."

"What did I hear you call us?" asked Aunt Yi Zhang Qing sternly.

"Father and Mother," Zhou Qin hurriedly corrected himself and bowed respectfully.

"That's better," said Aunt Yi Zhang Qing with a smile. "As long as you two love and cherish each other, we'll do whatever we can for you."

The day before the wedding Manzi's father, Changan, came home from Tongzhou.

Changan had not set up his own home in Tongzhou, but lived with his wife's parents. His wife had one daughter and was expecting a baby again. The father-in-law was getting on in years and his business was left more and more to Changan, who was easy-going, timid and rather weak. The shop therefore neither prospered nor went bankrupt. Changan was becoming rather fat and looking more and more like the law-abiding, amiable merchant that he was, rather than the peasant he was born.

He came home to visit his parents once a year as a filial son should. He also brought presents for his father's friends such as Ji, Zheng and Liu. Although he despised Beangreen and Du Si, he still paid them a courtesy call when he returned, as they were next-door neighbours.

This year, when Changan came home, he did as always but reserved the finest present for Wang Ri Lian. He bought her material for a blouse and a pair of trousers, two pairs of cloth shoes, a tea set, a mirror and a beautiful box for combs and pins.

Despite their son's coming home to see them, Changan's parents were rather apprehensive, and Manzi was not very happy to see his father either. Learned and Aunt Yi Zhang Qing knew that this time he was going to take Manzi away from them. He was to go to school in Tongzhou. Manzi's going would be like taking a big part of their lives away. Manzi did not relish the thought of leaving all the people he loved either. It meant leaving the canal and the village and his carefree life. He felt he was going to be put into a cage.

Changan sensed that his arrival had diluted the merry atmosphere and that his presence hung like a cloud over everyone. Though unambitious, he was not entirely dumb. He felt the tension and to relieve his awkwardness, he decided to divert the attention of all.

"Oh, I nearly forgot!" he suddenly exclaimed, clapping his hands. "Zhou Qin, my brother-in-law has been accepted by Yenching University. He's passed the entrance exam. Herc is the notice of admittance." He brought out a large red envelope from his pocket.

"This is happiness upon happiness!" exclaimed Learned, and, forgetting about local customs, called out to Manzi, "Go and invite your Uncle Zhou Qin over here." Then he continued, "He has brought honour to our tiny village and to our humble house. Landlord Dong has wide fields and a string of brats and yet not one of them has even been admitted into the middle school in Tongzhou! His days are numbered!"

"That is why I think Manzi must go to school this year," Learned's son quickly pointed out. "He should follow in his uncle's footsteps."

"Absolutely, absolutely," agreed Learned, nodding.

"But the boy is still so young. Don't push him," protested the grandmother.

Manzi arrived with Zhou Qin.

"Congratulations!" cried Changan, standing up and shaking his clasped hands before him. "Let me be the first to congratulate you on your double happiness."

Zhou Qin took the envelope without even looking at it and stuffed it into his pocket. "North China probably hasn't room now for a desk. I haven't decided whether I'll go or not."

"And here is something else for you," said Changan, taking out another envelope and handing it to Zhou Qin. "It's a letter from Shanghai together with the remuneration for an article of yours."

"What's that?" asked Manzi.

"Your uncle has written an article and it has been published and he is being paid for it. That is what it is," explained his father. "You must study and go to college and learn to write and you'll get payment for your articles too."

Then turning to Zhou Qin, he said, "I met the new police chief on the ferry. Named Yin. Captain Yin. He sends you his regards."

"How come you mix with such people?" Learned asked Zhou Qin.

"He's one of us," Zhou Qin answered in a whisper.

The next day, the bride was fetched in a sedan-chair carried by four stout men accompanied by two trumpeters. They did without the *suona* players, gong beaters and drummers. When the bride arrived at the groom's house a string of fire-crackers exploded and the wedding ceremony started. It was as merry as one could wish.

Ji and Zheng, as match-makers for the couple, were there to witness the marriage. Zheng Er was master of ceremonies, not in play this time, and his wife, He Niu, had the bridal chamber decorated and ready. In the middle of Liu's courtyard burnt two large red candles. The groom and bride bowed to the orders of Zheng Er and then they were escorted to their chamber, together holding the same long piece of red silk before them. Manzi, dressed up in a bright red vest, finely embroidered by Wang Ri Lian, was told to roll about the bed. The boy did more. He did somersaults and handstands and tumbled about wildly.

Suddenly, Manzi heard his grandpa and his father quarrelling. Their voices floated over the fence into the newlyweds' room.

"I have to get back before they shut the city gates. I must get back to my shop," Manzi heard his father say. "The boy must go to school this autumn. I have to take him and prepare him for school."

"But he's still too young. I'll be worried about him," his grandmother said in a choked voice. "Wait another year or two until he's a little taller. Then no one will bully him at school."

"But, Mother! . . ." Changan pleaded desperately.

Manzi saw fate ahead and got off the brick bed and ran in the direction of the canal. He fled like a startled bird. He first hid himself in the reeds where Zhou Qin and Wang Ri Lian had once played the wedding game. Then feeling still unsafe he dived down among the stunted willows at the water's edge where Wang Ri Lian used to bathe. The water came over his head. He dared not paddle, so he floated and then carefully trod water noiselessly. He saw the little red birds looking down at him from the trees and fish gliding past him. Then he heard footsteps and someone say very quietly, barely audible: "From now on, you're Zhou Qin's only contact. Look after him well."

"I will, I can promise you that, Wenbin."

"When they set up the underground armed resistance against the Japs, you must try to give them legal status."

"I'll do that. Leave it to me."

Manzi turned slightly and peered through the willow branches and saw two young men, one in police uniform, the other had a square face and was about thirty or so. They shook hands and parted.

Manzi guessed that the younger man in uniform must be the new police captain. But who was this Wenbin? It was getting dark and Manzi felt a little frightened, alone in the water among the willows. He dared not go back for his father would surely take him away. He felt terribly wronged and lonely. Tears rolled down his cheeks into the water.

"Manzi! Manzi!" He heard his Aunt Wang Ri Lian calling.

"Aunt!" Manzi climbed out of the water and flung himself on her and began to cry his heart out.

Pressing the wet boy to her, she picked him up, comforting him, "There's a good boy. Come home with me."

"I'm not going home. Ever. Father's going to take me away with him." Manzi tried to free himself, but Wang Ri Lian held him tightly.

"Your father's not going to take you anywhere," said Wang Ri Lian, smiling. "And your Uncle Zhou Qin is not going away either. He's going to start a school here in the village and you can learn there."

"Was it that man called Wenbin who told Uncle Zhou Qin to stay here?" asked Manzi.

"How did you know?"

"I saw him talking with Uncle Zhou Qin here," announced Manzi. "But why does Uncle listen to him?"

"He's an old schoolmate of your uncle's."

"Then he must be Zhou Wenbin!" cried Manzi in excitement. "Will you take me to see him?"

"He's gone."

Manzi gave himself a resounding slap on his bald head and cursed himself.

He rode home on Wang Ri Lian's back. They found Aunt Yi Zhang Qing and Manzi's father standing outside the gate. When his grandma saw him, she waved him away.

"Go and stay with your Aunt Wang Ri Lian," she said.

"I wasn't coming anyway," sniffed Manzi.

Wang Ri Lian carried Manzi to her home. The house was very quiet. He Niu was doing the cooking in the outer room which served as the kitchen.

"Where are they?" asked Wang Ri Lian.

"In the east room. They're talking about setting up a civil defence corps," He Niu spoke in a conspiratorial whisper.

Wang Ri Lian put Manzi down and, picking up a bowl, filled it with steaming millet and then another with chicken.

"Here, eat this," she told him. "Tomorrow you start learning characters from your uncle."

"I'm not going home tonight. I'm going to sleep here with you and Uncle Zhou Qin."

Wang Ri Lian blushed and tried to dissuade him.

"But your father hasn't seen you for more than six months. You must go home and sleep."

"I won't! I won't!" cried Manzi, throwing away the chopsticks. "I'm going to sleep with you and Uncle."

"Oh, let him," He Niu put in with a giggle. "Let him warm your bed and I can guarantee you'll have a big chubby boy next year."

He Niu apparently had not forgotten her secret formula.

"Get away with you!" Wang Ri Lian gave her a playful slap, her face glowing from the reflection of the warm fire.

Translated by Alex Young

The Budding Lotus

1

YU Wenqian always had to return home no matter how harsh the weather was and July downpours were nothing to him. Riding his "Eternity" brand bike, he moved as swiftly as lightning. It was seventy-two *li* along the Beijing-Tianjin Highway from his college, situated by the Tonghui River, to Flower Street Village on the east bank of the North Grand Canal, and this country-bred student made the round trip every day.

He had been at the college three years now but he still remained the simple, straightforward youth from Flower Street. Among all the bright colours, his rustic dress was like a camel in a herd of sheep, more noticeable than all the long side-burns, large sunglasses, tight shirts and bell-bottoms.

Early every mid-summer morning, he would cycle hard along the highway. His mud-stained feet bare, he wore a conical bamboo hat, a threadbare jacket covered in dew and blades of grass, and a pair of patched trousers rolled up above the knees. On his bicycle he carried a large, two hundred *jin* bundle of fresh grass. Since he was studying foreign languages, he would recite as he rode along, thirty-six *li* in English and the other thirty-six in Japanese. Having memorized both an English-Chinese dictionary and a Japanese-Chinese one, he would always get full marks in written exams, but was, as many country people are, too shy to open his mouth and so had not reached a pass in his oral work. As soon as he spoke, his thick local accent made the whole class rock with laughter and he came to an abrupt halt.

After crossing Eight-*li* Bridge, he headed to a dairy farm and once the grass had been weighed, went to clean up in the farm's bathroom. Then, out of the bulging satchel suspended from his handlebars, he took some clean clothing: a deep grey dacron shirt, a pair of metallic grey rayon trousers and black, thick-soled plastic sandals. In the morning light, neatly-dressed and with a pair of large eyes beneath bushy brows, a round head, square face, fan-shaped chest and a figure like a ridgepole, he was considered by the villagers to be a handsome youth.

Each day he would tidy up the schoolroom before his town classmates arrived.

His college consisted of only one single building which rose up amidst thick vegetation. Since it had no dormitory, the students sprawled on their desks to take their noon siesta. But Wenqian would go up instead to the banks of the Tonghui River outside the college gate, spread out a plastic sheet under the green shade of a weeping willow and lie down to take a sound sleep.

Now, with that same plastic sheet draped over his shoulders as a raincoat, the conical bamboo hat fastened under his chin, he leaned forward over the handlebars like a wind-beaten stalk, unaffected by the pelting rain.

Following his afternoon classes, he flew home on his bike like a shooting star.

The old Flower Street was now gone. Its remaining

traces were only dimly discernible in the Yus' house, a hut left by his grandfather and father with a tiny courtyard fenced in with willow branches. Even the gate, which was changed every three years, was in the old style.

As soon as he walked into the courtyard, he threw the satchel through the window on to his *kang* and then went out again with a wicker basket and a sickle to cut grass on the river bank outside the village.

The grass there was green, tender and succulent, and the farm bought as much as he could gather. He worked without stopping until the moon hung from the willow tips and swarms of mosquitoes bit his hands. Basket by basket, he carried the grass home and scattered it on either side of the fence. Then, rising at dawn, he tied it in a bundle which he fixed to his bicycle. He would sell the grass for three yuan on his way to college.

Labouring in this way for the three months from June to August would earn him around two hundred and eighty yuan and, together with his monthly twenty yuan state grant, his income exceeded his whole year's production team dividend before going to college.

At home Wenqian had only a widowed mother whose feet were bound and who was old and ailing. Working only now and again, she couldn't earn many workpoints in a year, and so he had to earn the grain ration for the two of them while going to college at the same time.

The white sheets of rain blurred the sky and the land. There were no pedestrians on the road and cars and carts were sparse. Hardly opening his eyes and nearly out of breath, he was forced to keep his head down. Crossing the bridge, he arrived at the east bank of the Grand Canal. From the bridge's end to the village, the three *li* of yellow muddy road was like a pot of thick gruel. The bike would not move an inch.

For the first sixty-nine *li* Wenqian had been on his bike, but the final three would mean carrying the bike through the mire.

The ruts through the mud, like flowing streams, carried away flowers beaten down from the wistaria vines twining around the roadside willows. Suddenly ahead Wenqian saw something which seemed like a lotus blooming behind the curtain of rain. He halted, wiped the rain from his face and took a closer look. Lying in the road was a pale pinkish raincoat. A bulge underneath it made him wonder whether some passerby had fainted in the heavy rain. Putting down his bike, he staggered over and picked up a corner of the coat. Underneath was a broken-down moped.

"Hey!" he shouted. "Whose . . . moped is this?" He was the only person who could hear the question. The rain pouring into his mouth made him splutter.

He looked around. To the east was a field of tall crops, to the west a watermelon patch on the edge of which, beneath a willow tree, a small shed shook in the fierce storm.

Since he couldn t find the moped's owner and couldn't bring himself to leave it behind, he hoisted its considerable weight onto his shoulders, planning to put it in the shed.

Suddenly a girl rushed out from behind a green curtain and, tugging at his plastic sheet, shouted, "Put my moped down!"

Looking over his shoulder Wenqian was startled to see Hua Bilian standing there looking like a drowned rat.

2

On a piece of land eight *li* east of the village, between the county highway and a creek, stood the Beijing-Flower Street Shirt Factory, jointly run by the commune and a clothing company in Beijing. The commune, whose Party secretary had been chosen as chairman of the factory's board, provided the land and labour to build the factory and was in charge of its personnel and security work, while the clothing company offered capital, machines, technicians and administrative personnel to look after supply, production and marketing. One of the company's assistant managers was concurrently a director of the factory. The profits were split fifty-fifty between the two parties.

After testing their qualifications, the commune recruited four hundred young women workers and a hundred men from thirty-six brigades. It had a ready market for its goods all over the country and even exported one-third, and in two years the commune had made a net profit of two and a half million yuan.

Bilian worked in the factory's cutting workshop. Her father Hua Siji, a master mason, made a living moving from job to job with his trowel. Her mother whose nickname was Qiao'er, was an infinitely resourceful woman who had liked acting as a matchmaker ever since she was sixteen. She had a tongue so glib she could make the dead turn over and in the past thirty years had drunk enough nuptial wine to open a distillery.

Bilian had inherited her father's skilful hands and her mother's silver tongue, as well as her father's astuteness and her mother's good looks.

Small and delicate, she was both nimble and clever

with her hands. Whether transplanting rice, harvesting wheat or doing any other kind of farm labour, stronger women could only lag behind no matter how hard they tried to catch up with her. She worked rhythmically, taking her time, leaving behind a faint scent of lilac wherever she went.

Though as lovely as a flower or a piece of jade, and with a mother who was a veteran matchmaker, she still had not succeeded in finding an ideal marriage partner.

There was nothing particularly strange about this. Bilian had high expectations, her mother was over-cautious, and her father experienced and astute — each had a different set of standards. How could any young man successfully pass through all of these three barriers?

An excellent character, a good education, intelligence and ability, eloquence, as well as a good class background were Bilian's five conditions for a husband. And not a single one of these could be dispensed with.

All the same her mother was unable to set her mind at ease.

Qiao'er was forty-six now and had long been called Aunt Hua by the village's young people. For most of her life she'd acted as a go-between, using her glib tongue to give extravagantly colourful and fabricated descriptions of prospective spouses. So, even if it were her own brother, anyone who wanted to act as a matchmaker for her daughter would automatically be regarded by her as a weasel paying respects to a hen — not acting with the best of intentions. Even if her daughter was satisfied with the proposal, she herself would not give her assent without first giving the young man a thorough going-over.

Hua Siji had wandered here and there and seen the world. No one could fool him since he always looked before he leapt, and didn't make decisions until he had all the facts to hand. He'd worked hard for most of his life and refused to rashly marry off his only daughter like tossing out a basin of water. Though a man of few words, he was head of the family, and had the final say. He planned to find a son-in-law who would marry into the family and live with them, and did not want some incompetent who was only willing to change his family name.

Three pairs of eyes, like six searchlights, scanned far and wide, but missed what was under their very noses. No one had thought of Yu Wenqian.

The Yus were the only family in the village with this surname and, as they had settled there later than others, were considered vastly inferior in social position to the older residents from large clans. Misfortunes never come alone. As luck would have it, Wenqian's father had died early, leaving behind an orphan son and a widow who were poor and looked down on by others. Born in 1956, Wenqian's pet name was Qian'er. He was three to five during the successive famine years, and had only three meals of thin gruel a day. Underfed, he was sallow and emaciated, with a neck as thin as a withered cane, a head the size of a gourd, a small belly like a drum which boomed when beaten, and skinny ribs which resembled a washboard. Even his own mother had dared not hope that he would pull through. Later, at school, he shared a desk with Bilian. A kind-hearted teacher bought him a new suit of clothes and a pair of shoes and he in turn brought credit to this benevolent teacher, coming first every year in the examinations. During his three years in primary school he always wore the same clothes, and they gradually became too small and threadbare. The year 1966 saw a huge upheaval throughout the country and this same teacher was placed under detention and criticized. All the children no longer went to school. All, that is, except Qian'er. Each day, he climbed over the enclosure wall from the date tree outside and crept into the bleak and gloomy schoolyard to see his teacher through a back window in the detention shed. Tears rolled down his cheeks when he found the man with hair dishevelled and a face beaten black and blue. Three years later, both he and Bilian received notices informing them that they should go to middle school. It was winter then and the classroom was as cold as a freezer. The desks and chairs were broken and there were no textbooks. Qian'er was the only pupil willing to endure such hardships. Seeing that their daughter was becoming as beautiful as a peach blossom, Hua Siji and his wife were afraid that she might make the sort of mistake that would cause lasting sorrow if they slackened their vigilance for a moment. To guard against this they bolted the door as soon as it was dark. During those years Siji's trowel became rusty, since he was not allowed to earn extra money with his skills. But when the team leader wanted to take a wife, he still had to ask for help from Aunt Hua. So she used the money she got from her matchmaking to buy a sewing-machine and kept Bilian tied to it.

Of the young people in Flower Street, there was one other who hardly ever went out in the evenings. That was Qian'er. He was infatuated by books, too engrossed at times to notice that there was nothing in the pot or unaware that he'd eaten his fill after downing eight cornmeal dumplings with vegetable stuffing. His poverty, plus his countrified appearance, made Aunt Hua wager that even a blind girl would not be foolish enough to choose this boy as her husband. But never judge a person by looks alone. When the weather changes there is no telling which cloud will produce rain. In 1977, a year or so after the downfall of the "gang of four", universities and colleges resumed classes and began recruiting students. The young people of Flower Street were too nervous to try their luck. Only Qian'er entered his name for the entrance examinations. Unfortunately, he was notified that he had failed. All the same, he was only a hair's breadth under the admission line although he seemed barred as if by a mountain. He tried again the following year and this time was admitted to the college by the Tonghui River outside Chaoyang Gate. From then on, he was no longer referred to by his pet name Qian'er but addressed as Wenqian, his proper name. An early spring blossom ushers in a profusion of blooms. His successful example provided an impetus for other young people in the village. Several of them threw away their playing-cards and took up textbooks instead. Two were admitted to technical secondary schools in 1979 and 1980. Encouraged, Bilian set out on her sewing-machine the textbooks she had used so many years ago. Her entry into the shirt factory as a worker had not been through any sort of pull, but through an open and aboveboard test of her abilities. During his three years as a day student, Wenqian left home early in the morning and came back at dusk while Bilian worked the three different factory shifts in turn. Each had a different schedule and took a different route. They seldom met and had not seen each other for a long time.

As the saying goes, fate brings people who are far apart together. Whoever would have thought that it would be a rainstorm that would cause them to meet again. It seemed that it was preordained and that the rain was acting as their go-between.

Putting the moped down, Wenqian joked, "Bilian, when did you buy this 'electric donkey'?"

"Three days ago," she replied smugly. "It cost me six month's wages and my bonus."

"But it's like a servant who bullies his master, refusing to work halfway through the journey." He winked at her and added, "It looks as if you still need to buy a whip too."

Bilian burst out laughing. "After the second shift it began to drizzle. I thought I could do this eight *li* in no time on the moped. I never expected it would break down in the middle of nowhere. So I just sat beneath the runner beans to get out of the rain and hoped some passerby would come to my aid. Fancy meeting you here. Isn't that just my good luck?"

"You ought to have carried it to the shed over there."

"That's Qiukui's contracted melon field. I was afraid that Little Iron Du would be watching the field for his sister and would have that wolfhound of his tied up in the shed."

"So that means I have to act as a porter, does it?"

"Oh, Qian'er, thank you!"

A peal of laughter trailing behind her in the rain, the girl darted towards the shed.

3

Since Beijing people love eating watermelon on hot summer days, a melon shortage occurs every year. In the past, Flower Street had long been famous for its particular strain of melon known as "Red Number One Scholar". Red-fleshed and black-seeded, it was sweet and refreshing if eaten immediately on purchase. If taken home, the colour and taste kept for seven days and a replacement was guaranteed if it lost any of its quality.

However, some years back grain was the crop to be grown in the countryside. The watermelons of Flower Street were uprooted and the village teenagers had only seen them in pictures. It was only in 1979 that the ban on growing them was lifted. After looking back over the records, purchasing agents from fruit companies in Beijing swarmed into Flower Street, visiting every household and bowing to their hosts. They wished they could hang this small hamlet with its eight hundred *mu* of land in mid-air and grow watermelon on all six sides of it. Unfortunately, some of the veteran melon growers were now dead, some were old and the rest had grown rusty. It was necessary to "pick a general from among the dwarfs" — to choose the best person available. So Bold Fellow Du, unknown to the public in the past, now unexpectedly became a master grower.

Du himself did not have any extraordinary skills. Depending entirely on the secret methods handed down by his ancestors, he grew one plot of an early variety and one plot of a late type and thus could sell his products at high prices.

His nickname, Bold Fellow, was actually a result

of his cowardice. A bag of bones, he had been prone to illness since childhood. To save his life he had made a vow to Buddha and for three years had been a little monk in a temple, where he had been frightened out of his wits by the wood and clay idols. After returning to secular life he still shivered with fear when night fell. He grew watermelons together with his old father but dared not keep watch in the shed at night. After his father died, he and his wife Erduo lived on the three-*mu* field. Now he had to watch over the field himself, he took his wife to keep him company. At midnight, those intent on stealing melons or doing mischief imitated the howling of ghosts and the crying of nighthawks around the shed. Bold Fellow was so frightened that he left his wife behind and fled home, refusing to spend a night in the shed ever again. Annoyed with her cowardly husband, Erduo, broad-shouldered, solidly-built and much bolder, went in a fit of annoyance to watch the field by herself. A sharp, shiny fishing spear in hand, she sat in the shed every night, her eyes wide open till dawn. One rainy night two young hooligans barged into the shed to try and rape her. She yelled for help. Woken by the noise Hua Siji shouted over to Bold Fellow Du, who lived next door, "There're some villains in your melon field, brother. You better go quickly and rescue your wife!" But instead Bold Fellow shut all the windows and doors tight, not daring to go out. Shivering in his shoes, he whimpered, "Brother, please. . . . Would you go for me?" Siji picked up his mulberry wood shoulder pole and rushed out to the field. By then, Erduo had already been stripped and her hands tied behind her back. Siji arrived just in time and drove the villains away, but he himself got stabbed and fell in a pool of blood. Only at daybreak did Bold Fellow Du rush to the spot. Seriously wounded, Siji was confined to bed for over a month. He was still single then and Erduo, grateful for his rescue, brought him food and soup every day. Gradually, as they got to know one another, they fell in love. When Erduo again went to keep watch in the field, Siji would always be with her to keep her company. Only after Bold Fellow Du joined the agricultural co-op in 1955 and Erduo no longer went out at night did Siji marry Qiao'er.

For the past two years, Bold Fellow Du had again contracted to look after ten *mu* of watermelon, but there was no longer any need for Erduo to keep watch over it herself. Their son Little Iron could do the job perfectly well with the wolfhound.

Some years back, only a few months after Qiukui was married, her husband was sentenced to ten years' imprisonment. An investigation had proved that he had murdered someone during the "cultural revolution" when he was the head of a rebel gang and a looter. So she moved back to her mother's home and looked after herself. She also contracted to be responsible for two *mu* of watermelons and entrusted her brother with the job of keeping watch for her.

A poky, squat affair, Qiukui's shed could hardly be considered even a pigeon house; it was more like an upright chicken coop. As soon as the last month of the year arrives, villagers coop up their non-laying hens or unwanted cocks in a special cage to be fattened for New Year feasts. The cage is like an instrument of torture in the old days and the chickens have only enough room to stand motionlessly after being fed.

This is the best method of producing tender flesh. Since awards were given to those who exceeded the production quota, Qiukui wanted to plant more vines in her two *mu* field and begrudged using too much land for the shed. As a result, the one she built was merely a makeshift shelter from the wind and rain.

Bilian halted two or three paces from the shed as she suddenly remembered Little Iron's hound, and turned back with a shriek. Hiding herself behind Wenqian's back, she walked cautiously, tugging at the hem of his jacket.

The tiny tottering structure contained neither canine nor human. Bilian had been the victim of a false alarm.

Relieved, she bounced into the shed, followed by Wenqian carrying her moped. He then returned to the muddy road to fetch his bike.

Qiukui was calculating. The shed was not even as big as a bed mat, and there was just enough room to sit down. If you wanted to lie down you would have to simulate a dried shrimp. With Bilian sitting on the tattered mat, its thick layer of straw underneath and her moped by her side, there was no room left.

Carrying his bike on his shoulders, Wenqian poked his head in to have a look and stood in the doorway.

"You take shelter here, Bilian," he said. "I'm going on home."

"No, don't go!" Bilian cried out. "I'm afraid."

"This shed can't hold two people."

"Then let's stand side by side."

Stepping into the shed, Wenqian suddenly held his breath. In the torrential rain earlier, he had had no time to look at her. Now he was able to catch a glimpse. Her permed hair straggling over her shoulders, she was wearing a bright terylene shirt with a high neck and short sleeves, which clung to her body to reveal her narrow brassiere. Her cream-coloured tapered slacks seemed glued to her legs and her high-heeled white sandals were covered in mud. She was not the Bilian of three years ago, but more like a heroine in a romantic film who had walked down from the screen into this heavy rain.

"You'd better sit down again," Wenqian urged. "You'll get tired standing like that. I'll stand guard for you by the door." He leaned against the shed's front post, half of his body exposed to the rain.

"Mind you don't catch cold."

"Summer rain won't do you any harm. This is like having a shower."

"Put on my raincoat then."

The bright pink raincoat was too small for him and he placed it over his head.

The rain gathered strength and splattered endlessly, arousing feelings of loneliness and confusion.

"Wenqian. . . ." Bilian called softly. "They say . . . you have a girlfriend . . . in the college?"

"Nothing of the sort."

"Hmph, don't try to hide the truth from me! Her father's a senior cadre."

"You must have seen too many love films and learned how to cook up stories."

"Is there a girl in love with you?"

"I don't think so."

"And you haven't taken a fancy to anyone?"

"I never even think about it."

"Well, a man has to get married after all, and you're not too young any more."

"I'm up to my neck in lessons. I'm really too busy for romance. Besides, I have to gather grass to sell."

"How many more years to go before you graduate?"

"One."

"What are you planning to do after graduation?"

"I wanted to start work as soon as possible, but our department director wants me to continue studying for a master's degree."

"Oh, so you're like a sesame stalk, blossoming notch by notch!" He sensed jealousy in her voice. "You're going up step by step and won't think of us country people any more."

"I'll never change my ways as long as I live." He hung the raincoat over a rafter and made for the willow grove close by.

The rain gradually subsided. Bilian stepped outside to find Wenqian returning carrying a bundle of wistaria vines.

"What are they for, Wenqian?"

"To deck out this 'upright chicken coop'," he said, smiling, "and beautify the environment."

A sullen look flashed across her face as she asked again, "You still can't forget Qiukui?"

Looking down, he replied after a pause, "Of all of us who grew up together, she's the one who's . . . suffered most."

"Let me give you a hand." She put on her raincoat and came out to help.

One after another, she straightened out the vines and passed them to Wenqian as he buried their roots by hand at the foot of the gables and by the back wall. Then he pulled them up onto the roof.

In no time at all the prison-like shed was transformed into a bridal sedan-chair.

4

Qiukui was the only daughter of Bold Fellow Du and Erduo, but both her parents disliked her because she was a girl and had been born in a sheep year, thus violating a local taboo.

According to a bad old custom still prevailing along the banks of the canal, a girl born in the year of the sheep or the tiger, no matter how pretty, would cost her parents dearly in her trousseau even if she were married out as "substandard goods". Those born in the year of the sheep are fated to poverty and those in the year of the tiger are fierce. Who would be willing to take in a poor sheep or a fierce tiger? The sheep-year-born creatures are again divided into three categories. Those born in spring, when sheep have grass shoots to eat, are thought of as having some possible way out of their poverty and so are placed in the middle category. Those born in summer and autumn, when the grasses are lush and the sheep fat, belong to the first category and are described as "fortune in poverty". Those born in winter, when it is cold and the earth is frozen and the grasses withered, will live in abject poverty and are naturally considered the lowest category. Even to this day some people still believe in this nonsense.

Qiukui happened to be born on that very day of the nineteenth solar term — the Beginning of Winter in a sheep year and, even worse, at *weishi,* the period from 1 p.m. to 3 p.m., which is considered the exact point at which winter sets in. Upset by this terrible timing, the Du couple refused to accept the fact and named their girl Qiukui — Autumn Sunflower — deceiving both themselves and others. But, with guilty consciences, they were uneasy whenever they thought about it and were permanently depressed.

If Qiukui had been an only child, Erduo would have had to love her, since she was, after all, her own flesh and blood. Who would have thought that only a year later she would have had a son by the lover with whom she kept watch in the shed. The boy became her priceless treasure. Misfortune henceforth befell Qiukui. Because her fortune and her brother's were mutually destructive, her mother chose the name Iron Lock for her brother and detested her even more.

Iron Lock was like a gold egg placed high atop his parents' heads and Qiukui, as well as receiving her parents' contempt, was bullied and humiliated by this brother. Ever since childhood, they were treated differently. All the good food in the family — the sesame oil, wheat flour, eggs, melons and fruit — was given only to the boy; Qiukui did not have even a mouthful. As the old song *Little Cabbage Blighted in the Field*, which is popular in areas round Beijing, goes: ". . . Brother eats noodles, I drink soup. Holding my bowl I stare at it with tears in my eyes. . . ." It tells how a stepmother mistreats the daughter of an ex-wife. But Qiukui and Iron Lock were born of the same mother. During the three famine years, when the villagers dined in the brigade's mess hall, Iron Lock scooped out the thick goodness from the porridge that was brought back. All Qiukui got was sweet potato-leaf broth. Driven by hunger, she went with Qian'er to the woods to hunt birds, catch fish and shrimps in the river, wild water chestnuts in the grass and pick wild jujubes on the sand-banks to fill her stomach. Acting as a maidservant to her brother, she had to take him out to play when she was only four. If anything was against the boy's wishes he would kick or bite her and she dared not hit back. Whenever her mother heard the boy crying, she would give her a good hiding with a broom. When he went to school shouldering his small satchel, she had to carry a wicker basket to gather food for their pigs by the river or grass for their sheep, wearing shabby clothes abandoned by her brother. Never having been to school, she didn't know how to read and write. Other girls in Flower Street had some amount of schooling but she was the exception, sent by her mother at the age of eleven to earn workpoints in the production team. After working in the fields she then had to gather bundles of firewood. She was also forced to go back and forth dozens of times to fill the water jar early in the morning and water their small vegetable patch every evening, carrying two large wooden pails on a shoulder pole, stopping to catch her breath three times on each trip.

Standing up to the hard work whatever the weather, she was a strong girl by the age of sixteen, as tall as her mother and could earn workpoints as an able-bodied labourer. As she was not given to preening and never picked and chose in work, the village women were all fond of her. Since to her, her home was as cold as an icebox and the field as warm as a brazier, she liked to get up at dawn or work an extra shift at night so she could avoid the hateful looks of her parents and her brother. Extra shifts also meant more workpoints;

Erduo was pleased to let the bird out of the cage, but she was too greedy to bear in mind that sorghum fields and pitch-black nights were dangerous for young women.

In the village there was a boy of poor-peasant origin by the name of An Tianbao. When An Tianbao was a child, his father had been press-ganged by the Kuomintang and then, less than three months later, captured by the People's Liberation Army, which he subsequently joined. In a battle to take an important city, one of his arms had been blown off while trying to scale the outer wall. He was awarded a first class merit citation and demobilized as a second-grade disabled veteran, drawing a pension from the county civil administration section every month. A hot-tempered person with a strong sense of justice, he was loyal to his friends, willing to risk his life for them, and ready to help the weak. During the chaos of 1966, it made his heart ache to hear that a veteran senior officer had been labelled a "Cliquist", beaten, and paraded in public. He raged against this and was consequently beaten to death, leaving no end of trouble to his family. As a result, his son thus became a blacklisted "son of a bitch". No girl would have him even though he was handsome and as strong as an ox.

But men are after all different from plants; no one can live without love. Tianbao quietly lost his heart to Qiukui.

Brought up surrounded by humiliation, Qiukui by nature never looked down on or bullied anyone. She treated Tianbao as her elder brother. He was eight years her senior, good at farm work, and had a gentle disposition. Never had she thought of him in any other way, nor was she wary of him.

Channel digging, dike building, wheat harvesting and brick making are four tiring jobs that need skill. Qiukui was strong enough to do them but not particularly quickly or steadily. So Tianbao took her in hand and taught her how. The girl was unaware that when she squatted down or bent over, Tianbao would, from time to time, take a furtive glance down her unbuttoned collar at her full, round breasts, since she wore only a loose-fitting army jacket left by her brother and faded from washing.

One moonless night there were a few young people on late shift watering the paddy fields by the river bank. Qiukui was the only girl. Since Tianbao was one of the targets of discipline, he had to turn up to every night shift.

None of those young men had any real intention of working. They just came to build up a few workpoints. All they had to do was to keep the irrigation ditches from overflowing and open up new ditches to each field. They divided themselves into two groups; one stayed behind to look after the work, while the other crept into the vegetable garden at the edge of the village to steal cucumbers and tomatoes. Then, following a low whistle, they would slip into the dense willow grove, eat their fill and, stretching out their limbs, lie down to have a sound sleep. Tianbao, helped by Qiukui, had to bustle about attending to the water pump and making his rounds on the irrigation channel.

It is certainly difficult staying up and working all night. Exhausted, you fall asleep like a felled log. Soon, thunderous snoring was heard from the distant willow grove. Qiukui couldn't hold out either and yawned continuously. His heart aching for her, Tianbao told her to find somewhere to get a little sleep. "That's awfully kind of you, Brother Tianbao!" she laughed. With this, she planted her spade in the edge of the channel and started off, a plastic sheet under her arm. She took the winding path along the river bank and found a patch of white sandy ground amidst some osier bushes at a bend in the river.

Her clothes were caked with sweat and so, under the cover of night, she took a bath in the river and also gave her things a good scrub. Back on the bank, she spread them over the osiers to dry. It was the height of summer, and the midnight air was hot and still. There was not even a hint of rain and the river breeze carried no moisture. Her clothes would dry before dawn. She fetched an armful of dried leaves from the sorghum field and spread them on the sandy ground. The plastic sheet covering most of her body, she lay down and peacefully went to sleep.

In the meantime, Tianbao, agitated, sat by the river keeping watch on the water pump. On other night shifts, when girls and married women worked together, he did not have the courage to move closer to Qiukui. Now she was alone it was a good opportunity for him to pour out his heart. But, afraid that he would stir up a hornets' nest, he rose to his feet and sat down again many times, unable to make up his mind.

A slight breeze swept across the osiers and grass on the bank of the river. Then, suddenly, he saw a dark lump drifting down river. He reached out to catch it. To his surprise it was Qiukui's army jacket. His heart thumped wildly at the thought that he might actually have an excuse to start a conversation with her. This golden opportunity could not be lost. Straightening his back, he jumped up to look for Qiukui, the dripping jacket in hand.

He finally reached the white sandy ground at the river bend. As he moved closer, a white figure immediately came into view. The plastic sheet covering Qiukui's body was clean and transparent. His heart missed a beat and, rooted to the ground, he felt his throat contract as he stared blankly for a time before stuttering, "Qiukui, your jacket must have fallen into the river. . . ."

The sleeping girl remained motionless.

Waiting a minute, he decided to wring out the wet jacket and hang it up before he left. Shaking the jacket after squeezing it, he woke Qiukui up. Though as tall as her mother, she was as timid as her father. Still in a daze, she caught sight of a massive dark figure and cried out in alarm.

Tianbao quickly threw the jacket down and raced away, stumbling now and again, vanishing into the darkness.

Qiukui's shouting brought forth no response, for all the young men were dead to the world. Throwing them into a pot of hot soup wouldn't have woken them up. Nobody came to her rescue.

Qiukui, frightened out of her wits, gradually calmed down. Rubbing her eyes, she thought that she'd had a nightmare. Putting on the wet jacket and dry trousers, she took the same path back to the channel wondering why the trousers had dried but not the jacket?

"Brother Tianbao, I dreamed that a tiger wanted to

eat me. . . ." she said as she approached the water pump.

But Tianbao was nowhere to be found.

The young man was afraid that Qiukui would lodge an accusation against him and that he would be labelled a "bad element" and beaten and paraded through the streets. He would have no way of staying on there. Remembering that in the past people usually fled to somewhere east of Shanhaiguan when they had stirred up trouble, he rushed home, took some money and grain coupons, as well as his father's certificate of merit and his household registration booklet, and escaped that same night.

Several days passed before it dawned on Qiukui that what she had dreamed of was probably not a large tiger but the kind-hearted Tianbao. She regretted that she had shouted so rashly and made him become a fugitive. For many days after that she secretly felt sad.

After graduating from senior middle school, Yu Qian'er returned to the village and took over Tianbao's job.

Honest and straightforward, he never took advantage of others. A novice, he was slow and unskilled in his work although strong enough to cope with it. By then Qiukui had become a veteran. It was her turn to take Qian'er in hand and teach him the skills. Two years his senior, she treated him as a younger bookworm-ish brother, not eager to marry or to try and peek inside her jacket.

The pampered Hua Bilian was fond of being in the limelight and found herself ostracized by the girls in the village. By contrast, Qiukui was on intimate terms with all of them. So Bilian kept in with her, giving her two brightly-coloured cast-off suits and a second-hand violet scarf. But, as she was plumper than Bilian, the clothes were too tight for her. Seeing the curves of her own body in the mirror, she was bashful and covered her face with her hands, exclaiming sheepishly, "*Aiya,* I can't go out like this!"

"Qiukui, I always thought you were such a wallflower!" Bilian teased. "Tell me, who's going to be the lucky boy?"

"Who would want an illiterate like me?" Qiukui seemed upset. "What's more, my mum wants me to earn workpoints for another few years. . . ."

Bilian rolled her eyes and then suddenly giggled, "You and Qian'er are made for one another."

Qiukui, confused, blushed. After a long pause, she shook her head and said with a wry smile, "He can't afford to marry me. My mother wants at least eight hundred yuan for betrothal gifts alone."

Bilian had made the suggestion in jest but it had struck a chord in Qiukui's heart. From then on she thought always of Qian'er. When they were on night shift watering the paddy fields, she went out of her way to urge Qian'er to take a rest on the white sandy ground in the bushes at the bend in the river. Time flew and 1977 began, but Qian'er remained unresponsive.

But just then Siji's wife, Aunt Hua, came to act as a matchmaker for Qiukui.

Not long after Aunt Hua married Siji, the gossip about the affair between Erduo and Siji found its way to her ears. For more than twenty years since, she and Erduo had been rivals. With her guilty conscience, Erduo had to keep Aunt Hua at arm's length. Now

Aunt Hua was making a visit, and in consideration of the fact that she was being deferred to, Erduo, all smiles, invited her guest in.

Bargaining over the marriage issue ensued. Erduo's pampered son Iron Lock, now known as Little Iron Du, had grown up and was a prize catch. Planning to marry out her own daughter in return for a daughter-in-law, Erduo demanded 1,000 yuan as a betrothal price when they began their discussion, as well as 18,000 grey bricks and 3,500 red tiles. The price was indeed exorbitant. Beyond Erduo's expectations, the matchmaker agreed quickly, fully complying with her conditions. With a few words, they clinched the deal.

On hearing the news, Qiukui was upset. Abandoning her work in the paddy fields, she went in the middle of the night to rap at Qian'er's back window.

Qian'er was working on his lessons for the college entrance examinations. After what seemed like an eternity, he raised his head, "Who's that?"

"I. . . ." Qiukui replied, a sob choking her throat. "My mum's decided to exchange me for 1,000 yuan and 18,000 bricks and 3,500 tiles. . . . Please, save me!"

Qian'er emerged and said firmly, "I'll go with you to the commune office to ask for protection."

"I'm afraid my mother will skin me alive. . . ."

"What else can I do for you then?"

"But you . . . you're my sweetheart!" She threw herself into his arms. "Can you bear to see me dragged off to a living hell?"

"I couldn't produce ten yuan even if I went through my boxes and chests, and I've got hardly any bricks and tiles even if I pull down my house. . . ." Then, with determination, he bit his lip and continued, "Try to get it delayed a little until I get into university. Your mother won't ask me for money then."

"Bless you!" Qiukui's tears soaked his chest.

However, Qian'er failed his examination and the young man came with the required sum, the bricks and the tiles, and bought Qiukui, taking her away like a sheep before the unsuccessful candidate's helpless eyes.

Several months after Qiukui's marriage, her husband was arrested and brought to trial. He was not only sentenced to ten years in prison but was also required to pay compensation for what he had unlawfully taken. Qiukui was three months pregnant when her divorce came through and had an induced abortion at the commune hospital when she returned to Flower Street.

By then her parents had built a big, new five-roomed house with the bricks and tiles they had received as her betrothal gifts. The 1,000 yuan had been squandered by Little Iron Du, who frittered away the ten yuan banknotes, one after another, on his girlfriends. He still had not obtained a wife.

When, the following year, Qian'er was admitted to college, he took the admission notice to show Qiukui, never imagining he would bump into a crestfallen Tianbao emerging from the Dus' after meeting with a rebuff.

Tianbao had fled to the northeast and worked as a temporary labourer on a state farm where he had learned a lot from an old agricultural technician and saved several hundred yuan. Now he had returned in glory. Shortly after putting down his luggage, he had heard about Qiukui's misfortune and had gone without delay to her house to make an offer of marriage. Erduo immediately agreed and only asked him for half the sum — five hundred yuan — to marry off her daughter. Qiukui however had hardened her heart and simply refused to marry again. Her mother, angry, drove her out.

As he was planning to build a new house, Siji took Qiukui in to look after the old house for him.

Over the past two years Qiukui's contracted field had been like a magic tree that sheds coins when shaken. Every year she made a profit and soon became well-off. But she was still too timid to keep watch by herself in the field at night and too ashamed to publicly sell watermelons in the market. Little Iron Du saw the advantage of undertaking these jobs. He sent his hound to keep watch in the field and took thirty per cent of the profits from selling the products.

The rain began to subside, and Qiukui could not sit still any longer, worried that her watermelons might burst open in the sun after becoming waterlogged.

Now that she had a full purse and was her own mistress, she tried to retrieve the youth she had lost. Beaming with satisfaction she walked proudly, wearing a red printed tunic under a green raincoat, and a pair of galoshes. In the distance she spotted a man and a woman pulling wistaria vines over her small shed. Her hand shading her eyes, she recognized Wenqian and Bilian, and hurriedly took cover in the sorghum field. She was suddenly seized by a great sadness and began to cry.

Wenqian carrying the moped and Bilian the bike, the pair walked past the sorghum field chatting and laughing without noticing Qiukui. But their image remained with Qiukui for a long time.

5

They were now a short distance from the entrance to the village.

Flower Street was a small village with several dozen households scattered along its three streets, each of which was separated by a creek. Along the banks of these creeks scrub brush had been cut down and replaced by fruit trees — peach, plum, apricot, pear and apple. Around the village clustered thick groves of poplar, willow, mulberry, date, elm and locust trees. From the outside you could not glimpse a figure by day nor could you see any lamplight by night.

Wenqian lived in the village's front street and Bilian in the back, and they had not been in touch with one another for years.

"You take the moped home, Wenqian. . . ." Bilian halted, hitting on an idea. "Let's make an exchange."

Unaware of what she was driving at, Wenqian laughed, "You can't run a moped unless you've got the money. I couldn't afford it."

"But you rescued it in the rain. I wouldn't ask you for money."

"That sounds like highway robbery."

"No, I mean it," Bilian declared, tenderness and love in her eyes. "You have to travel one hundred and forty-four *li* from home to your college and back every day. Every moment is precious to you. You'll save two hours on the moped. It's only eight *li* from here to my factory, so I could get there and back earlier than you even if I took a broken cart pulled by an old bull."

"I'm not high enough to own a moped." Wenqian

made a wry face. "What's more, I don't have enough pull to get the petrol."

"Don't worry about that!" she assured him, smiling broadly. "A lot of the drivers on the north-south route are friends of Little Iron Du's. He can get enough to open a filling station."

"Petrol mixed with theft might make the environment even more polluted," Wenqian said, half-joking, half-serious. "I advise you not to ride your moped any more. Its wheels are turned by a foul wind."

"You're as stubborn as a mule — you won't budge an inch even if you're beaten!" Bilian sulked, arrogance and petulance creeping into the corners of her eyes. "You have to make the exchange whether you like it or not!"

She got on the bike and made for the village, leaving Wenqian behind as her porter.

Crossing the small bridge and the two creeks she dismounted before reaching her own home.

The Huas were the richest family in Flower Street. Its three members earned incomes from three different sources. With her wages plus bonus, Bilian got more than seventy-seven yuan every month in the shirt factory while her father, a grade-seven worker in charge of the commune's capital construction team, got over a hundred with a bonus and various allowances. Her mother's income every year was not a small sum either, since she raised chickens, fish and martens at home. She also got extra money every month acting as a matchmaker. In recent years, as the peasants had become better off, the sum for betrothal gifts had increased accordingly and matchmakers consequently re-adjusted the fee for their services. Aunt Hua earned a considerable figure from hers. With their accumulated wealth they had built a large, tile-roofed brick house consisting of ten rooms and a courtyard enclosed by a brick wall. The arch over the gate-way was decorated with an impressed copper coin pattern and the two red door panels with their brass knockers were in the style of the big mansions of old Beijing. The place would certainly have given a start to city dwellers living in cramped rooms, who would wonder if they were seeing a mirage.

There was an even more astonishing sight inside. Facing the gate was a large screen wall with a huge, brightly-coloured picture of spring flowers, painted in the style of the Yangliuqing New Year pictures, by an artist who had been invited from the county cultural centre and paid a substantial fee. Behind it was an artificial hillock with green rocks and emerald mosses. Under the canopy on the hillock was a row of eighteen small, exquisite marten cages. When the martens grew big enough, the male ones would be worth one hundred and twenty yuan each and the females ninety-six. That was another source of income. The most marvellous thing, however, was the fish pond, about one *mu* large, which had round lotus leaves unfolding over dark green water and sending forth a delicate fragrance. Only crucian carp were raised in it. On New Year's Day or on other festivals, when the big ones reached two to three *jin* in weight, and the smaller ones five to six ounces, they were sent to the market to sell. At the base of the eastern and western walls stood two rows of chicken coops with two hundred hens which altogether produced about a hundred eggs every day.

The ten red-crested cocks were like a chorus when they flapped their wings and crowed.

When asked how much the building had cost, the host would smile without saying a word, for he was a master mason with nearly a hundred apprentices to call on. Once he issued an order, they would all come over to pitch in without asking for a cent. Besides, he also had pull at the brickyards, the kilns and the carpenters, all of which conveniently opened their doors to him. This explained how his large house could rise up from the earth in what seemed like no time at all.

A rumour had long been spread that Siji would one day get into trouble, although at the moment he could travel through any pass. But he remained unconcerned, believing that, in his later years, he had found good luck. What sin had he, a man of nearly sixty, committed by flaunting his wealth and enjoying a happy life for a few years?

These few days he was at home on leave. Cooped up indoors by the rain, he sat cross-legged on the *kang*, playing cards with his wife to while away the time. Seeing through the window that the rain was petering out, he threw down the cards and went outside to limber up.

Hawk-nosed and vulture-eyed, he was a tall fellow with long arms, a shiny shaved head and a moustache. His dress was compatible with his status as the wealthiest man in Flower Street and gave him the air of the veteran craftsman: a front-buttoning jacket made of Hangzhou silk. He didn't like pullovers, and his sleeveless white cotton undershirt was also in the same style. His loose black silk trousers were tied around his ankles, and on his feet he wore a pair of black cloth shoes with two decorative lines running from the tip to the throat.

Ten years his junior, his wife had been a beauty when young. Although over forty, she still did not look her age. Her arched brows, bright, intelligent eyes and ruddy lips still retained their old charm, and her hair, still completely black, was in an elongated bun. She saw her husband as a tree propping up the sky and herself as an ivy twining round it. She followed close on his heels and they stood by the pond watching the fish playing beneath the lotus leaves.

"Dad, mum," called Bilian sweetly as she came around the screen wall.

"*Aiyo,* why did you come back in this heavy rain?" her mother cried affectionately, seeing her soaked to the skin. "You'll ruin your health like that!"

"I missed the two of you!" Bilian giggled, pushing the bike into the yard.

"Where's your moped?"

"I've exchanged it with someone." Bilian carried the bike into the shed and locked the door.

"Who with?" pressed her mother. "How much did you get?"

Throwing her mother a surreptitious smile the girl replied, "With Yu Wenqian, one for one."

"What? . . ." The older woman blinked. "With that . . . Yu Qian'er?"

"He's been at college for three years now. Won't you call him by his proper name Wenqian?" The girl turned and walked into her own room.

The room was neatly furnished with a wardrobe, a dressing table, a double bed, a standard lamp and some chairs. Casting off her wet clothes, she opened the wardrobe and took out a dark green pleated skirt and a white silk blouse, both produced by her factory. Then she kicked off her mud-stained, high-heeled sandals and put on a pair of azure blue plastic slippers.

"Why should you let that Yu Qian'er get things on the cheap?" Aunt Hua yelled outside her daughter's room.

"He's called Wenqian!" Bilian laughed. "We both . . . took shelter from the rain in Qiukui's shed in her melon field. . . ."

"Did he . . . take liberties with you?" Aunt Hua was alarmed and pushed into the room.

"I intend . . . to marry him. . . ." Bilian stammered coyly, sitting on the edge of her bed.

"Why are you so stupid as to take a fancy to him?" Her mother was upset. "That three-roomed pigeon coop of his with a yard the size of your hand would suffocate you."

"Couldn't an old couple like you share five or so of your big rooms with us?" Bilian cast a sidelong glance at her mother.

"He's an ugly duckling," her mother teased. "I can't see anything lovable about him."

"That's because he always works so hard in his study." Bilian smiled. "After three years at college, he's become very clever and sounds a lot more sophisticated than he used to."

"But as a college student he'll probably go the way they say: 'In their first year, they keep to a simple and plain way of life. In their second, they pick up bourgeois habits. In their third year, they reject their working class parents.' He'll forget about you."

"I trust him."

"How much will he get after graduation?"

"Forty-six yuan a month in the first year and fifty-six from the year following. Including allowances, he'll get more than sixty."

"*Aiyo,* still a dozen yuan less than you get!"

"I'm not short of food or clothes or money. What I lack is. . . ." The girl paused, raised her head, then continued, ". . . a man who'll give me a bit more prestige."

Her mother snorted, "It's not up to me or you to make the decision. In our family your dad has the final say." With that she left, long-faced.

In the outer room, Siji was sitting watching TV in an armchair by the electric fan. His wife turned down the volume and, frowning, whispered something in his ear.

"That suits me fine!" he exclaimed, slapping his thigh. "I've placed an order for a refrigerator and a washing machine but I still feel I'm missing something important. What I need is a college graduate for a son-in-law."

Since the old man had given his consent, Aunt Hua, as though she had received an imperial edict, beamed with joy. "I'll go to the Yus after supper," she said.

"No, not you, mum!" Bilian rushed out of her room. "You can't go yourself. You've got to find someone else."

"Think about each household in Flower Street," sneered her mother, "and see if there's anyone who's a match for me as a go-between."

"Different keys for different locks," countered Bilian. Thinking for a moment, she continued, "An Tianbao is a good friend of Wenqian's. Go and ask him for help."

At that very moment there was a voice from the gate, "Aunt Hua!"

By a curious coincidence, it was An Tianbao himself, stepping into the yard with the moped.

Aunt Hua, smiling, came out to greet him, "Hello Tianbao, how is it that our moped is in your hands?"

"I met Wenqian on my way here. He asked me to return it to Bilian and get his bike back." Tianbao usually had a glib tongue, but suddenly he stuttered, "Auntie, I've come to ask a favour of you. . . ."

"Come on in and have a seat!" Aunt Hua's face was wreathed in smiles. "You need to plant two poles to build a fence, right? As the saying goes, neighbours are dearer than distant relatives. There's no one who doesn't need help from others."

6

Tianbao was still single.

He had built a three-roomed house with the money he brought back from the northeast. When his father's mishandled case was redressed and he got eight hundred yuan of retroactive pension money from the county authorities, he added two more rooms and built an enclosure wall. Crying over a husband who had been persecuted to death, and missing a son with a broken heart, his mother had died of grief three years after he had fled. Now his large, desolate compound was badly in need of a female presence.

Supported by the villagers, he was elected leader of

the rice and wheat team, made up of a score of people who had contracted three hundred *mu* of land to grow rice and wheat and harvested 1,800 *jin* in two crops. They had also taken on two creeks and now produced nearly 10,000 *jin* of fish a year. In the slack seasons they made ropes, and wove straw curtains and hats to sell. The profits and bonus each member received equalled Bilian's income.

It wasn't that no one had wanted to act as a matchmaker for him. Aunt Hua had approached him a dozen times but each time he just shook his head without saying a single word. Nobody could guess what was in his mind.

Tianbao's heart was as clear as a mirror except for one single black spot. He couldn't think of that moonless night eight years earlier, when he had frightened Qiukui, without feeling guilty. It seemed that Qiukui's misfortune in marriage was also somehow his fault. Consequently, he was resolved to marry her and bring this miserable girl a sweeter life.

However, Qiukui was as cold as ice, and gave him a wide berth. All he could do was wait for the day when spring returned to her heart.

With money in their pockets, the other young men in his team vied to purchase wrist watches, bikes, TV sets, electric fans and the like, but Tianbao spent over seven hundred yuan on a refrigerator and over two hundred on a washing machine. With these appliances, he could cook ten days' food at once and ease the laundry burden. But they were still no substitute for a woman in the house. The cuckoos landed on the pear tree outside the wall as usual with a cry which sounded like "A bachelor's life is hard".

The village was so small that he and Qiukui ran into each other almost every day.

Qiukui knew only that growing watermelons was profitable but was unaware that it needed skill. She stealthily watched and mechanically copied her neighbours bedding, fertilizing, sowing and watering their crops. But when the sprouts sprang out of the earth, she did not know what to do next, for she couldn't follow this stage in the process just by watching others. She went to her father for advice. He gave her a few tips but was too busy to do the job for her.

One day, as she sat at the edge of the field worrying about what to do, Tianbao came over to see what was bothering her.

Having established the reason, he grinned, "What a happy coincidence!" He rolled up his sleeves. "I'm semi-expert at growing watermelons."

"But you weren't even ten when watermelons became extinct in our village." She refused to believe him.

"Yes, but I learned how from someone when I worked at that farm in the northeast. He was a real Shen Nong,* that old man, but it's a pity that I only learned the basics."

"Since you know how, why haven't you contracted a watermelon field?" Women are exacting; Qiukui was still dubious.

"You can't feed people on melon juice alone." Tianbao laughed. "I prefer to produce two crops a year, rice and wheat."

Any doctor is worth a try if you're critically ill. Qiukui had no choice but to ask Tianbao for help. As they

* The ancient Chinese god of agriculture.

moved along the furrows Tianbao told her what to do, their heads together, their bodies close. Qiukui was now like a thoroughly ripe fruit, her bosom fuller than eight years earlier. But this time Tianbao did not look sideways, nor try to steal a glance at her body.

When the harvest season came, Qiukui's field was full of watermelons, bigger even than her father's, thin-rinded and delicious. She bought two bottles of liquor and a box of cakes and waited in the field for Tianbao to arrive.

"Brother Tianbao," she greeted him, holding the gift out with both hands, "I should have shared the profits fifty-fifty with you, but I knew you wouldn't agree to that. Please accept this gift as a sign of my gratitude."

Mistakenly thinking that the time was ripe, Tianbao, his forehead dripping with sweat, refused to accept the gift and said haltingly, "Qiukui, we two. . . ."

"Oh, off with you!" Qiukui shouted, as her amicable expression froze. Having got the snub he'd asked for, Tianbao, miserable, left.

For the next year Qiukui again contracted a melon field, assuming that she had learned all she needed to know and did not have to ask for any more help from Tianbao. Unexpectedly, there was a lot more rain than usual after the wheat harvest. Qiukui was compelled to turn to Tianbao once again. Tianbao responded, paying no heed to the previous occasion when he'd been cold-shouldered.

As soon as the rain had finished Tianbao went to inspect his team's paddy fields. Then, worried about Qiukui's watermelons, he made a detour to her field to have a look. To his surprise, he found Qiukui sitting in her shed, which had been spruced up like a bridal sedan-chair, her eyes as red as a pair of fresh peaches in May.

"One gets admitted to college and puts an end to all those years of suffering. . . ." she whimpered. "The other's been her parents' beloved daughter since childhood, always lucky. Only I . . . I was born under an unlucky star. Even after I die, I will just be a forlorn homeless ghost wandering in bitterness." She buried her face in her hands and sobbed.

Only when Tianbao caught sight of Wenqian and Bilian walking side by side on the muddy yellow road did he realize what had happened. Bracing himself, he strode into the shed and consoled her, "There, there, don't cry, Qiukui. Let's work together to change things. Happiness comes after suffering. Take a step forward and enter my house!"

Qiukui looked up, startled at first, and then shook her head. "No, you're a person of exceptional ability. You must have been possessed by demons if you've taken a fancy to a shameful, ill-fated woman like me."

"But I've been in love with you for a long time. . . ." Tianbao stammered, the sweat standing out on his forehead. "Eight years ago in the grove on the river bank that night, I . . . wanted to say this . . . to you."

Qiukui's sobs increased. Seeing that she hadn't absolutely rejected his offer, Tianbao felt confident and rushed back to the village to look for a matchmaker. He met Wenqian at the entrance to the village and went to Siji's house with the moped.

Aunt Hua invited him in and before he had even finished his request, she congratulated him, "It's genuinely a happy match! You can depend on me. My word on it!"

"Better not to ask for trouble!" Bilian stared at her mother. "By trickery and force you made Qiukui marry that murderer and ruined her last time. She's certainly got a grudge against you."

"If Aunt Hua doesn't take this up, who else is qualified to?" Tianbao asked anxiously, wringing his hands.

Pointing to herself, Bilian smiled, "I'll do the job in my dad's name."

"Fine, fine, fine!" Aunt Hua exclaimed listlessly, her face flushed. "Looks like I've got a successor indeed!"

Bilian was anxious. She gulped down her meal and hurried to their old house to find Qiukui.

Qiukui usually bolted the door and went to bed at dusk, without seeing anyone. When Bilian approached the house, she had just returned from the field and was driving the chickens into their coop. After checking that they were all there she would bolt the gate.

Bilian helped her to shoo the chickens into the yard. It was clean and neat, with a well-established grapevine and some fruit-laden trees. The main hall was locked, the windows on the west wing were shut, and moxa coils had been lit to smoke out mosquitoes. The stove was cold, for Qiukui did not usually cook supper for herself. Her meal consisted of a cold steamed bun.

Over the enclosure wall was Bold Fellow Du's courtyard, from which a hubbub of voices mingled with the smashing of pots and bowls was heard.

"What's going on with that old couple?" Bilian asked in a low voice.

"My mum has given Little Iron the family savings

to pay his gambling debts." Qiukui sighed. "Spare the rod and spoil the child. My mother's very partial to my brother and is paying for it in this life."

Putting an arm round Qiukui's shoulders, Bilian whispered, "My dad has sent me to ask if he could act as a go-between for you."

"Uncle Siji's a little late," Qiukui said with a frosty look. "I've already found someone myself."

"Who?" Bilian was taken aback.

"Guess." Qiukui's eyes shone teasingly.

"I can't. . . ."

"One of the best in the village. . . ." Qiukui left the sentence unfinished.

"Who? . . . Who?" Bilian's face was as white as a sheet.

Qiukui finally disclosed the riddle's solution. "An Tianbao."

"Oh dear!" Bilian felt as though a great weight had been lifted from her. "You must have read my father's mind."

"And you and your father are satisfied with that?" A rigid smile was suspended at the corners of Qiukui's mouth.

"Congratulations!" said Bilian exultantly.

Qiukui declared with a straight face, "But it'll be like drawing water with a bamboo pail – all in vain."

"Why?" Anxiety gripped Bilian once again.

With a wry smile Qiukui explained, "Little Iron has gambled away all the family savings and my mother will certainly ask Tianbao for a sum twice as much as before as a betrothal gift. I don't want to be sold once again."

"Well, fight it then," retorted Bilian. "My mother

tried to arrange my marriage too, but I defeated her plans one after another."

"But I dare not. . . ." Qiukui was overcome by a feeling of misery.

"Don't be afraid," Bilian declared. "My father can handle your mother. . . ." She suddenly realized she had put her foot in it. There was an abrupt silence. Both she and Qiukui knew something about the early relationship between Siji and Erduo.

Qiukui was not angry with her, however. Biting her lip for a while, she then nodded and said, "Bilian, would you please take a message to Uncle Siji. Ask him to deal with her and help me out."

7

Hua Siji swaggered through Bold Fellow Du's gate and gave a cough as loud as the first giant firecracker set off on New Year's morning.

Compared with his ten-roomed new brick house, Bold Fellow's medium-sized courtyard was hardly worthy of admiration. A narrow walkway separated it into small vegetable gardens fenced in with sorghum stalks, in which cucumber, eggplant, capsicum and green beans were grown. Little Iron and his mother could only produce these common vegetables to earn a little extra cash.

The scuffle was over; a deathly silence reigned over the pitch-black courtyard.

Responding to the cough, a sturdy figure hurried over from beneath the grape trellis. A flustered Erduo greeted the visitor.

Over fifty, her face lined, Erduo was still very strong,

able to carry two hundred *jin* sacks. She had formed the habit of sleeping in the open when keeping watch over the melon field and preferred to sleep out in the yard in order to avoid the summer heat in the stuffy house. Beneath the grape trellis a rain-soaked door panel served as her bed, a plastic sheet and a rush mat spread on top. With her thick hair bound into a haphazard bun, she was naked to the waist and wore only a pair of baggy shorts. Still boiling from the squabble, she was waving a large palm fan.

"Why, the rain's only just stopped and you're out already!" she scolded Siji, both pleased and petulant at seeing him.

According to local custom, it was essential that a sister-in-law and her husband's elder brothers use a respectful form of address to one another. Erduo was a sister-in-law whose husband was younger than Siji, and yet she was not only stripped to the waist but talked to him in an audacious manner. After a heavy rainfall, mosses as well as mushrooms appear.

"People don't visit temples without a reason," Siji replied in a carefully modulated voice. "I've taken an interest in someone's business and have to come to ask for some help."

"Well, out with it then!" Erduo stood up, hands on hips. "If something suits me, I always nod my head, but if I don't like the sound of it, I'll kick you out."

"Where's Bold Fellow?"

"On the *kang,* sleeping like a dead man," Erduo fumed. "I must have done something bad in a former life that I have the punishment of being married to this jellyfish."

"I've come to act as a go-between for An Tianbao and Qiukui," Siji declared solemnly. "You must grant me this favour."

"I gave it the nod three years ago, didn't I?" Erduo laughed. "It was only because Qiukui behaved like a broken wheel and refused to move along the lane I made for her that Tianbao's been sleeping on a cold *kang* for three years."

"And you've got the nerve to say so!" Siji flared up and continued even more sternly, "The first time you married Qiukui out, you asked for betrothal gifts; the second time you demanded money again. You're more like a trader than a mother."

"I'm not giving away an able-bodied labourer for nothing. I want a straight cash deal. Give me the money and I'll hand over my daughter."

"How much if I want to buy you?"

"Buy me and make a shrine to me in your home for your Qiao'er to worship every day. Have her kowtow to me three times in the morning and burn joss-sticks to me in the evening!" Erduo taunted him. "I'll just wait and see how much you ask from the bridegroom's side when Bilian marries."

"Not a cent," Siji assured her, thumping his chest. "On the contrary, I'll give them a thousand yuan or so."

"That's because you're marrying into a family with a higher status."

"No, I only want it to be balanced in terms of family background."

"But I have a devil of a son to take care of. You don't have to bother about him anyway. . . ." A slightly acid note was mixed with sadness in her voice. "The ten *mu* of land is contracted in the name of three family members but Little Iron never does a stroke of work. He sends his dog to keep watch over the field and pockets all the money from the sale of the watermelons. I don't begrudge the cost of the food and clothing and cigarettes which he is so fastidious about. But he's addicted to gambling, and loses two or three hundred yuan at a time. A dozen households in this village have already got TV sets, electric fans or washing machines. How can I see all of this without being jealous? He's up to his ears in debts he hasn't paid off although he's taken away our 2,000 yuan savings. I don't have a cent to my name now."

"It's your own fault for spoiling that little beast!" Siji snorted.

"Is he my son alone?" Erduo started sobbing. "I hate that father of his who only thinks about himself and keeps in the background making snide remarks." Her words were aimed at Siji.

"Pipe down!" Siji warned. "Hand him over to me and I'll straighten him out in three years and a season."

"Do you . . . mean . . . what you say?"

Siji heaved a long sigh, "Bilian's a girl and she works at a clothing factory. Her lily-white hands have never been near a clod of earth. If I don't pass on what I know to Little Iron, who else is there? Should I let outsiders have the advantage?"

"Thank you very much for your kindness, brother!" Bold Fellow Du interjected, turning on the light. He had been keeping an ear close by the window.

"Don't treat me like a stranger, you," Siji turned to

the window. "Just think of him as our son. But Erduo, you mustn't ask for money from Tianbao. If you make me angry enough, I'll take my skills to the grave with me."

"No feelings can equal the affection between father and son. Go ahead and take that rotten devil in hand!" Erduo cried, overjoyed. She gave Siji a shove despite the eavesdropper's presence.

There wasn't the slightest hint of the peasant child in Erduo's pampered son. Neither male nor female in appearance, he looked more like a goblin than a human with long sideburns, permed, curly hair, clad in a bright checked shirt and bell-bottoms. He thought he looked very stylish in his creased and greasy knocked-off clothes from the free market.

"You dirty little swine!" Siji grabbed Little Iron by the hair and spat at him.

"You old fogey, why poke your nose . . . in my business." Little Iron struggled, clenching his fists to attack.

"Your mother's already agreed!" Siji roared as his large hands gripped the boy's arm like a pair of pliers. "If you dare refuse to obey, I'll nab you and have you charged with insubordination."

With this he gave Little Iron's arm a slight twist. The boy dropped it in pain, uttering a sharp cry. An amateur orthopaedist, Siji had dislocated a joint.

After he'd dragged Little Iron home, Siji transformed the boy's appearance. The following day he took him to the capital construction team to commence his three-year-and-one-season apprenticeship for a thorough remoulding.

8

Tianbao shuttled between the front and the back of Flower Street.

Bilian accompanied him to see Qiukui, then to the Du couple next door and finally returned in triumph to Siji's.

Siji and his wife were enjoying the cool air by the fish pond with a closely-cropped and clean-shaven Little Iron sitting beside them. On the table before them lay a large watermelon and a sharp knife. They were waiting for the triumphal return of Bilian and Tianbao in order to start a melon feast.

"Uncle Siji, Aunt Hua," called out Tianbao as he came around the screen wall, bowing with every step. "I'll never forget your great kindness as long as I live!"

"We're old family friends. Cut that out or we won't be as close as before." Aunt Hua's remarks were music to the ear. "Anyway, we'll have to trouble you to run around over Bilian's marriage."

Little Iron, who was a year older than Bilian, wagged his head and teased, "Sister Bilian is a senior middle-school graduate who's seen the world in that garment factory. There's no dog watching the door in the Yu household. Why not go for yourself and tell Wenqian face to face that you love him? That would be superb!"

"Who could be as shameless as you — your skin's so thick an awl wouldn't pierce it."

Aunt Hua pulled a long face, "We country people shouldn't go too far. To cross a river you have to walk over a bridge and to climb up to the roof you have to first position the ladder."

Tianbao scratched his head. "It's my first time acting

as a matchmaker. Since you're a veteran you should pass on some of the tricks of the trade to me and tell me what to say at the Yus' house."

"It's similar to a deal in the free market." Slicing open the melon, Aunt Hua continued unthinkingly, "First you ask the price, then you bargain to get your profit."

"Mum!" Bilian cried, stamping her foot. "Love can't be bought or sold. The main thing is that we are compatible. To talk about terms and conditions is downright vulgar."

"No, we must make everything above-board," said Siji, his face taking on a grave expression. "That'll save a lot of trouble in case anybody some day changes his mind."

"You have your say first then!" Tianbao fired back.

Stroking his beard, Siji laughed, "My little finger is worth more than a Yu's waist. What interests me is that Wenqian has a lot of potential, not his meagre belongings."

"What do you say, auntie?" Tianbao turned to Aunt Hua.

"I . . . I. . . ." She tried to take her cue from her husband. "The old man is boasting and I'm not going to be mean either. I'll be perfectly content provided Wenqian is faithful to Bilian and knows how to honour this old couple."

Tianbao turned to Bilian and smiled, "You should say something too, sister."

The girl lowered her head, and fiddled with the hem of her tunic for a few minutes before opening her mouth, "There's no limit to learning. I want him to listen to the advice of his department director and sit the post-graduate exam. That way he'll be able to work in Beijing and become somebody."

"Anything else?"

". . . He should pay a bit more attention to his appearance and not lag behind the city students. Everyone is equal, aren't they? Why should we country folk be outshone?"

"Well?"

". . . I've told him that from tomorrow on he should use my moped to go to college and . . . tell him not to gather grass to sell any more. That'll hold up his work and affect his health."

"I'm an impatient sort of person," Tianbao said as he picked up a slice of watermelon. "I'm doing this matchmaking the same way I'd produce a rush crop of autumn wheat. See you later!" He headed off.

There was a shortcut to the front street but he took the path skirting around the enclosure of Siji's old house instead. He halted at Qiukui's gate and listened carefully, but heard no sound from inside. The courtyard was quiet, disturbed only by the rustling of the peach tree's leaves. Reluctantly, he walked away.

Crossing two small bridges, he arrived at Wenqian's creek-facing house. With its tiny willow-fenced courtyard, it was too small to be compared to Siji's mansion. However, the large old willow by the gate was a favourable omen, its foliage sheltering half the courtyard like an umbrella. The tree had withered and then revived several times. For the last two years it had been green and luxuriant. Wenqian's father had died when he was three. A fortune-teller had alleged that the boy would destroy his mother five years later unless he arranged for a godmother to replace her as a victim. They were being asked to do the impossible. Where could they find such a martyr? But a fortune-teller can always find a way. Pointing at the willow tree, he said the godmother was already standing at the gate. So with three offerings of joss-sticks, a cup of wine and two feet of red cloth draped over a branch for the ceremony, the boy knelt down three times and made nine kowtows to acknowledge the tree as his godmother. Thus it seemed that the tree felt a concern for the mother and son; it kept them in its shade in the summer and provided firewood for them in winter. Many a time when they had nothing in their pot, they went hungry rather than sell it.

Approaching the tree, Tianbao saw a light in the west wing. Wenqian was doing his homework, while his mother was sewing beneath the window outside.

As his was a one-man family, Tianbao often felt lonely. Having spent many years with the old agronomist at the state farm in the northeast, he liked the company of educated people. That was why he frequently visited the Yus. But he never disturbed Wenqian when he was busy, and only chatted with his mother.

"Auntie, Wenqian," he yelled, stepping into the courtyard, "I've come to congratulate you, and you should do the same to me."

"Why are you showing off like that?" Wenqian's mother asked, handing him a rush cushion. "What good news have you brought?"

"I've become engaged to Qiukui!" Tianbao announced, radiant, then added with pride, "And I've acted as a go-between for Wenqian."

Unable to keep still, he stood up and grabbed the

window ledge to look inside the room, his eyes fastened on Wenqian.

The tiny room held only a narrow *kang*, a table and a chair. Perspiring profusely, Wenqian was working out maths problems under the lamp. On the wall facing the window was a reproduction of the oil painting *Father*, by the young artist Luo Zhongli. Since his father had died very early and there were no photos of him, Wenqian could not remember his appearance. This oil painting, which he had seen in a magazine last April, a portrait of a peasant who had survived the hardships of the old society, had brought tears to his eyes. It seemed to be the image of his father he had seen hundreds of times in his dreams. So he had cut it out and pasted it on the wall facing his seat. When occasionally he slackened in his work, he would feel ashamed as soon as his eyes fell on the deeply wrinkled face.

"Whose daughter is it?" the old woman was eager to find out.

"Oh, you've seen her around," Tianbao tried to keep mother and son guessing. "She's a girl from a wealthy family in our village."

"I'm a straightforward woman, and don't like beating about the bush." Wenqian's mother was impatient. "Tell me her name. Quickly. Don't keep me guessing."

Tianbao pursed his lips, "Your son already knows perfectly well."

"Who is it, Wenqian?" She tapped on the window.

"Hua Bilian!" replied Wenqian, throwing down his pen. "But I don't want to have anything to do with that family."

"Why? Now that you're a college student, you turn your nose up at them?" Tianbao loyally defended the

Huas since he was grateful to them and wanted to return their kindness. "You won't find any other girl as good looking, clever and skilled, nor with as considerable a trousseau as Hua Bilian!"

"That father of hers is insatiably greedy and her mother's a trader in girls!" Wenqian grumbled.

Tianbao had talked himself hoarse with Wenqian's mother, but her son stuck to his guns. At his wits' end, Tianbao sullenly returned to the Hua family to report the outcome.

However, when he saw Bilian pacing back and forth at the gate anxiously awaiting good news from him, he couldn't bear the thought of pouring cold water on her hopes. He immediately forced a smile, and tried to look happy.

"What did Wenqian...?" she asked uneasily.

"He said he had to think it over first," Tianbao hedged and hurried in.

Siji and his wife were in the courtyard watching Little Iron repair the moped under the bright lamplight. The scoundrel had become friendly with a few drivers and, apart from stealing petrol for Bilian's moped, had also learned how to repair motor cycles. Now he was flaunting his abilities in front of the old couple.

"Tianbao's back!" Aunt Hua hailed. "That mother and son must be grinning from ear to ear."

"Wenqian's a good son-in-law. He asked me to tell you. . . ." Tianbao decided to falsify his report, "He's a college student and knows more about the policies of the government than we do. He said that those who benefit themselves at the expense of the public interest would in future be severely punished; to act as a matchmaker violates the new marriage law and such people will be convicted on charges of trading in human beings. It's not a laughing matter. You two had better trim your sails, or you'll capsize."

"I don't need to be reminded by him. He's no cleverer than I am," Siji guffawed. "Now my mansion's finished, there's nothing else I want. Greed sooner or later bites your hand and you lose face and ruin yourself."

"It's wise of you to say so, Uncle!" Tianbao complimented him. "Wenqian will have no more objections then."

Pointing to the one-*mu*-sized fish pond, the chicken coops under the west wall and the marten cages on the artificial hill, Aunt Hua said, "I could hardly manage more than this if I was a thousand-armed Buddha. I'd rather sell my fish, eggs and marten pelts than go in for 'trading in humans'! From now on I'm not going to act as a matchmaker any more even if somebody sends a limousine for me."

"Auntie, you're even more far-sighted than Uncle Siji," Tianbao joked.

"What message did Wenqian send?" Bilian followed Tianbao in and demanded.

"He deliberately changed his tune this evening and set himself against us!" Tianbao was furious. "You wanted him to become a post-graduate student but instead he's insisting on applying to work in the shirt factory right after graduation. He says he wants to devote himself to helping develop industry in the countryside."

"All he can see is what's directly under his nose. He

doesn't have any lofty ideals." Bilian ground her teeth in hatred. "It's true that the countryside needs this modernization of industry, but you can't do much with just a few years' college education."

"You told him he should pay attention to his dress, but he said he couldn't afford it."

"I'll buy his clothes for him!"

"He wouldn't accept your moped."

"In that case I won't ride it either."

"He said the state stipend he got was not enough. He has to gather the grass to sell."

"I'll allocate him another stipend! Forty yuan for him and his mother and I'll still have more than thirty-seven left."

Tianbao turned around and went out again, murmuring to himself, "If you . . . still don't agree, Wenqian, I'll . . . break off our friendship!"

Sensing the confusion in his words, the suspicious Bilian tailed after him.

Just as she arrived at Wenqian's gate she heard an argument going on between Tianbao and Wenqian.

". . . Everyone has feelings!" There was a whining note in Tianbao's raised voice.

"I don't mean I dislike her. . . ." Wenqian was both anxious and annoyed. "All she cares about is dressing herself up like a butterfly and never finds any time to study and prepare for the entrance exam for the TV University!"

"But how could I pass it?" Bilian's patience was exhausted. She burst into the courtyard like a gust of wind. "Help me make up the lessons I've missed when you come back from school every day and I'll take the exam eight years from now."

"Why eight years?" Turning to the girl Wenqian said furiously, "Why?"

"You already know the answer! I've only had three years of proper schooling. . . ." Bilian wept.

Translated by Kuang Wendong

An Encounter in Green Vine Lane

I

FOR twenty-five years I've lived in Green Vine Lane.

My home is situated in a small separate courtyard, with five date trees inside and four scholartrees outside, all of which have been there since the Qing Dynasty. The five rooms under these date trees changed their occupants six times in succession, though they were built less than half a century ago.

At first this small courtyard was used as a back-yard. As far as I know, the original owner of this mansion was a dandy, a descendant of the Qing royal family. With a legacy of about a dozen or so residences inherited from his ancestors, he led a life of debauchery in this big mansion together with his wife and two concubines. In order to entertain his guests, he later added a back-yard with three additional rooms on the south side and two on the east according to the location of the date trees, and used it as a place to play mahjong, smoke opium, sing Beijing operas, hold feasts and so on. After Liberation, in spite of his advanced age and ailing like a candle guttering in the wind, he failed to overcome his addiction to opium and was arrested for buying the drug on the black market. As his health had been completely ruined by alcoholism and his licentiousness, he died soon after he was sent to jail. A fight immediately began involving his wife, two concubines and twelve sons and daughters, and the feud was so fierce that even his burial was postponed for nearly a month. Finally, acting as a mediator, the local court made a decision that each member of the family should share equally the money accumulated from auctioning his more than ten residences. As a result, in order that the house should fetch a higher price, a wall was quickly erected between the back-yard and the main front buildings so that the five additional rooms formed a separate courtyard. But when I bought this small courtyard, it had already become dilapidated.

Usually, a person would hold a house-warming party when he moved into a new home, but in my case it was different. Soon after we moved in something unfortunate happened.* Everyone in my family, young or old, fearful and nervous night and day, kept to the house most of the time. Then I was sent to Tongxian to do physical labour in the countryside. For twenty out of the twenty-five years, I lived alone in a thatched cottage in a small village along the banks of the North Canal. Every month, whenever I took a few days leave of absence to go home, I always returned when it was dark and stayed indoors. I never went out of the small courtyard. In recent years, though I have lived in the city since my rehabilitation, I've still no time to go out in the streets. Instead, I keep myself busy reading, writing or entertaining guests. Unlike those years in the village along the banks of the North Canal, where I was on intimate terms with every villager

---

* This refers to the anti-Rightist movement in which the author was wrongly labelled as a Rightist.

and could recognize which hen of which household had just laid an egg upon hearing it cackle, I know no one here in Green Vine Lane, not even my nearest neighbours living in the next courtyard separated by only a wall.

One morning in June this year, while leaving to attend a literary forum, I spotted an old man sitting under the dense shade of the scholartrees. No sooner had he heard the creak of my gate than he turned his face in my direction and watched me cross the threshold. He stood up immediately, bowed and greeted me with a broad smile. "Are you going downtown, sir?"

He was in his seventies, thin, with grey hair, long eyebrows like those of the God of Longevity, smiling eyes and a few wrinkles, all of which suggested that he was a genial sort. Dressed in a small jacket with buttons down the front and a pair of black silk trousers with legs as wide as lanterns, he held a folding fan more than a foot in length. Though physically small, he had quite a large mouth and a loud, husky voice.

Unable to recollect if I had seen him somewhere before, I thought he was just a talkative old man. Out of politeness, I replied, "Are you enjoying the breeze here?" With that, I nodded courteously and left in a hurry to go to my meeting.

Little did I think that when I came back at noon, he would still be sitting under the dense shade of those scholartrees. Having spotted me from afar, he rose to his feet and greeted me again, "You've come back!" Though somewhat hoarse, his voice had a pleasant ring.

"And you're still here enjoying the breeze!" I answered with a smile. Since I didn't want to appear rude, I stopped to exchange a few words with him.

"May I know your name, sir?" I asked, handing him a cigarette.

"Thanks, but I'm not a smoker or drinker." While speaking, he stood there gracefully. "Don't be so formal. My name's Wang Jiekui."

I noticed the calluses on both his hands and felt closer to him. Then I asked, "Are you from the countryside?"

At this, he grew more relaxed and replied smiling, "Mr Liu, I was born at Green Poplar Village and so have the honour to be one of your neighbours, separated only by the canal."

"Have you known about me for a long time?" Upon hearing him speak my surname, I felt even closer to him.

"I've watched you on TV several times." He narrowed his eyes and smiled broadly. "Besides, I enjoyed listening to your novelette *Catkin Willow Flats* on the radio."

"I hope you won't spare your criticisms," I said quickly.

"I really don't deserve this." He grew serious. "May I ask you: Did you ever hear or see the woman ballad singer Yun Zhe Yue you mentioned in your story?"

"Yes, I saw her in my childhood." The old man's inquiry reminded me instantly of that brave, pretty woman, who had led a wanton life as a travelling entertainer. "Later, I heard that the Japanese and the puppet government's secret police had posted a reward to arrest her on a charge of advocating resistance against the Japanese. She died in prison at Tongzhou. I haven't the heart to go on writing about her."

"It was very kind of you to make her a character in your work. She was my junior fellow apprentice. Now her name will live in history." Tears welled up in his eyes. "If she were alive today, she'd be sixty-nine. As far as I remember, she was born in the year of the tiger."

"Are you a ballad singer too?"

"I've been a story-teller for thirty years."

"Where did you perform?"

"At Jade Spring Teahouse in Nanxiaojie Street, inside the Chaoyang Gate."

"In 1948, while studying in Beijing, I used to go to Jade Spring Teahouse almost every Sunday."

"I related the complete novel *Cases of Prefect Bao*."*

"But I remember that was Liu Jingting Junior's performance."

"Liu Jingting Junior was my stage name." The old man chuckled. "Are you . . . are you that young scholar 'Ten *Jin* of Beancurd'?"

This rarely-heard nickname brought back long forgotten memories. Events from thirty-four years ago flashed into my mind.

2

At that time, I was twelve years old.

Soon after I passed the entrance examination that year and obtained an official tuition grant, I left my home and came to Beijing to attend middle school. However, my scholarship always came late, never once on time, leaving me no choice but to find a way to fend for myself. Having handed in a five-dollar note borrowed from a classmate, the son of a rich family, as my cash

---

* Prefect Bao was a just official in the Song Dynasty.

deposit, I began work as a newspaper boy after school. In those days, more than twenty newspapers, large and small, circulated in Beijing, varied in form and bad in content. As a matter of fact, the success of a newspaper at that time relied solely on its distribution, which was controlled by a handful of men. Each manipulated a number of distributors who were in charge of selling a certain number of newspapers, while every distributor in turn controlled a group of newspaper boys running all over the city. The biggest group had scores of boys, whereas the smallest only ten or so.

In order to collect the newspapers in time, I had to get up at three o'clock every morning, and then run from my school to Dengshikou, where I would stand in a line in front of the Jianguo Dongtang Theatre. Only after the newspaper boys had waited there for a long time was a creaking sound heard in the distance, and then a tricycle and trailer appeared loaded with ten or more bundles of newspapers and pedalled by our boss, the distributor. As the heavily loaded tricycle zigzagged under the dim street lights, it still took some minutes to reach the top of the queue. Then our boss would distribute the newly printed newspapers to us one by one. Those who stood in front could pick any best-seller, but their quantity could not surpass their cash deposit.

At the very beginning, as I had handed in five dollars, I was allowed only one hundred and fifty newspapers. Before long, I increased my deposit to fifteen dollars after making a small profit, so the distributor permitted me to get more than three hundred and fifty copies. Once the newspapers were in my hands, I clutched them under my arm and ran as fast as I could, shouting all the way at the top of my voice: "Hey, today's newspaper! *The World Daily*! *The North China Daily*! *The Beiping Daily*! *The Xinsheng Daily*! *The Xinmin Daily*! . . . Read all about the huge robbery at Dong'an Market in broad daylight, about the case of a strange corpse discovered in a trunk at Qianmen Railway Station!" I used to finish this at one go like a prolonged tune.

At that time each newspaper boy had his own route. I went from Ganmian Lane to Chaoyang Gate, running along the big streets and small lanes within that district. As a rule, customers liked to read newspapers as early as possible, while we newspaper boys did our utmost to sell them quickly since the price varied with each hour. For instance, a newspaper worth four cents could sell for twenty cents a copy at four o'clock in the morning, fifteen cents by five o'clock and ten cents by six o'clock. By seven o'clock we neither made a profit nor loss, but after half past seven, the remainders were worth nothing, fit only to light a stove. Every Sunday, in addition to the newspapers, I could sell fifty magazines. My income thus doubled.

I was born and raised in the countryside. At five or six years old, I began to chase wild rabbits, and at twelve, I could run as swiftly as the wind. Because I ran fast, I could sell all my newspapers before half past five. Every morning, in Nanxiaojie Street on my way back to school, I would usually go into a small restaurant where I would order either a bowl of noodles with beef-ribs or seasoned millet porridge with two deep-fried fritters. Then, with my stomach fairly full and sweat streaming down my face, I would go to school to attend the morning self-study class.

This small restaurant was run by an ugly, fierce-looking woman in her forties who wore gaudy clothes and heavy make-up. Her lover was none other than my boss, the newspaper distributor Zhang Deshou. By then, Zhang was around twenty-two years old. He suffered from acne and had two gold teeth. While speaking or walking, he tried to imitate the coy, coquettish style of the well-known actor Xiao Cuihua.*

The majority of customers in this small restaurant were poor — those who pedalled tricycles, water carters, vegetable sellers who carried a pair of baskets on a shoulder pole, peddlers who sold peanuts, watermelon seeds and cigarettes in small baskets, fortune-tellers, and chemists with trade banners selling rat poison. There were also the occasional peasants who drove their loaded animals to the city, and poor students enjoying a feast. Whenever the woman couldn't manage the business by herself, Zhang would give her a hand, playing the role of waiter, either carrying plates or adding up the bills.

In my school, the food was revolting and the menu monotonous: steamed maize bread with vegetable soup. Sometimes meat wasn't served for a couple of months at a time. Consequently, I was unable to bear it and decided to give myself a feast in the restaurant.

Although I had my breakfast there every morning, I hardly ever ordered a meal inside, and what's more, I usually ate standing at the entrance and then left in a hurry as soon as I'd put down my chopsticks.

One rainy day, when I stepped into the restaurant, I

---

* A Beijing opera actor noted for acting the roles of young women.

found no customers there except the woman and her lover Zhang. Sitting facing each other, they were having their meal: fried pork and pancakes and an egg soup.

"Hurry up, the food's getting cold!" Zhang urged his lover after he had eaten and drunk his fill, while picking his teeth with a match sliver. "As Manager Liu has ordered a plate of *shijin* beancurd, I've got to take it to him quickly."

Just at that moment, I entered the restaurant.

"Oh, Little Scholar, what do you want to eat?" the woman asked while chewing the pancake.

"Shi Jin of beancurd!" With Zhang's voice ringing in my ears, I posed as an expert and ordered the same.

"Ten *jin* of beancurd! How the hell can you eat that much?"* Alarmed by my order, the woman widened her cherry-like eyes, straightened her neck and stopped swallowing the food in her mouth.

"If that fellow Liu can eat such a large amount of beancurd, so can I!"

Upon hearing this, the woman laughed so much that she spat her food all over Zhang's face. Splitting her sides, she exclaimed, "Good heavens, what a joke! Ten *jin* . . . of beancurd, like a mountain. It'll surely ruin your . . . small, white belly."

After hurriedly cleaning his face, Zhang was so angry that he turned to me, his teeth showing, snorting in contempt and smiling coldly. "What a shame! Fancy a little scholar like you, mixing up your words whenever you open your mouth. Remember, it's *shijin* beancurd, not *shi jin* of beancurd. . . !"

---

* The words *shijin* (mixed flavoured) and *shi jin* (ten *jin*) sound almost the same in Chinese, so the author mistook the name of this popular dish, ordering the quantity ten *jin* of beancurd.

"Little Scholar. Ten *Jin* of Beancurd! Little Scholar. Ten *Jin* of Beancurd!" Clapping her hands and stamping her feet, the woman proprietor rocked with laughter.

Blushing, I fled. From then on, I was nicknamed "Ten *Jin* of Beancurd". Only after I finally left that place, did I succeed in ridding myself of it.

Opposite the small restaurant was Jade Spring Teahouse, which consisted of a couple of rooms without a partition holding twenty-eight square tables. The teahouse could seat more than one hundred customers at the same time. Born into an old official family, the owner of this teahouse knew the rudiments of writing and took an interest in reading newspapers. Since I used to give him a free copy of a paper every morning on my way back to school, he allowed me to sell magazines in his teahouse. At the entrance hung a blackboard posted with playbills, announcing that there were two performances every day. The one during the day featured the *Cases of Prefect Bao* performed by the celebrated Liu Jingting Junior, while at the night show *Strange Tales of Liaozhai* were recounted by the master story-teller Zhao Yingpo. The popular name of *Strange Tales of Liaozhai* was *The Stories of Ghosts and Fox-fairies.* Zhao was good at telling ghost stories and his narration was horrible and bloodcurdling. Some, while listening to his performance at night, would more often than not be so frightened that they would rather pee in their trousers than pluck up their courage to go outside. Nor did they dare go home without someone to accompany them. In a small alley, they would panic at the mere rustle of leaves in the wind. However, whenever Zhao performed in this teahouse, the audience, under the spell of his mastery, would never miss a chance to listen, even at the risk of peeing in their pants once again.

I had been addicted to listening to stories since I was six. Nearly every Sunday, immediately after I had sold my newspapers and magazines, I would spend my spare time in Jade Spring Teahouse.

As a rule, before the performance began, on a small stage in the teahouse's hall stood a desk on which lay wooden clappers and a folding fan. When the old wall clock began to strike eight o'clock, a waiter went on to the small stage and hung in front of the desk a red curtain embroidered with the performer's name in big characters. As soon as he withdrew, there came a loud cough behind the curtain at the entrance to the stage, and then the noise in the hall instantly died down. As Liu Jingting Junior raised the curtain, making his appearance on stage, the audiences applauded. Then, with a broad smile, he walked up to the front part of the stage, making a deep bow to the audience, polite and relaxed. After that, he raised his head, straightened his back and quietly took his seat at the desk. Picking up the wooden clappers in two fingers and holding the folding fan in his right hand, he composed himself and cast a sweeping glance around the entire hall. Shortly afterwards, with a sudden strike of the wooden clappers on the desk, he commenced his performance in a tone neither fast nor slow, neither high nor low.

"Last time, the narration was suspended when I came to. . . ." On account of his clear pronunciation and elegant tune, every word was uttered with emotion, touching the hearts of the audience.

Craning my neck to look at the stage, I saw a man of about thirty-seven years old with an emaciated appearance and short hair, dressed in a rather worn cloth gown. To tell the truth, there was really nothing extraordinary about him. He looked like an ordinary person.

In front of me, Zhang suddenly whispered in a low voice, "Amazing! This yellow-skinned skeleton has such a golden voice!" I saw that, sitting cross-legged, Zhang had fixed his shifty eyes on something behind the story-teller. Following his gaze, I spotted a young woman aged about twenty on a bench near a teapoy in front of the entrance to the stage.

Her skin was fair, her eyebrows drawn elegantly and her small mouth painted scarlet. She combed her hair backward in a banana-like style quite fashionable at that time. Her lotus-pattern short jacket was unbuttoned as she nursed a baby girl, changing her breasts, as big as gourds, from right to left. She did it casually as if no one else was present.

"Who is that woman?" I asked Zhang in a low voice.

"Master Liu's wife," Zhang whispered in my ears slobbering. "She's called Sweet Sister, the daughter of the teahouse owner. She's made Liu Jingting Junior earn a lot of money for her father."

Usually, whenever the first performance came to a close, Liu would leave the stage to take a rest, and then, rising to her feet, Sweet Sister would go to collect money from the audience with her baby in one hand and a small bamboo basket in the other.

"Is there anyone here who feels like being the first to give money?" In contrast to Master Liu's voice, this young woman sounded affected and sweet in spite of her big build.

Whenever I listened to Liu's story-telling, I noticed that it was always Zhang who first offered money generously. Smiling and grimacing, Zhang chucked a big banknote into the basket and said to her, "Take it and buy some tonic for your man!"

Sweet Sister spat at him on the spot, yet Zhang, shaking his head, seemed quite pleased, as if she had spat perfume.

Once the small basket was filled with coins and paper money, she would go back to her seat and count it. Then Liu would resume his performance.

Sometimes, when the collection was taking place, some mean fellows would slip away and a few others would try to follow their example, throwing the entire hall into confusion.

"Now, now! Those who have money should help us, whereas those who have forgotten to bring any should assist us by standing still." In an attempt to maintain order, Sweet Sister went on explaining at the top of her voice, "So, gentlemen, you needn't be nervous even if you really haven't any money. Just sit still!" At this point her voice suddenly became sharp and hoarse. "Of course, that gentleman who left a moment ago had his reasons. Though as frightened as a stray cur, he is, in fact, a dutiful son. He hurried off to buy medicine for his sick mother. However, I think he ought to leave here openly. There was no need for him to slink out as he did. Otherwise, when he dashed out of the entrance, he might have collided with a tramcar."

Jade Spring Teahouse was located at the entrance to Nanxiaojie Street and a tramcar was approaching with its noisy bell along the route inside Chaoyang Gate.

With a kind of irresistible magic force, Sweet Sister's words nailed the audience to their seats, though some of them had planned to steal away.

"Look at that woman. What a sharp tongue she has! She has cursed those stingy fellows in an ingenious way!" Zhang thought highly of her eloquence, and smiled broadly.

On one occasion, when the collection happened to be lower than usual, Sweet Sister insisted on keeping the audience waiting till they offered a bit more. Though Liu tried to go on stage several times, he was driven back by his wife's glowering looks.

Feeling sorry for him and impatient to listen to the rest of the story, I fished out the money earned from my magazines that day and handed it to Sweet Sister.

"Thank you very much!" she said as she beamed at me. "Just look, though he normally stands to listen, this little scholar is so generous that he would even cut off his own flesh if necessary. I dare say he'll become a Number One Scholar or obtain a doctor's degree!"

Upon hearing this compliment, I was so embarrassed that sweat beaded my face.

I was about to leave after the performance when Liu called out suddenly, "Little Scholar, wait a minute, please!"

"What's the matter, Master Liu?" I asked him, halting.

He took out a banknote from Sweet Sister's small bamboo basket and walked up to me, saying, "Take your money back! Keep it and buy some books for yourself." Though Sweet Sister rolled her eyes, he pretended to have seen nothing.

Greatly embarrassed, I hurried away.

"Ten *Jin* of Beancurd! How can you be so ungrateful to Master Liu!" Zhang grabbed the money from the story-teller. Catching up with me, he grasped one of my hands, urging, "Quick, let's go and have a plate of *shijin* beancurd!"

Zhang pulled me along till we reached the small restaurant, and the money thus landed in his lover's wallet.

On the following Sunday, I went to the teahouse again. At the sight of my entrance, Sweet Sister nodded, giving me special treatment: she not only invited me to sit next to her, but also poured me a bowl of strong tea. When the first performance came to an end, she put her daughter in my arms, saying, "Little Scholar, please hold Rong'er for a while!" Then, taking up her small bamboo basket, she began collecting money from the audience.

Rong'er, whose pet name was Niuniu, had a small pigtail standing upright in the centre of her head and a pair of lovely round, dark eyes, looking like two fresh grapes. Oddly, the baby didn't react to me as a stranger. But she eventually wet my pants, and they were soaking as if they had just been washed.

On that day, I played the role of Sweet Sister's babysitter, so that she had time to give her father a hand pouring tea, boiling water or soliciting customers.

It was getting darker and darker. As Rong'er, a plump infant, was as heavy as a small stone roller, I grew exhausted and dizzy. Then Liu's loud voice suddenly boomed into my ears, "Immediately after his master, Prefect Bao, had ordered tea, Bao Xing went out of the chamber with a teapot in his hand. Walking through the winding corridor, he came to the kitchen. But as soon as he pulled aside the door curtain, he exclaimed, '*Aiya*!' If you want to know what happened next, please come again tomorrow, and I'll explain it in detail." With a flourish of his wooden clappers, Liu ended his performance.

This episode made me nervous. Bao Xing had gasped when he raised the door curtain. What had he seen? Was there an assassin bursting through the window with a sharp sword? Or did someone throw a man's head into the kitchen, the blood still dripping?

"Master Liu, what did Bao Xing see?" I inquired impatiently when the story-teller left his seat and came down from the small stage.

However, instead of answering my question right away, Master Liu took the towel handed him by Sweet Sister and cleaned his face calmly. Beaming, he replied in a low and soft voice, "Don't worry, Little Scholar, it's nothing serious!"

As I insisted on being told, Sweet Sister, a bit annoyed, snapped at me, "He's just stopping the story at a climax to keep the audience in suspense. Don't spoil our business!"

I had no choice but to go back to school with a distracted mind.

That night, I tossed and turned: The first half I suffered from insomnia, while in the latter half I had a nightmare. I wasn't even calm when I came back to school soon after selling my newspapers, so I asked leave on the pretext of having a stomach-ache. No sooner had the bell begun to ring than I sneaked out of the school gate.

As I reached the entrance to the teahouse, I heard Liu had just begun to return to his story. "Last time, I'd stopped at the point where, ordered by his master Prefect Bao to make some tea, Bao Xing went to the kitchen with a teapot in his hand, but, no sooner had he raised the door curtain than he exclaimed in alarm, '*Aiya*!' Well. . . ." Blinking his eyes, Liu paused for a while as I entered.

All at once, my heart sprang into my mouth.

What did he mean? What had happened? Staring at Liu, I thought over and over again that it must be an assassin, or a man's head dripping with blood.

To my surprise Liu answered the riddle, "The water on the stove hadn't boiled yet!"

At this, the whole hall rocked with laughter. Some, overwhelmed with admiration at his superb skill, thumped the tables and shouted "Bravo", whereas I felt as if I had been made fun of. Greatly disappointed, I left the teahouse, returning to school with tears streaming down my face. What lousy luck! When I reached school, the supervisor was standing in front of the gate looking stern. He questioned me, and I confessed my misconduct. I had made a fool of myself. It was noted down that I had cut two classes and I was publicly warned at morning assembly. From then on, I avoided the teahouse, and I never met with Master Liu, Sweet Sister and their daughter Niuniu again.

After thirty-four years, I felt that past life belonged to another world.

3

I stood under the shade of the scholartrees together with Master Liu, who was now seventy years old.

"What have you been doing all these years?" I asked him impatiently.

"It's hard to explain in a few words!" He sighed and his shining eyes suddenly grew dim. "When you have some time, I'll tell you in detail the story of my family's separations and reunions over the years."

"Please visit me at home after four o'clock!" As I crossed the stone step in front of my door, I halted, adding, "I've finished another novelette entitled *The Lotus in the Breeze*, in which both Yi Tai Xi and Huo Shao Yun are mentioned."

"Oh, them. I'm quite familiar with them!" A trace of a smile appeared on the old man's sad face. "Yi Tai Xi was my senior fellow apprentice, while Huo Shao Yun, who took Yun Zhe Yue as his teacher, calls me uncle."

"Be sure to come this afternoon!" After urging him once more, I entered my courtyard.

When I awoke from my noontime sleep, there was no one else at home, for all the others had gone either to work or school. The branches and leaves of the five date trees in my courtyard were so thick that they looked like an umbrella. I placed two rattan chairs and a round table in their shade and prepared a pot of green tea before I watered the flowers as I waited for Liu's arrival.

At four o'clock sharp I heard footsteps outside my door. I hurried to welcome him, but instead of Liu my visitor was a woman of thirty-five or so.

Tall and slender, with a pale complexion, sad eyes and two pigtails, though her hair had been permed, she wore a white blouse embroidered with light golden flowers and a black skirt. She seemed to be in mourning, but for whom?

Before I had time to open my mouth, she smiled shyly, asking, "Are you Comrade Liu?"

Nodding my head, I asked in reply, "May I know your name?"

"I'm Xu Rong." She was on the verge of tears. The daughter of Liu Jingting Junior.

"So you're Niuniu!" I exclaimed.

"Yes, I am." She lowered her head bashfully. "My father told me that when I was a baby you used to listen to his story-telling and hold me in your arms."

"Come in and sit down, please!" Recalling the old days, I was deeply moved. "Why hasn't your father come with you?"

"Oh, he's gone to hospital to see my mother." Standing motionless, Xu Rong lowered her eyes. "He said he would come to visit you tomorrow."

"What's wrong with your mother?"

"Cancer of the esophagus. She may not live till tomorrow."

I was startled to hear this. I sighed and asked her sadly, "Did your mother suffer a lot in the countryside these past years?"

"She divorced my father twenty-five years ago, but she's been living all the time in the city. . . ." While speaking, Xu Rong looked miserable, tears streaming down her face.

"Why did they divorce?"

"My mother got involved with a scoundrel, and then it was too late."

Then Xu Rong made to leave. As I did not like to press her to stay, I had no alternative but to see her off. While walking with her, I asked her, "Where are you working at present?"

"At a street-run toy factory."

"What does your husband do?"

"He died long ago."

Upon hearing this, I felt sad again. Who would have thought that little Niuniu, whom I used to hold in my arms thirty-four years ago, would have met with such a tragic fate!

When we reached the door of a neighbouring courtyard, Xu Rong took out her handkerchief to wipe away the tears from her eyes. It had not occurred to me that my little Niuniu's home was so close to mine.

That evening, concerned about Liu, Niuniu and her mother Sweet Sister, who was probably also fifty-eight years old now, I crossed the threshold of a neighbouring courtyard for the first time in my twenty-five years in this small lane.

The appearance of this courtyard had changed completely. There were small, low houses that looked like dovecotes, and it was difficult to find a way through them. The whole place was full of children weeping, adults shouting, the clatter of dishes and bowls, the raucous mixed music of Beijing opera, *pingju,* a TV play, assorted songs and a chorus from TV sets, radios and tape recorders. What a row! When I inquired where Xu Rong lived, someone indicated with his lips, indicating that she lived in a side room at the back of the courtyard.

The side room was, in fact, a very small, narrow and shabby one hidden in an innermost corner. Yet despite the small size, Xu Rong had set up in front of her home a wire fence and a wooden gate. The fence was sparsely covered with ivy which brought a bit of vitality to the place.

"Is Comrade Xu Rong at home?" I inquired, standing at the gate.

"Who's there?" The light in the house was suddenly switched off.

"It's me, Old Liu."

"Oh, wait a minute!"

"Has your father come back from the hospital?"

"No. He didn't want to leave my mother."

"Then I'll come again tomorrow!" As it was suffocating in this crowded compound, I hurried back to the street, breathing the fresh air.

Once out of the north entrance to Green Vine Lane, I turned into Fuyou Street. Instead of returning home right away, I proceeded to stroll along the pavement under the dim streetlights slanting down through branches and leaves of the trees by the roadside.

Before I could walk far, Xu Rong chased after and finally caught up with me.

"I'm going to the hospital." While buttoning up her blouse, she ran with quick, short steps. "Would you like me to give a message to my father?"

I stopped and said, "What worries me most is your mother's condition."

"I'm afraid she won't last the night!" Xu Rong was choking with sobs. "When my father arrived at her bedside, she was already unable to speak, let alone raise her hands. She just weeps."

Then we began to walk together.

"Why did they get divorced?" I asked.

Xu Rong sighed. "Soon after Liberation, my maternal grandfather died, so Jade Spring Teahouse became my mother's property. Originally my father had made up his mind to join a folk art troupe, but my mother disagreed with him, insisting that the teahouse would profit by his remaining there. Being progressive in his views, my father decided to tell a story reflecting contemporary life. But, the novel from which he adapted this story was written by a writer who later was labelled a Rightist. So my father got involved in this problem, and was punished along with the writer. Fearing that the teahouse would be confiscated and that we would lose our livelihood, my mother readily placed her confidence in a scoundrel and divorced my father. As I was only eleven the court decided I should live with her."

"How did your father end up at Green Poplar Village?"

"He sought refuge with his apprentice He Chuansheng, and ever since then he has lived there, more than twenty-five years in all."

"Why didn't I ever hear about this?"

"In 1951, when my father went on tour to several places, he accepted He Chuansheng as an apprentice, but my mother mistreated him, so the boy left before his apprenticeship was finished."

"Are there any others at his home? As an outsider, how could your father stay there all the time?"

"Chuansheng was an orphan. Only his grandparents lived with him. When my father went there, Chuansheng got a father and his grandparents another son. All four got on very well together."

"This He Chuansheng seems a loyal friend." I praised him, but after thinking for a while, I realized there was something strange about it. "With only four of them that means He Chuansheng never got married?"

"He was married, but out of consideration for my father he divorced his wife." At this point, Xu Rong began to sob once again. "She was so selfish and used to snub my father, banging bowls down loudly or hinting bad things about him. Unable to endure it any longer, Chuansheng decided to divorce her."

"I'm going back home the day after tomorrow, so I'll go and visit your friend Chuansheng."

"But he's in Beijing at present."

"Where's he staying? I'll go and see him right away."

"Since he accompanied my father here, he's been staying at a small hotel in Xiheyan Street outside the Qianmen Gate." Xu Rong paused and then went on, "He's worried about my father so he's keeping him company at the hospital. I'll tell him to call on you as soon as possible."

"Your father's a fine man!" I sighed. "He's not bitter and still tries his best to be with your mother on her deathbed. You should show more respect for him than even He Chuansheng has."

"Oh, no, it was my mother who wanted to see my father." Xu Rong wept some more. "Realizing she was dying she longed to see my father once again. As soon as they received my telegram, my father and Chuansheng rushed here, arriving the day before yesterday."

"But why did they meet only today?"

"Because my stepfather forbade them to meet before."

"How narrow-minded of him!"

"He's a beast!" Xu Rong snapped. "The dirty swine made a false charge against my father twenty-five years ago, and then he mistreated me eleven years later."

My heart pounded. "What happened?"

"Several years ago while working as a buyer for a street-run factory, apart from having some political problems before Liberation, he was also guilty of corruption. So in an attempt to join a so-called revolutionary organization during the 'cultural revolution', he forced me to marry its head, a man twenty years older than I."

"When did your husband die?"

"Soon after he was promoted to leader of the public security section of the industrial administrative office of our district, the people's government discovered that he had murdered three people in the past, so they went to arrest him. Frantic with worry, he died from a cerebral haemorrhage within a few hours."

"Then how was the reunion of your parents arranged today?"

"Chuansheng gave my stepfather one thousand yuan, so we bought the right to their meeting!" Filled with anger and hatred, Xu Rong trembled. "You know that scoundrel pretended that because of my mother's hospitalization he had spent one thousand yuan in medical bills, so if my father wanted to meet her, he should pay it all back. Chuansheng was furious but went home, got all his savings, which he'd accumulated bit by bit to build a house of his own, and gave them all to that rat."

"But you should stand up to him!"

"He's an ass-licker and his superiors think highly of him."

"Anyway, you can take him to court. I'll find a lawyer for you."

By then we'd reached the north entrance to Fuyou Street and a trolleybus was about to halt at its stop. Xu Rong ran to board one going to the hospital. Gazing after her, I felt very upset. Liu, He Chuansheng and Niuniu had been bullied by that bastard, yet, I, an outsider, would never stomach such treatment. I am a born meddler. Sure enough, once a lawsuit was filed, we could settle matters in court.

4

The next afternoon I was sleeping on my bed. All of a sudden, I was awakened by someone pounding at my door. Putting on a jacket, I rushed to open it.

Xu Rong was there, wearing a black armband.

"Is your mother. . . ? Though it was to be expected, I was upset when I saw her in mourning.

"Please help us sort things out now!" she asked in tears. "That beast insists on keeping my mother's ashes."

Hurriedly buttoning up my shirt, I went to the neighbouring courtyard again.

At this, the inhabitants of those honeycomb-like houses poked their heads out of their windows and stared at the small side room. Close behind me, Xu

Rong dared not raise her head, and she seemed to tremble.

"My master wants to have the ashes of my mistress!" An angry voice exclaimed from the window of the side room. "Are you going to give them to him? Yes or no?"

"Help!" someone shouted in a voice just like the squeal of a pig about to be slaughtered.

Xu Rong gave me a push and we rushed to the gate together and saw a middle-aged man brandishing a kitchen knife in one hand and grasping the front of a wretched old man's jacket with the other.

"Let him go, Chuansheng!" Xu Rong shouted. "Here's Comrade Liu. He'll settle the problem fairly. Let him judge the case for us!"

The middle-aged man put the kitchen knife down on a chopping block.

"I don't care who's here. If a person has an offensive weapon, it's proof enough that he wishes to resort to violence. Let's go to the police station!" Picking up an oil-stained handbag, the old man rose to his feet, ready to go.

"Don't move!" He Chuansheng barred his way.

"Sit down! None of you is allowed to raise a hand to fight!" I shouted from the fence. "There's a saying, 'With justice on your side, you can go anywhere; without it, you can't take a single step.' Now, who wants to speak first?"

"How ashamed I feel!" Standing woodenly, Liu wept. "While on her sickbed, Rong'er's mother often said that, after her death, her ashes should be given to me. But . . . but Zhang Deshou wants more money for them."

"Zhang Deshou? Zhang Deshou?" Pulling aside the ivy, I put my head through and looked around.

"That's me!" the old man answered, nodding his head.

In spite of his changed appearance due to age, I recognized at first glance from the speaker's crafty eyes and gestures that this was none other than my old newspaper distributor. I smiled coldly and asked, "Zhang Deshou, do you recognize me?"

"What's your name then?"

"Ten *Jin* of Beancurd!"

"This man's an out-and-out scoundrel!" Filled with indignation, He Chuansheng declared. "He forced my master to pay him one thousand yuan for medical expenses, and now he wants five hundred yuan for the ashes. Is there any humanity in him?"

"Anyway, Sweet Sister was my wife, alive or dead!" Trembling on his sorghum-like thin legs, Zhang stamped his feet. "If I give him her ashes, that means I'm a cuckold. No. I won't do it for nothing!"

"But, Zhang Deshou, you're going too far!" With that, I turned round to ask Xu Rong, "Did your mother leave a will?"

"A few days before she died, I borrowed a tape-recorder and recorded all she said."

"Good! Play it right now."

Xu Rong went into the inner room and returned with a tape-recorder. As soon as she put the cassette in the machine, the conversation that had taken place several days ago between Sweet Sister and her daughter was heard.

"Niuniu. . . ." The sick mother gasped for breath at almost every other word. "I'm dying. . . . Probably,

I can't live much longer. . . . You see . . . I've so much . . . to say to you!"

"Mum, don't worry, you take it easy and stay here, and you'll get better soon," Xu Rong cried in a low voice.

"Everybody must die. Now, my time has come. . . ." The old woman struggled for words. "All my life, I've only done one thing that weighs on my conscience. I treated your father unfairly. . . . Do you still remember him?"

"How can I forget my own father?"

"Try to find him for me! I want to see him. How I wish that he could beat or curse me! This is the only way I can die in peace."

"But no one knows where he is."

"I think . . . perhaps, he might have gone to He Chuansheng's home. But I'm not sure if he's still alive."

"Why do you think he went to live with him?"

"Because Chuansheng always respected his elders and superiors. How sorry I am now that I. . . . You see, I thought he was stupid, so I used to beat him. . . ."

"Where does he live?"

"At Green Poplar Village along the canal."

"I'll write to him immediately."

"Hurry! . . . I miss your father so much. I long to see him. . . . Give him my ashes. . . ."

"I'll send him a telegram right now."

As Sweet Sister gasped, the tape made a noise.

"What a damned bitch! Uttering a pack of lies even as she lay dying!" Zhang butted in, taking advantage of the pause.

"Shut up!" yelled Chuansheng.

"Rong'er, after I pass away. . . ." The old woman resumed her speech with difficulty, "You must go back to your father! Zhang Deshou . . . is a beast, simply a beast!" The speaker stopped to catch her breath. "When he fell out with that woman who owned the small restaurant immediately after Liberation, he came to kowtow to us, begging us to hire him as a waiter in our teahouse. Your father felt sorry for him and agreed. Who would have thought that . . . in 1957 he lied to hurt your father, and later on, with sweet words tricked me? He did us all great harm and broke up our family."

"Damned bitch! Damned bitch!" Zhang grabbed the machine, exclaiming, "I'll smash this along with the ashes of that damned bitch!"

"Give them to me!" Xu Rong shouted grieved. "Give me my mother's ashes!"

When He Chuansheng turned round to pick up the kitchen knife again, I stopped him with one hand and pointed at Zhang with the other. "How dare you behave like a brute? Once Xu Rong files her lawsuit, I'll be her witness in court!"

Zhang smiled wryly, saying, "Rong'er, if you want the ashes, how can I refuse you? But, you must give the tape to me."

"All right! All right!" Xu Rong promised him, confused.

"No, don't!" I told her. "This is proof of his crimes."

"Give it to him and get him out of my sight!" Waving his hand, Liu spoke in a weak voice. "If he remains here longer, I'll die with disgust."

So an exchange was made of the tape for the ashes.

"Comrade Liu, thank you for helping us!" Zhang

bowed and smiled in a sinister way. "We've been friends for decades. If you have time, will you do me the honour of visiting my humble home for a chat? I'll entertain you with a dish of *shijin* beancurd, with a true Beijing flavour like in the old days."

With that he left.

"Comrade Liu, thank you for coming to our rescue and settling the problem!" His eyes brimming with tears, He Chuansheng clasped my hands.

Silence reigned in the narrow, small courtyard. Only then did I take a long look at He Chuansheng. He was five or six years younger than I. Though he was a peasant, his appearance and manners were more elegant than mine, perhaps because he had once been apprenticed to a story-teller. He acted just like a country school teacher both in speech and manner.

Ashamed at his gratitude, I hastened to say, "Don't mention it. I only put in a word or two for you. I'm a writer, with no power, so what great role could I play?"

"In fact, even if you hadn't appeared, I wouldn't have dared kill him." He smiled. "I just wanted to frighten the bastard, but if he was obstinate, I'd have given him the five hundred yuan in my pocket."

"It seems that your family is the most prosperous one in Green Poplar Village, otherwise how can you afford to throw your money away like that?"

"That's not true. But in the past two years, we villagers have all become richer. My family's just average."

"You've proved a loyal friend," I praised him, patting him on the shoulder. "I'll urge the county broadcasting station to interview you."

"Oh no, don't do that, please!" He blushed at once. "In fact, if you'd like to visit us and see how Mr Liu has been a good son to my grandparents, you'll realize I've still a long way to go."

"Learn all the fine skills of your master."

"You know I was only his apprentice for less than two years. I can't learn all his skills completely." Shaking his head, He Chuansheng took out the five hundred yuan from his pocket. "I've wanted for a long time to buy a tape-recorder and some cassettes to record all my master's skills so they won't be lost for ever."

"That's a good idea!" I exclaimed in delight. "I'll ask the county cultural bureau to get some cadres to help you write them down."

"There's no need for that." He spoke as if they had already a careful plan. "I can do it by myself."

"But your education. . . ." I wondered whether he clung to the traditional idea that a performer in the old society preferred to keep his own rough manuscript to himself rather than hand it over to others.

"But Chuansheng has some education!" Sitting all the while with his eyes closed, Liu suddenly opened them. "Soon after being driven away by Rong'er's mother, he returned home and went to primary school and then junior middle school. But because I went to live at his home, he gave up his original plan to take the entrance examination for senior middle school. So he lost the chance to go to university. . . ."

"My master encouraged me not to abandon my studies." He Chuansheng blushed and added, "Old Liu, forgive me if I've offended you, but I've adapted your novelettes for story-telling."

"Wonderful. How kind of you!" I was overjoyed at this news. "When do you plan to return home?"

"Well. . . ." He Chuansheng exchanged a glance with Liu and went on, "We thought we'd leave tomorrow."

"Then, let's go together!" I issued an order. "Niuniu, you'd better ask for leave and spend some days in Green Poplar Village. It will broaden your horizons."

At half past eight the next morning, a Beijing jeep came to drive me to the countryside and I took Old Liu, He Chuansheng and Xu Rong with me as well. Leaving the south entrance to Fuyou Street, we passed Chang'an Street, Tiananmen, Wangfujing, the railway station and Jianguo Gate. As soon as we were beyond the city wall, the jeep sped along the highway from Beijing to Tianjin, taking only two hours to reach our destination.

Sitting in the jeep, I had time to think. Before getting out I had already made my decision.

Being meddlesome by nature, I liked very much the idea of playing the role of matchmaker!

Translated by Hu Zhihui

The Liuxiang Melon Hut

1

ON the eighteen *li* Canal Flats that spread like a lotus leaf in the blue-green water glittered a sparkling dew-drop, the tiny village of Liuxiang.

Beyond the village, by the canal, was a melon patch, eight punt-poles from east to west and ten from north to south, the rough wooden gate standing half closed between the willow-wattled walls. Outside the walls running alongside a row of river willows was a small dyke, half the height of a man. Entwined around the trunk of each river willow, green creepers drew the wild flower blossoms high into the trees, while in forks and on branches, high and low, birds' nests hung like inverted golden bells. Below the little dyke, the water had risen and the boats rode high. Skiffs glided to and fro in the shade of the willows.

Inside the melon patch, facing south, Liu Shaoqing and his daughter, Liu Yemei, had planted eight willow piles in the ground as uprights, and three feet above the ground had built a two-roomed melon hut. Tough pliable strips of red-barked water willow were woven into four walls which were plastered with mud and wheat husks as smooth and flat as a mirror, and so shiny that reflections could be seen in them well enough to distinguish male from female and old from young.

The ridged roof was thatched with rushes that father and daughter had cut from the canal side to top the hut with a pointed green bamboo hat.

The hut had two rooms. Liu Shaoqing lived in the outer room and Liu Yemei lived in the inner one.

The inner room had a door and a window. Beyond the back wall the weeping willows nestled close, so that when a gentle breeze blew it hung a waving curtain over the back window.

Underneath the hut was a wood stove with a six-sided chimney, next to which were stacked several neat piles of green firewood with bundles of wild sagebrush tucked in amongst them. When this was fed into the belly of the stove, the curling smoke wafted a faint fragrance through the air. On top of the stove was a much-patched iron cooking pot with red earthenware plates, jars, a black calabash dipper, blue-patterned rice bowls, a big-bellied salt pot and a slender-necked oil bottle arranged beside it.

Father and daughter whittled down willow branches to use as chopsticks. They ate chaff and wild herbs, drank river water and only ate meat when they caught fish and shrimps in the canal.

In front of the hut there was just enough space to stand in, and beyond that stretched row on row of melon seedlings.

The curling tendrils of the melon plants spread everywhere. Through layer upon layer of thick leaves, one could feel along the winding creepers to huge water melons like lapis-lazuli rollers lying in disorder all over the ground. A moment of inattention and they would send you sprawling head first to pick yourself up with a lump the size of an egg on your skull. If you didn't have the strength of an ox, you needn't think of making off with one.

"Behind every mountain is a bigger mountain, beyond heaven is another heaven and behind every able man is a man of even greater ability." At the Canal Flats, even Liu Shaoqing was not considered a master hand. His father had been the expert at growing water melons, not he. Liu Shaoqing's skill reached its height first with musk-melons and second with *mian* melons.*

His musk-melons were smooth, round and full-bodied. The white ones were like white jade, the yellow ones like gold. When he picked them he always left two green leaves attached to the stem which made them appear even more attractive. He would fetch two buckets of water from the canal, and squatting in the deep shade of the willows, put the musk-melons in to cool. An hour later he would scoop them out, and splitting a narrow strip off a reed, would use it to cut a light groove on the surface of each melon. It would then fall neatly into halves. The fruit was sweet, crisp and refreshing, oozing with honey-sweet juice that exhilarated the heart and refreshed the mind. His *mian* melons had thin skins and thick flesh, with great round bellies that split open to reveal white seeds and red pulp and a pot full of honey. There were melons like the painted faces of Beijing opera characters, melons with wry expressions and melons like simpletons, all quite ridiculous looking and delightfully charming. No one who had ever eaten Liu Shaoqing's *mian* melons had ever had enough. People came from hundreds of

---

* A type of melon which is softer and less sweet than the musk-melon.

miles away, their hearts tethered firmly to his melon seedlings.

Towards the end of April, melons were sown and beans were dibbled. As soon as the flowers in Liu Shaoqing's melon patch opened, thc sweet fragrance spilled everywhere, and when the melons were ripe, the earth was enveloped in a fragrant mist. The slightest breeze from the south would scent the air for miles around and travellers hurrying east and west would halt in their tracks, boats sailing north and south would draw close to the bank and melon eaters would swarm in like bees to their hive. Liu Shaoqing's hands were never idle. He would squat among the melon ridges pulling the thick leaves apart to select the melons, snap the stems and pick the fruit. Liu Yemei's feet never stopped. With a willow basket in her hand and scales on her shoulder, she would fetch melons and sell melons, moving back and forth at a trot.

But if the melons were not fully grown, not ripe to perfection, even if there was no rice for the pot, Liu Shaoqing would not pick them. No matter how one begged and pleaded, one could talk the skin off one's lips and Liu Shaoqing would merely sit cross-legged in the melon hut, eyes closed, as still as a stone statue. There was nothing he could do but gaze at the melon field with joyful sighs. It was as if he wasn't selling melons but waiting for the right time to marry off his daughter.

Liu Shaoqing was a little eccentric.

2

Melon king Liu Shaoqing had long since turned forty and was fast approaching fifty.

He was tall and gaunt with long egret's legs that carried him forward with great strides. His face was engraved with deep wrinkles like a bricklayer's cleaver and he had a dark smudge of moustache on his upper lip. His face was invariably bent downwards, eyes on the ground, not uttering a sound. Before summer had barely started he was stripped to the waist and barefoot, body folded into three as he squatted among the melon ridges, head and back baking in the fierce sun, beads of sweat splashing on to the melon leaves. His daughter couldn't bear to see it and picking a large lotus leaf inverted it on his head. She wove him a straw rain cape and when the great drops of rain came pouring down would take it to him and slip it over his shoulders.

When it comes to people's reputations, seeing for yourself is a hundred times better than hearing from others, but at a dispassionate glance, no one would guess that Liu Shaoqing was a master nurseryman; and even less would they believe that he was expert at martial arts.

Liu Shaoqing had learnt growing melons from his family, but his martial arts had been passed on to him by someone quite unrelated.

The year he turned ten — it was also in this melon patch the size of your palm — his father had hoisted a pair of huge woven baskets on a carrying pole on to his shoulder and set off to sell his melons, leaving Liu Shaoqing to watch the melon patch. He had climbed up into an old river willow and from there watched and listened to the movements all around him. On the canal, the passenger boats and big cargo boats with their tall masts and billowing white sails kept passing by, up to Beijing or down to Tianjin like clouds flowing over the water. Fishing boats shuttled back and forth, the fishermen singing melancholy fishing songs as they cast their wide nets. Suddenly a woman wearing handcuffs and with fettered ankles burst from the cabin of a closed government boat and jumped into the water. Shots from the mausers of the escorting soldiers thundered in his ears, beating on the surface of the canal like hail. Liu Shaoqing was so frightened that he pulled a willow branch across, through the air to the ground, and ran back to the melon hut.

There was the flash of a figure and he blinked his eyes and saw the woman who had leapt into the canal push a gap in the willow fence around the melon field and wriggle half-way through. Just at that moment their eyes met and she was caught in a dilemma, not knowing whether to advance or retreat, but he hastily signalled to her to wriggle in among the melon ridges and hide herself under the dense layers of melon leaves.

The government boat came in close to the bank and two soldiers jumped off and burst into the melon patch.

"Gentlemen! Officers! You want to buy some melons?" Liu Shaoqing jumped down from the melon hut and went to meet them with a beaming face.

"Young brat! Have you seen an escaped criminal — a woman?" the senior of the two shouted coarsely with a fierce scowl.

"To answer your question, sir, I haven't seen her." Liu Shaoqing continued to smile sweetly with an expression of unaffected innocence, "And my eyes are so sharp that if a midge flies past I can tell a male from a female."

It was almost noon and the weather was hot and

humid without a breath of wind. The scent of the melons was not dispersing and lay heavily concentrated inside the melon patch, making people as dazed as if they were drinking mellow wine. It was as if they were drunk, or half-witted.

"Pick a few melons to quench our thirst!" The saliva had long since been drooling down the senior's chin and he swaggered to the melon hut and sat down.

The other soldier was just about to walk in among the melon ridges when Liu Shaoqing quickly barred the way. "Sir, you can't tell which ones are ripe, let me pick them for you."

The fellow didn't feel inclined to move, so he also went to wait and rest in the cool shade of the melon hut.

Liu Shaoqing went in among the rows of melons, crawling along the ground, lifting the plants in search of melons. Holding a melon close to his ear he patted it with his open hand and listened to see whether it was ripe or not. Finally he bit through a dark green stem, picked a huge black-sinewed water melon and pushed it out along the row. He rolled it along the ground to the melon hut, the sweat pouring off his face.

The two soldiers grabbed the melon and seizing a melon knife slaughtered it on the spot, biting off great chunks and wolfing them down.

While the two soldiers were intent on eating, Liu Shaoqing took the chance to quietly slip along the rows to where the woman was hiding. Taking great care, he whispered softly, "Aunt, don't panic, and don't move. I'll get rid of them."

The two soldiers finished off the huge water melon and then gulped down two *mian* melons and a musk-melon. This turned them both into pot-bellied locusts, incapable of moving. How could they chase after a runaway convict?

"Put it on the account!" The soldiers stretched their necks, belched, and then, hands cradling their distended bellies, waddled off.

Liu Shaoqing waited while the boat cast off, turned back and moved half a *li* from the shore and then shouted towards the melon rows, "Aunt, come out!"

The woman who had jumped into the canal rose up from under a thick layers of leaves. She was about thirty years old, tall and sturdy, and although her hair was in disarray and her face dirty and she was obviously soon to give birth to a child, she was still pretty and charming and her eyes sparkled with courage.

"Such a brave and chivalrous young gentleman!" The tall sturdy woman went over to the melon hut and bowed deeply to Liu Shaoqing like a man. "Many thanks for your kindness in saving my life."

"Aunt, I don't deserve it!" Liu Shaoqing went into the hut and searched out the axe they used for chopping firewood. "Let me break your handcuffs and fetters."

The tall sturdy woman shook her head, saying, "Be so good as to give me two *mian* melons to eat, I'll build up my strength first."

Liu Shaoqing assented and ran off among the melon ridges. In a moment he ran back with a melon in each hand.

The tall sturdy woman had certainly not tasted rice or water for several days, and taking the two big *mian* melons, finished them off in a flash like a strong wind scattering wisps of clouds.

"Aunty, hurry up! Break your fetters and flee for your life!" Liu Shaoqing urged her anxiously.

"There's no need." The tall woman wiped her mouth, took a deep breath and clenched her teeth, summoning all the strength in her body. With a fierce shout, she stretched her shoulders, jerked her feet apart and, as he watched, every link of the iron chains on her hands and feet shattered into tiny pieces; then she drew the fingers of each hand close together and, as if they were soft and boneless, drew them out of the handcuffs. One stamp of her feet on the ground and her ankle fetters split asunder.

Liu Shaoqing stared stupefied, then cried out in astonishment, "Aunty, you've really got some strength!"

The woman smiled and asked, "Child, do you want to learn this *gongfu*?"

"Oh, yes!" Liu Shaoqing answered loudly and clearly.

"Then come with me!" She patted her pregnant belly. "Not only shall I teach you the heights of martial arts, if this is a girl, I'll make her your wife for nothing at all."

"I have to . . . ask my father . . . whether he'll let me. . . ." Liu Shaoqing was terrified and tried to beat a retreat.

"Come with me!" The woman's expression suddenly changed. Stretching out her hands, she grasped Liu Shaoqing's wrists.

Liu Shaoqing's whole body went numb and he couldn't move an inch. He opened his mouth to speak, but could only stutter, he wanted to shout, but no sound came out. The tall sturdy woman bent down, hoisted him on her back and set off with fast, vigorous strides.

When Old Father Liu came back selling melons, his son had long since been kidnapped. He looked for him everywhere; there was no trace of either him or his dead body, so he just had to resign himself to the will of heaven.

Several days later a government notice with pictures and diagrams appeared at ferry stages and intersections, on village walls and temple doors, offering a reward for the capture of the escaped Boxer convict, the great master of martial arts, Big Sister Wu.

Old Father Liu silently prayed to heaven to protect her. This Big Sister Wu could find a path through any mountain and a bridge over any river, and would always escape death by the skin of her teeth. Little did he imagine that it was just this Big Sister Wu who had kidnapped his son.

Though a tree grows ten thousand feet tall, the leaves still fall back to the roots. Liu Shaoqing was gone for thirty years, and then one day came back to the Canal Flats from north of the Great Wall, leading his thirteen-year-old daughter Liu Yemei.

Old Father Liu was still alive, already an old man of seventy or eighty. Liu Shaoqing took over the melon patch from his father and without a word continued his ancestors' profession, making a living by growing melons. About where he'd been for the last thirty years, he kept his mouth tightly sealed and even Old Father Liu could get nothing out of him. Every year he produced melons of the highest grade, and seeing that the skills of his ancestors had not been lost, Old Father Liu left for the nether world with a smile of contentment on his lips.

Liu Shaoqing was a morose character, but the melon

patch was far from cheerless and lonely. From morning till night it resounded with the merry echoes of Liu Yemei's laughter like a hundred birds larking in the forest.

Three girls together can perform an opera, but Liu Yemei alone was enough to command two stages.

3

When Liu Shaoqing was carried off by Big Sister Wu, they had headed for the Northeast, and in a grassy pasture along the way, sure enough, she gave birth to a daughter. Mother and children depended on each other for survival and continued to head north until they came to the banks of a vast river. There was no sign of a boat and even if they'd sprouted wings it would have been difficult to fly across, so they had no choice but to settle down in a tiny desolate village where they chopped down a tangled patch of sagebrush, built a simple hut and passed their days in anonymity.

When Liu Shaoqing was twenty-six and Big Sister Wu's daughter was sixteen, they consummated their marriage, and two years later Liu Yemei was born. But when Liu Yemei was three years old, her mother died, leaving her to grow up under the care of her grandmother. Ten more years passed and Big Sister Wu lay terminally ill. Dressed in her burial clothes, she lay on a bier of *kaoliang* stalks and hemp ropes, eyes wide open, staring at Liu Shaoqing, still refusing to breathe her last. The expression in his old mother-in-law's eyes made everything clear to Liu Shaoqing. He searched out a sharp, pointed knife and kneeling at the bedside made Liu Yemei take it and place the point on his heart. Between his tears he promised: "Mother, if your child ever dares to marry again, let him die beneath Yemei's blade." A fleeting smile passed across Big Sister Wu's face and two loving tears fell from the corners of her eyes. With a light sigh she departed this world.

A weary bird thinks of the forest and an old man's thoughts turn homewards. Liu Shaoqing buried his mother-in-law and brought his daughter back to his family home.

From the time Liu Yemei came gurgling into the world, she was doted on by her grandmother. Big Sister Wu had a bold and resolute character and a thunder-and-lightning disposition. When Liu Shaoqing spoke a word out of place, went against her wishes, or did something she took objection to, if she opened her mouth it was to curse him, if she raised her hand it was to beat him and if she lifted a foot it was to kick him. If Liu Shaoqing's hands and feet were the least bit tardy in learning the skills she was passing on, she would brandish a rattan whip, the back of a knife or the shaft of a spear and beat him fiercely and unrestrainedly until his whole body was black and blue. She called this "if you don't use the whip you won't get results". Big Sister Wu also took a great aversion to her daughter's weakness, hated her for being a wisteria flower that couldn't straighten its back, cursed her as a well rope that couldn't be pulled straight and for never putting up a good front since she'd been a child. But to Liu Yemei, Big Sister Wu was like the sun rising behind the western hills, as different from that iron-hearted, fire-and-brimstone character as if they were two different people.

It was as if in a past life Big Sister Wu had become indebted to her granddaughter and served her faithfully in this life to demonstrate her gratitude and requite the kindness. As her daughter lay on the brick bed, she personally lent a hand and delivered Liu Yemei into the world of men. The first cry of the downy little life fell on the ears of Big Sister Wu like the warble of the oriole or the twitter of a swallow; her eyes filled with happiness and tears of joy poured down her cheeks. And they were born to be together, for once Liu Yemei was a full month old, if her father or mother held her she would kick her little feet as if they were full of prickles and bawl lustily, but as soon as she got into Grandma's arms, the frowns would immediately vanish and a smile would appear on her face, the tear-drops on her soft, round cheeks appearing like spring rain on almond blossoms. From then on Liu Yemei was at her grandmother's side day and night. Big Sister Wu had always hated being tied to the kitchen, had always loved to be out in the fields working, whatever the weather, but now she could never put a foot outside the door. She looked after the house, cooked the meals, coaxed the child and was willing and happy to do so. As she gently rocked the cradle she would sing lullaby after lullaby in dulcet tones, coaxing Liu Yemei to sleep. If a cat in the courtyard yowled or a dog barked, or beyond the wall a cock crowed or a bird squawked, she would seize a watchman's cudgel and drive them away, fearing they would wake the child. If Liu Yemei had a headache and temperature, she would work herself into a fever of anxiety and if in a couple of days her temperature was still not dropping, she would knock her head on the ground at every step and go to the Temple to the Goddess of Mercy to kowtow and seek the advice of the oracle.

As a husband in his wife's home, Liu Shaoqing held the lowest position in the family. Even his daughter Liu Yemei's position was a head higher than his; so like a fruit on the mountain or a flower by the river, his daughter grew up as wild as a crazy melon vine, and he didn't dare to utter a word of protest.

Big Sister Wu was determined to cultivate her granddaughter's indomitable spirit, so from her infancy dressed her as a boy. She didn't grow plaits, but wore her hair in two tufts, nor did she wear bright colours or dab on powder and rouge. Each day they would practise boxing and martial kicking with flying knives and dancing spears. She on no account would teach her how to cook and sew, but instead let her play with the boys, climbing high in the trees and swimming in the river. When two tiny buds appeared on Liu Yemei's chest she still didn't know the difference between male and female. Only on the day she suddenly received her first "monthly letter" did Big Sister Wu awaken her with a mournful sign: "Grandma has been deluding herself, you are after all a jade maiden, not a golden boy. . . ." Thereupon Liu Yemei took off her boy's clothing and put on her girlish finery. Big Sister Wu scrutinized her from head to toe, from far and near. The romantic charm of pretty Liu Yemei's graceful bearing, courage and agility were the spitting image of hers when in the flower of her girlhood — so her despondency turned to delight.

Liu Yemei followed her father back to the Canal

Flats, their old home, but a lifetime of wildness was hard to change, and she found she didn't get along well with the girls who had grown up near the big city; her mouth knew no constraints and no subject was taboo; when she spoke she had no idea of the limits of propriety and frequently had those affected young ladies hiding their faces in embarrassment or blocking their ears. She felt awkward and constrained, so stopped mixing with her sour green apricot companions.

The square inch of land that made up the tiny melon patch lay in an isolated spot outside the village, and apart from people buying melons, there were seldom any visitors. Her father scarcely spoke a word all day, so Liu Yemei was bored to distraction. But her mouth could not stay idle, so she chirruped and twittered at her father's side, determined to get a noise out of this gloomy wooden fish.

One year a child and in another two years a woman, Liu Yemei had reached sixteen; the year her mother was sixteen she and her father had conducted their nuptials, but Liu Yemei had never thought of riding a festooned sedan chair and leaving the melon patch amidst the beating of drums and the clamour of music; yet she had the vague feeling that only when there was someone beside her to tease and amuse her would her heart be filled with delight and her days joyful.

Just at this time, someone came to call on Liu Shaoqing, asking to be taught martial arts.

Liu Shaoqing's melon growing was a skill handed down through the family. Not only was it not passed on to anyone outside the family, it was even kept a close secret from his own daughter. A daughter faced out of the family, and as soon as she was married off, she became part of someone else's family. To pass skills on to a daughter was the equivalent of opening another branch and not keeping things in the family, so passing on family skills had a rigid set of rules: they could only be taught to sons who remained at home and sons-in-law who lived with the family. Liu Shaoqing's skills had come from Big Sister Wu — her rules had been the same — it was only because Liu Shaoqing lived at his wife's home with the same status as a daughter-in-law that Big Sister Wu had passed her martial arts on to him.

Although Liu Yemei was always at her father's side, she didn't thoroughly understand the secrets of melon growing, and although she'd learnt a little boxing and sword-play from her grandmother, she hadn't been taught the consummate skills.

Although Liu Shaoqing was fading, he still had his own definite ideas; he was determined to wait until Liu Yemei brought a satisfactory son-in-law to live in his house before passing on the ultimate secrets of melon growing and martial arts. Then, without fear of any leakage, he would pass the secrets on to the young couple.

The young man wishing to learn martial arts found he'd run up against a stone wall, but he was neither angry nor despondent. On the contrary he came to the melon patch every evening to visit father and daughter and discuss events past and present with great wit and humour. He could also play a bamboo flute with a sweetness that was wonderful to hear. As the days passed, he won great favour with Liu Yemei and even Liu Shaoqing relaxed his vigilance.

This young man was also the son of a poor family in Liuxiang Village. His name was Wu and his milk-name Chenggou'er. He had been to school and had the formal name Wu Gou. At present he was a school-teacher.

4

At the entrance to Liuxiang Village, the canal branched off in a wide curve. On the bank next to a bridge was the little two-roomed, low-eaved, thatched cottage where Wu Gou lived with his family.

His family was poor, his mother widowed — how could he afford to get an education?

That Wu Gou could go to the city to study and become a school-teacher is a story in itself.

When Wu Gou was eight years old he had begun to work for a wealthy family in a neighbouring village as a cowherd. Each morning while the stars still twinkled overhead, he would drive the cattle to the Canal Flats and in the evening he would tread the moonbeams back to the village. The little boy, not big enough to fill a bamboo basket, would spend all day coaxing the great fierce, evil-eyed beasts, living on leftover soup and sour rice.

He herded the cattle for three years, then one day when he had just driven them into their shed and closed the gate, he was called to the accountant's office. He heard the steward shout out to him, "Chenggou'er! Starting tomorrow you are going to keep the young master company at lessons. You don't have to mind the cows on the river bank any more. Quickly go up to the house and kowtow."

This rich landowner had three wives and four concubines, but only at the age of sixty did he finally produce a precious son. From then on he threw himself wholeheartedly into rearing the stripling into a dragon. A huge sedan chair with eight bearers brought a scholarly old schoolmaster from Beijing to open the family school. Face to face with the landlord, the old teacher gave a solemn oath: he would guarantee to give the young master a good education. His knowledge was vast and he'd seen much of the world, they must find a whipping boy to study alongside the young master as they did in the palace when the young emperor attended classes, if the young master was not diligent or was disobedient, his schoolmate would be beaten in his place. This was called "killing the chicken to warn the monkey". The young master would then be an obedient student and not detest his studies.

The landlord exclaimed repeatedly, "Ingenious! Ingenious!" and then thought of the little cowherd Chenggou'er.

The classroom was set amidst flowers and trees in an elegant three-roomed, tiled pavilion in the back courtyard. Green bamboos waving gently before the windows added to the quaint antiquity of the tranquil surroundings. The old gentleman sat upright on his high platform, his long, sombre face lowered and eyes staring, fondling his long, sparse whiskers. On a long desk before him lay several scrolls of classics on yellowed silk and a three-legged bronze censer in which long, thin joss sticks of sandalwood smouldered. Behind this setting, he looked just like some clay or wooden figure brought here from the Temple to the City God. Three paces in front of his desk sat the young master and Wu Gou. The young master used a red sandalwood desk and a pearwood armchair padded with soft silk cushions. Wu Gou used a square table of white planks and sat on a long, broad stool with broken legs.

The old scholar's feet may have stepped into the Republic, but his brain was nevertheless still at the threshold of the Qing Dynasty. His main aim in life was to produce a number one scholar of the highest grade to carry on his name when he was gone. But this young gentleman's appearance was deceptive. He was dull and stupid, and though his eyes were cunning, as soon as he opened a book he became as stupefied as a wooden chicken. The old teacher was eager to achieve results, regardless of method, so he determined to apply the whip to the race horse. Although Wu Gou was so bright that he could recite a passage after the first reading, he had no choice but to suffer punishment on behalf of his classmate. Each day his head would be covered with purple bruises, his body laced with weals from the whip, and his bottom would be so swollen that he didn't dare to sit on his stool. Seeing there was someone to take his punishments for him, the young master was even less concerned about taking his studies seriously, and so to dispel his worries and relieve his boredom, he deliberately feigned stupidity, watching with pleasure from one side as Wu Gou was beaten. With every word he learnt paid for in tears, Wu Gou studied for four years.

The emperor had never again taken his seat on the dragon throne, but the young master had long since become utterly sick of "the odes say" and "Confucius said" and was only interested in getting into his marriage bed as fast as possible for a bit of amusement. The wealthy landlord, as if waking up from his dream, wanted only to see a house full of grandsons to keep the incense burning, and in a single year married three lovely daughters-in-law into his household. Thereupon, the old teacher who had been worshipped like a deity was cast out like a pair of worn-out shoes and sent back to Beijing.

The family school closed down and Wu Gou was sent back to doing odd jobs. He made inquiries about a county teachers' college in Tongzhou City where education and food were both provided and went to take the preliminary examinations; the wealthy man suddenly turned hostile, forcing him to guarantee to pay compensation for four years of tuition fees and meals. Wu Gou wanted to continue his studies, so he had no choice but to make out an official document acknowledging his debts.

After graduation, Wu Gou was assigned to work in the village primary school, but at the beginning of each month, his meagre salary was collected by the landlord's accountant. Not a farthing found its way into his own hand; after eight years he hadn't managed to pay back even half the principal and interest. He was already twenty-six and still unmarried.

Although Wu Gou was delicate featured, wore a long gown and had the gentle and cultivated air of a pure scholar, he was as strong as an ox and had two dextrous hands. As nothing remained of his salary, he had to rent a third of an acre of land on the Canal Flats to eke out a living for himself and his mother. Every day after school, he would take off his long gown, wash it, dry it in the sun, fold it neatly and place it under his pillow. Then with torso bare, he would go out to the fields. Everyone else returned home in the moonlight, hoe on shoulder, but he would head out in the moonlight, hoe on shoulder.

He took his bamboo flute to the Liu Family melon patch every evening for over two weeks.

Sitting on the floor of the melon hut amidst moonbeams and the fragrance of melons, Wu Gou played a melody for Liu Shaoqing and Liu Yemei, the notes floating away on the breeze from the canal.

"Wu Gou, why should a scholar like you want to learn martial arts?" One day, as the sound of the flute faded away, Liu Shaoqing suddenly lost his usual taciturnity and asked the question that had been perplexing him.

"The Japanese devils have seized the three northeastern provinces and want to annex China." Wu Gou's voice was low and there was a catch in his throat. "Everyone has a share of the responsibility when it comes to determining the fate of his country. I want to learn a bit of martial arts and teach it to the students so that some day they can put aside their books and join the army."

Liu Shaoqing smoked silently, not saying a word.

"Brother Wu, I'll teach you!" Liu Yemei suddenly shouted, "but I don't know if you respect a chit of a girl like me enough to call me your teacher."

Liu Shaoqing didn't put up any opposition.

"Some hear the truth before others, everyone has their own speciality, the adept are honoured as teachers." Wu Gou spoke in classical Chinese. It was a habit that had become natural to him. "I am willing to be Little Sister's respectful student."

"At the fifth watch, the first cock-crow, see me under the old river willow outside the melon patch!" Liu Yemei ordered him.

Wu Gou returned home. He still had to correct his students' exercises by the light of a tiny oil lamp; when he finally awoke next morning, it was to hear the cocks of the whole village lustily heralding the dawn. He hurried to the melon patch to find Liu Yemei, trousers rolled to the knees, filling water buckets from the canal.

"I'm late," he apologized profusely, "sorry, sorry!"

"Go home!" Liu Yemei angrily waved him away and went into the melon patch without looking back, slamming the gate behind her.

That evening when Wu Gou went to the melon patch, Liu Yemei had already forgotten her anger and pestered him to tell her classical stories. When one finished, she wanted another and it was midnight before she let Wu Gou go home, arranging once more to meet under the old willow tree at the first cock-crow.

Wu Gou was exhausted mentally and physically. The moment his head touched the pillow he slept until dawn was just breaking; he rushed to the canal bank to find Liu Yemei just washing her face and combing her hair.

"It was only because you kept badgering me to tell stories that I . . . got up so late." Wu Gou said in a low voice.

"Go home!" Liu Yemei was as cold as an icebox, unrelenting and merciless.

That evening Wu Gou went once more to the melon patch and as before Liu Yemei's bad temper had long since vanished. She pestered him to play his flute and he played until midnight before she let him go, arranging to meet next day at the same time and the same place. This time Wu Gou had got smart. He went home and had a word with his mother, then went back to the old willow on the canal bank and sat there waiting until dawn.

As the crowing of cocks drifted through the morning mist from villages along the banks of the canal, Liu Yemei came barefoot through the dewy grass, humming a soft tune. Wu Gou quickly stood up beneath the tree and smiled. "Little Sister, I have been waiting respectfully for quite some time."

Liu Yemei gave a tinkling laugh. "Ah, it's my three-act play called 'Teasing Elder Brother Wu Three Times'."

Wu Gou heaped up a small pile of earth and stuck three fragrant wormwood branches into it, saying deferentially, "Teacher, please sit down, your student wishes to pay his respects."

Liu Yemei spat on the ground and shoved him to one side. "Let's be blood brothers! You'll still be Elder Brother, but you have to call me Second Brother."

From then on, at dawn and dusk, Wu Gou went every day to the canal side to learn martial arts from Liu Yemei. Liu Shaoqing didn't put in an appearance, but he often hid himself among the distant willows, watching quietly.

One evening after they had practised several sets of movements and figures of sword-play, the two of them sat on the low dyke to rest. Liu Yemei was unaccountably perturbed. "Elder Brother, play me a tune — a sweet, peaceful one. . . ."

"OK." Wu Gou smiled. "I'll play the sweet fragrance of your family's melons."

As the tune died away, Liu Yemei suddenly asked in a despondent voice, "Elder Brother, why don't you get married?"

"I'm as poor as a church mouse, who'd want to marry me?" Wu Gou was suddenly desolate.

"Get a matchmaker to find you a wife," Liu Yemei suggested.

"And what would I thank the matchmaker with?" Wu Gou gestured with his empty hands.

"Ah! I'd really like to be your wife." Liu Yemei spoke in all earnestness. "It's just that you'd have to change your name and live at our house, and that would really be doing a wrong to a local sage like you."

"Preposterous!" Wu Gou's face became stern. "You and I are brothers, don't lose your head and get crazy ideas."

"Then I'll be your matchmaker!" Liu Yemei's whole body felt hot and dry. "If I wear out eight pairs of shoes in the process, I won't even ask you for a needle and thread." She finished speaking and jumped into the canal for a swim. Wu Gou, treating the whole thing as a joke, turned and went home.

5

On the canal there were many small boats like chicken coops that trafficked in human flesh. Inside the tiny cabins lay women who had been deceived, duped or plainly kidnapped, eyes blindfolded, mouths gagged and tied securely together with thick ropes like grasshoppers on a string. There was no chance of escape.

The little chicken coop boats didn't dare to make their appearance during the day, only in the dead of night when there was not a soul around did they quietly glide along close to the canal bank. This earned them the name of "yellow croaker rowboats".

At midnight, Liu Yemei, after listening for her father's snores, stealthily crept out of the back window. Grabbing the willow curtain, she glided out of the melon patch and squatted on her heels amongst the rushes at the canal bank, waiting for a boat to pass.

And this time one came.

The tiny boat came floating stealthily down the canal like a piece of duckweed, the cabin like a battened-down hen coop. At the stern stood a man working a creaking oar, while melancholy sobbing reached her from within the cabin.

Liu Yemei didn't ask any questions. With a flick of the wrist, she hurled a stone that caught the oarsman directly on the head. With a cry of pain, he tumbled into the water clutching his skull. As the little boat began to spiral in the water, she waded in, pulled it to the shore and moored it to a willow tree.

She opened the door of the chicken coop and a dark shadow burst out. Pulling at one of its hands, she said, "Don't be afraid! I've come to rescue you." But the dark shadow turned and bit her savagely and ran to hide among the willows.

Liu Yemei was furious and caught up in a couple of strides. With a swing of her leg she sent the shadow sprawling on the ground. Liu Yemei felt her way to a long plait and grasping it in her hand, led her captive back to the melon hut.

Liu Shaoqing had been awakened by the noise and lighting a hurricane lantern asked, "Yemei, what's going on?"

"I attacked a flesh trader's boat and rescued someone." Liu Yemei pulled the black shadow into the lamplight.

The girl was about twenty with thick curly hair and a pretty peach blossom face. Garnet earrings dangled from her ears and her waist was as slender as a willow branch. She was wearing nothing but a cerise petticoat embroidered with buds and lotus flowers that embraced her two white shoulders and clung tightly to her chest, doing nothing to hide her ample bosom. But her slanting eyebrows and her flashing, aggressive beanpod eyes made her appear extremely artful and cunning.

Liu Shaoqing turned his face away and asked, "Girl, what's your name? Which village are you from? How did you come to be kidnapped and put on the boat?"

"My name is Hua Sanchun and I haven't been kidnapped and sold by anyone!" the sly woman shouted venomously. "I was going with my father to fish in the lower reaches of the canal. Why did your young wench stop us and steal our boat?"

"Yemei! You're really one for finding trouble where there isn't any!" Liu Shaoqing lost his temper. "Take this girl back fast and apologize to her father."

"But . . . but. . . ." Liu Yemei also began to have misgivings, "but why was she crying in the cabin?"

"I wasn't crying!" Hua Sanchun flared up.

"Oh no! There's still someone on the boat!" Liu Yemei suddenly awoke to the truth.

Hua Sanchun shivered like a jelly. Liu Yemei seized her plait again and marched her to the canal bank.

At the canal bank there was no sign of the chicken coop boat. By the look of it, the injured oarsman had climbed onto the bank, cast off the moorings and stolen away with the boat.

"You old sinner!" Hua Sanchun began to howl. "You don't even care about abandoning your own daughter, all you care about is currying favour with the boss."

"Just what are you?" Liu Yemei grasped her plait even more tightly and demanded sternly.

"Let go of me. I . . . I'll tell you the truth. . . ."

Only then did Hua Sanchun reveal the true situation: The oarsman was her father, Hua Zijin, who did the running around for a big flesh merchant from Tianjin specializing in "flying falcons". Through abduction or deceit, he had gained control over a group of women whom he sold to single men specially sought out for the purpose. Whether they were peasants, boatmen, porters or fishermen, they all bought their wives at bargain prices. At first the women seemed to know their place, to be sensitive to their husbands' emotions and both on the brick bed and in their daily tasks were diligent and painstaking. They gradually captured the hearts of their menfolk and were given control of the money, rice and firewood. Then it was time to make their move. One day when the man came home from work, he would push open the door to find the room empty and his wife long gone with all his movable property. Only then would he realize he had been taken in. The falcon had seized its prey and flown.

Some women, either because they couldn't extricate

themselves or because they had fallen in love with their husbands, didn't return to the nest on the appointed day. Then someone would come to the house and circle the courtyard whistling and throwing pieces of tile over the walls. The woman would know the falconer's underling had arrived and after contacting him secretly, would either escape with him or beg for a few days' grace to pick up a bit of profit. If the woman avoided contact, thinking of breaking clear of her master – if the falcon couldn't be retrieved — the boss's underlings would come and carry her back by force, not even stopping at murder. This was the work that Hua Zijin undertook, while his daughter kept watch and lent him a hand. This time the two women in the chicken coop cabin had cut their own kite strings. Their menfolk cared for them sincerely and wholeheartedly; they were pregnant and wanted to change their evil ways, wash their hands and start anew. Hua Zijin was adept at luring the tiger from his lair and sent Hua Sanchun to entice them out of their village with sweet words. There they were kidnapped and put on the boat. Who would have guessed that Liu Yemei would fight her way in when they were half-way home and throw their plans into disorder?

"So you're just a seductive vixen that feeds with the tiger!" Liu Yemei ground her teeth in rage and furiously slapped Hua Sanchun on the face. "I'm going to make sure that this time you've gone for wool and come back shorn. You were out for cheap profits but I'm going to make sure you're a double loser."

Now that Hua Sanchun's true colours had been revealed, she didn't dare to try any trick, but asked pitifully, "Young Aunt, how are you going to deal with me?"

"I'm going to cut off your wings and shut you in a cage!" Liu Yemei laughed coldly. "Find you a master on the Canal Flats." Hua Sanchun cast her eyes down and put on a coy expression, but said glibly, "Young Aunt, I'm a blossoming lotus, attractive and accomplished. What kind of man have you betrothed me to? If it's a talented man well matched to my beauty, I'll go with him, but if it's some idiot even a pig wouldn't eat and a dog wouldn't bite, I'd rather take a bit of rope and hang myself from the nearest tree than be badly done to for a lifetime."

"I've found you a gentleman schoolteacher," Liu Yemei said angrily, "with an outstanding character and exceptional talent. It's a come-down for him and a lucky break for you."

"But I still want to see him for myself." Hua Sanchun said with a delighted smile. "The matchmaker says she's bringing a saint and brings a demon instead; it's not that I don't believe your intentions are good, you have kind intentions, but I'm afraid you've never been beyond your own gate, let alone inside anyone else's. You haven't the experience to know what you're talking about."

Liu Yemei wished she could give her another couple of good slaps, but one look at that fragile body, delicate skin, soft flesh and attractive peach-blossom face, and she didn't have the heart to raise her hands again.

By the time she'd dragged Hua Sanchun back to the melon hut by her long plait, the day was already dawning bright and clear.

Hua Sanchun spent all that day locked into the dark

room of the melon hut, nibbling at musk-melons, wolfing down water melons and eating *mian* melons until the fragrance scented the corners of her mouth; although her body was held captive, she was nonetheless more radiant and charming than ever.

Liu Yemei waited impatiently until dusk and, as the sun set, ran helter-skelter straight to Liuxiang Village, over the little bridge and into Wu Gou's house. Wu Gou had just returned from school, taken off his long gown and was about to put it into the soapy washing water. Liu Yemei grabbed the gown out of his hands and tugging at his arm ordered, "Come with me!" then she turned and went.

"Second Brother, what is it?" Wu Gou stumbled along, mystified.

Liu Yemei didn't answer, but in the twinkling of an eye had pulled Wu Gou all the way to the gate of the melon patch where she finally halted. Then she put the long gown over his head, smoothed the sleeves, straightened it up front and back, and looked him over carefully with a burst of laughter. "I've caught a beautiful, artful-tongued, white-bellied waterbird and shut it in a cage. Go and look."

Wu Gou didn't understand what she was talking about and said stupidly, "That must be a feast for the eyes."

Liu Yemei drove him up into the melon hut.

After the time it takes to eat a meal, Wu Gou came out of the melon hut. Liu Yemei inclined her head to one side and asked, "Does it take your fancy?"

Wu Gou blushed scarlet, "I'll go along with whatever you arrange."

Liu Yemei leaped up into the hut and went into the dark room. To her surprise she found Hua Sanchun leaning against the back window weeping as copiously as a rainstorm on peach blossoms.

"You're a wild duck set to fly with the swans and you still think it's not good enough for you?" Liu Yemei shouted, her face blanching in fury. "What's the matter, do you object to his poverty — you want someone rich, do you?"

Hua Sanchun shook her head and said through her sobs, "To marry a wonderful man like him would be the luck of a lifetime."

"You've got a guilty conscience." Liu Yemei pressed her relentlessly. "Come on, out with it."

"I'm scared . . . I'd be the death of him." Hua Sanchun shivered, her face tragic, "Our boss's young gentleman Tang Sanyuanzi has already picked me to be his concubine. If I marry Mr Wu, we can't fly away into the sky or dig ourselves into the ground. Tang Sanyuanzi will come looking for me and then Mr Wu will be lucky to get away with his life, and I'll be taken off to flying falcons!"

"If they send a man, I'll kill a man!" Liu Yemei ferociously knotted her brows. "If they send two, I'll kill the pair of them!"

"If three come, then I'll lend a hand too." Outside the window Liu Shaoqing spoke with unhurried calm, then gave a laugh and added, "You can spend your life with Wu Gou without having to worry."

The moon was bright and full. Liu Yemei plucked a wild flower from the willow fence and hastily tucked it into Hua Sanchun's hair, then she pushed Wu Gou and Hua Sanchun down to kneel on the ground where they did obeisance to the moon and so became husband and wife.

6

For several days, Hua Sanchun was terrified of the daylight, longing for the night to fall. She and Wu Gou sported among the pillows, warm and affectionate. Although Hua Sanchun was a virgin, she had grown up among the flying falconer's coquettish vamps, spoilt and facetious. There had long since been no role she had not learnt to play. Wu Gou was a simple, honest peasant's boy and a conventional scholar and understood nothing of the subtleties of relationships. Although he felt Hua Sanchun was a bit too frivolous, he still adored her good looks and pitied her unfortunate lot, so he didn't pick fault with her, but was attentive and kind.

Early one morning, Wu Gou awoke to find the glow of sunrise already filling the window. He hastily threw on his clothes and got up.

"Don't . . . go to school today, stay with me." Hua Sanchun, face pallid, couldn't bear to see him go.

"I didn't ask for the day off yesterday." Wu Gou looked disconcerted. "I can't let the kids down."

"Then . . . go!" Hua Sanchun sighed. "See if you can come back early."

Wu Gou hastily left, not noticing that Hua Sanchun was distracted, avoiding his glance.

According to the custom of the Canal Flats, a new wife couldn't leave the house until she'd been married for eighteen days. Morning and afternoon, Wu Gou's mother took her hoe and went to the fields while Hua Sanchun did the cooking in the courtyard.

As the sun set, Hua Sanchun stood at the stove mixing flour and water into noodle dough. She had just lit the fire when suddenly a shrill whistle from the canal side beyond the courtyard wall pierced her ears — three long notes followed by two short, then two short notes followed by three long. Then the whistler gradually moved off into the distance.

Her face deathly pale, Hua Sanchun threw down the rolling board, piled firewood into the stove and ran into the house. There were three tattered quilts on the brick bed, a few books on the windowsill, a few old clothes in the wardrobe, and a little grain in a vat. Apart from that there were a few chickens and two goats. If she stole the goats they wouldn't bring anything, and she didn't have the heart to anyway; she looked at the sky to guess the time and hurriedly left the house, following the sound of the whistle to make contact with the man who'd been sent to find her.

Wu Gou was worried about Hua Sanchun, so he dismissed his students and came home early, looking forward to a meal. But when he opened the gate, he discovered the pot burning on the stove, chickens picking around an overturned flour bowl and the goats bleating in their pen. The courtyard was deserted.

"Sanchun!" he shouted.

No one answered. Wu Gou searched the house and courtyard but found no trace of Hua Sanchun. Panic-stricken he ran to their fields by the river, but only his mother was there hoeing the ground, so he turned and ran to the Liu Family melon patch.

"Oh no!" Liu Yemei fidgeted with anxiety. "One of the runners must have enticed her to leave."

"Go quickly and make a thorough search for her!" Liu Shaoqing stamped his foot.

Wu Gou and Liu Yemei, following the canal through groves of willows on the bank and tall rushes in the shallow water, suddenly heard the sound of cursing, beating and struggling coming from a patch of wild hemp growing at the canal bend. . . . Liu Yemei grabbed at Wu Gou with one hand and continued onwards on tiptoe.

The setting sun was like blood. A scrawny old man with arms and legs like matchsticks was screaming at the top of his voice, "He had it in you, but you haven't taken a single thing of his, you cheap little baggage."

"Papa, he's penniless. . . ." came Hua Sanchun's mournful voice.

"You expect me to believe he didn't have a single grain of rice?"

"How could I make them starve?"

"And not a single quilt? Half a mattress? No clothes we could sell as patches or rags?"

"How could I have the heart to let them freeze?"

"By the look of things, you've fallen for him, haven't you?"

"Papa, have a heart. . . ." Hua Sanchun sobbed. "What's done can't be undone, show some mercy and let me go back to him."

"Cheap bitch!" Hua Zijin began to punch and kick. "The boss's son doesn't mind that you're soiled goods, he sent me and Jia Erhaba to take you back. He'll dress you in silk and satin, deck you in silver and gold, feed you with the best, but you can't bear to part with an impoverished peasant without a catty of rice to his name."

"Papa, you can wash your hands and turn straight too!" Hua Sanchun held tightly onto her father's legs, begging plaintively. "Come and live at the Canal Flats, spend your days here with me."

"Crap!" Hua Zijin shouted shrilly. "Can that poverty-stricken man of yours afford to give me two pouches of tobacco a day? Can he give me *erguotou* spirits with every meal? Can he give me. . . ."

"Hua Zijin, don't fucking well waste your time blathering!" Jia Erhaba leapt out from among the wild hemp. "Truss her up and carry her off." He untied a length of rope from around his waist.

"No one's carrying anyone off!" Liu Yemei got into the action with Wu Gou close behind her.

"Mind your own business, you skinny little faggot!" Hua Zijin gave a sinister smile. "If you annoy me, I'll take you along too. Cherries and mulberries can be sold in the same basket."

"Papa, run! Fast!" Hua Sanchun shouted. "That girl is an expert at martial arts. You can't afford to provoke her."

"Animal can conquer vegetable, and a man can handle any woman." Hua Zijin took up a posture like a hungry wolf about to leap on a lamb.

"Papa!" Hua Sanchun wailed. "Just take a look, behind the girl is your own son-in-law, he's a man in a million. You couldn't find one like him if you went looking."

"I'll tear the penniless bookworm to pieces, then you'll have to forget the whole thing." Hua Zijin lunged at Wu Gou like a mad dog.

But it was Liu Yemei who stepped forward to meet him. Tripping him neatly with one foot, she grabbed one of his wrists and threw him rolling across the ground. With a cold smile she told him, "For the sake of Brother Wu and Sister-in-law Sanchun, I won't get violent."

Catching them off guard, Jia Erhaba pulled out a dagger and sent it glinting coldly through the air at Wu Gou.

No one could have imagined the speed of Liu Yemei's eyes and hands. She plucked the dagger out of the air by the handle and hurled it back straight into Jia Erhaba's thigh. He gave a scream of pain and staggered away, writhing in agony. Liu Yemei didn't pursue him.

Hua Zijin lay curled up in a ball on the ground, twitching in terror. Liu Yemei walked over to him and, mixing severity with compassion, gave him a kick and spat at him. "You get out of here too! I don't know how an inhuman father like you still has the face to come and see his daughter."

Hua Zijin clutched his head and scuttled off like a frightened rat.

Liu Yemei tossed the unconscious Hua Sanchun on her back and carried her home for Wu Gou.

Not long afterwards, Hua Sanchun became pregnant and was due to give birth the following year when the wheat flowers were setting.

As usual, Old Mother Wu worked in the fields while she stayed at home cooking the meals, and as before it was one evening when she was mixing dough that the whistle sounded from the canal bank outside the courtyard. Her heart leapt in fear, but she didn't panic like last time. She took a few deep breaths and pulled herself together. She extinguished the fire with two ladles of water, put the plate of dough inside the pot and weighed the lid down with a grindstone. Then she locked the door and set out for the Liu Family melon patch in search of help.

The path to the Liu Family melon patch was a wide

willow-lined lane, but Hua Sanchun, wanting to get there quickly, decided to take a short cut. She followed a narrow track that led up and down desolate hillocks and through bramble thickets that reached high above her head. Tiny woodcutters' tracks led off in all directions, crisscrossing in and out. Hua Sanchun had never cut firewood, and since the time when she had almost been tied up and carried off, she hadn't dared to leave the house. She wasn't familiar with the main roads and even less sure of her way along the tiny tracks, so after entering the Canal Flats in a flurry, she became totally confused and lost her way. She took this turning and then that one, twisting and circling until she came to a fork in the path.

"Sanchun!" Jia Erhaba leaped out of the thicket. Standing on one leg, he showed his teeth in an evil grin. "I've come back to fetch Your Majesty."

After the fellow's thigh had been gashed by Liu Yemei, he'd returned to Tianjin and been immobilized for a good three months. When he'd finally got up from his bed, one leg was markedly shorter than the other, he walked with a lopsided gait in leaps and hops, and to stand upright he had no choice but to prop himself up on one leg.

Hua Sanchun turned to run, but found the boss's son, Tang Sanyuanzi, standing in the path, blocking her escape.

Tang Sanyuanzi was a licentious profligate, slick and dandified, a smiling face hiding a vicious, evil heart: a man with the soul of a beast. He wore leather boots, a silk gown and silk trousers drawn in tightly at the ankles with silken ribbons fastened with bows. His unbuttoned, close-fitting shirt was sewn with a double row of loop fasteners, and tattooed on the white skin of his chest were a pair of ferocious dragons sporting with a pearl. At a casual glance he reminded one of a patterned white snake that had just slithered out of the grass.

"Sanchun, I've missed you." Tang Sanyuanzi leered at her from the corner of his eye. "Come with me!"

"Young Master, where . . . to?"

One look at the lecher's red lips and white teeth and Hua Sanchun, scared out of her wits, felt her legs go weak.

"I have a fast boat moored at the bank, I'll take you back to Tianjin to live like a goddess." Tang Sanyuanzi sweet-talked her in a honeyed voice.

"Young Master, please be lenient with me." Hua Sanchun sank to her knees. "I'm more than nine months pregnant with Wu Gou's child, I'm a wilted flower, past my bloom, let me free. Please."

"If you won't listen to good advice, don't blame me if I have to get rough with you!" Tang Sanyuanzi's expression suddenly changed to murderous spite.

"Bring Hua Zijin here!"

"Yes sir!"

Jia Erhaba pulled Hua Zijin out from the long grass like a mangy dog and threw him down in front of Hua Sanchun.

"Sanchun, go back and have a good time with the young master." Hua Zijin was snivelling and his eyes watered.

"I'll never go back to that life!" Hua Sanchun straightened her back and stood erect. "I'm determined to stay with Wu Gou till the end of my life."

"Are you coming with me or not?" A double-edged

dagger flashed coldly in Tang Sanyuanzi's hand as he slashed open Hua Zijin's shirt. "If you won't come I'll finish off your old man."

"No one can be closer than a father and daughter, Sanchun. Save papa's life!" Hua Zijin pleaded.

Hua Sanchun hardened her heart and gritted her teeth. "Alive or dead I belong to Wu Gou, I don't recognize any other relations."

Tang Sanyuanzi's brows met in a scowl as he plunged the blade into Hua Zijin's chest. Flicking his wrist back and pushing down, he slit Hua Zijin from chest to belly.

"Murder!" Hua Sanchun gave a shrill, desolate scream and began to run along the tiny path through the brambles. "Uncle Liu, Sister Mei! Help!"

Tang Sanyuanzi caught up in a few strides and kicked her to the ground. Jia Erhaba sat astride her body ready to truss her up like a chicken. Hua Sanchun fought desperately, struggling and flailing, all the time shouting at the top of her voice. She clawed Jia Erhaba's face with her nails and when Tang Sanyuanzi tried to put his hand over her mouth, she bit him sharply on the finger.

From the melon patch, Liu Shaoqing had seen a fast boat moor at the canal bank and two sinister strangers leap off, look carefully around and then quickly disappear. His suspicions roused, he stood for a long time lost in thought, then closed the wooden gate and set off in pursuit. Liu Yemei was cutting dry grass for kindling when Hua Sanchun's cries floated down to her on the wind. Sickle in hand she also ran up. Father and daughter met by chance on the path and continued on together.

Seeing that Hua Sanchun could not be taken by force,

Tang Sanyuanzi pulled out his double-edged dagger and raised his hand to stab her. Liu Shaoqing, still too far away to wrest it from him, shouted fiercely, "Stop!" The furious shout from the usually quiet old man resounded like a clap of thunder. Tang Sanyuanzi's hand trembled and the knife fell to the ground.

As soon as he caught sight of Liu Yemei, Jia Erhaba gave a ghastly shriek: "Young Master! This little brat is not to be messed with. Quick! Run!"

Father and daughter watched the two hoodlums flee in panic, wetting their pants in terror, but made no attempt to pursue.

Hua Sanchun had lost consciousness, and began losing blood. There was a gurgling cry and her baby came into the world.

7

Hua Sanchun committed herself unreservedly to Wu Gou and settled down at the Canal Flats.

This woman produced children like a lotus flower producing seeds, but when she'd given birth she was just as pretty and enchanting as ever. It was really strange. As she lay between life and death among the brambles on the canal bank, she had given birth to a boy whom she named Moyu'er. When Moyu'er was just a hundred days old, she became pregnant again. She had already given birth to a precious son and, as if she'd won great distinction in battle, became overweeningly particular and treated Old Mother Wu with great disdain; but the moment she saw Wu Gou she became fastidious in quite a different way, petting and fussing over him until she had him kneaded as smooth as the mud walls of Liu Shaoqing's melon hut.

During Hua Sanchun's second pregnancy, if she wasn't demanding to eat something sour, she was clamouring to eat something hot. The eggs that the family's chickens laid were meant to be swapped for oil or bartered for salt, but they all disappeared down her greedy throat.

Liu Yemei loved Wu Gou and his mother dearly. When the apricot season was over, she went to the canal bank to pick wild berries for Hua Sanchun and brought her baskets of chilli peppers so that she could eat to her heart's content. She also caught carp from the canal and set nets among the willows to catch quail to build up Hua Sanchun's strength.

For the thirty days of Hua Sanchun's confinement, Liu Yemei served her with unstinting care.

"Sister Mei, you're really my lucky star! Every day I pray to the old matchmaker under the moon to send down a golden boy to be your husband."

Liu Yemei could neither quarrel with her, nor get angry. "*Pei*! I'll cut out your tongue and slit your mouth!"

"If I was a man, I'd come with three bands, flags, gongs and parasols and carry you off in a sedan chair with eight bearers to be my wife. Then I'd make a Buddha niche for you, ten feet high, and worship you in it." The glib words rolled off Hua Sanchun's tongue as if she was chanting a folk ballad to the accompaniment of wooden clappers.

"If I was Brother Wu, I'd whip a layer of skin off you every day," Liu Yemei scolded with a laugh. "You're a greedy, lazy good-for-nothing. Whoever heard of a wife like you?"

Hua Sanchun's laziness was even worse than her greed. Ever since she'd given birth to Moyu'er, she'd had a reason for not giving in on any account. She didn't work the grindstone, didn't cook, didn't fetch water, didn't collect firewood and adamantly refused to work in the fields. All the labour inside and outside the house fell to Old Mother Wu who had to hobble in and out on her tiny bound feet as best she could. All Hua Sanchun could think of was decking herself out to entrance Wu Gou so that he wouldn't be tempted to seek his pleasure outside the home. She had no osmanthus oil for her hair, so she brought fragrant wood shavings from the carpenter, soaked them in a dish and then rinsed the water through her soft, raven-black hair until it shone with a brilliant lustre. Her peach blossom face naturally glowed with health, but she insisted on gathering handfuls of pink balsam flowers, squeezing out the juice and daubing it on her cheeks and lips. She couldn't afford patterned material, but fortunately she was intelligent and skilful. She bought coloured embroidery silk on credit from a passing pedlar and covered her coarse white cotton jacket with rich embroidery. Wu Gou came home from school to find everything in the house topsy-turvy and the water vat dry as a bone. Old Mother Wu was coaxing the howling children on one hand, and on the other feeding the chickens and beating the dog. Hua Sanchun meanwhile was admiring herself in half a broken mirror beside the window, smoothing her hair and posing in the last rays of the setting sun. Wu Gou's temper inevitably rose and he scolded angrily: "How can you bear to let things get like this?" Hua Sanchun made no attempt to argue, but turned her eyes on him with an enchanting smile. All Wu Gou could do was sigh, hang the water buckets on the shoulder pole and set off for the river.

At the riverside Liu Yemei was washing clothes. Seeing Wu Gou hurrying along the path to draw water, she immediately began to tease him. "Elder Brother, you've really spoilt Sister-in-law Sanchun rotten!"

"It's all your fault for setting the snare – I was really taken in!" Wu Gou joked. "You sent me a beautiful, artful-tongued, white-bellied waterbird, attractive and useless. I can't get rid of her even if I want to."

Liu Yemei lowered her head and silently scrubbed away at the clothes, not saying a word.

The next day when Wu Gou came home, he found the vat full of water and two full buckets standing beside it. "Who fetched it?" he asked Hua Sanchun who was admiring herself in the mirror by the window.

"Your good little sister, my virtuous sister-in-law," Hua Sanchun answered with a careless laugh. "Sister Yemei is just like one of the family."

Wu Gou turned and went out. He was on his way to the Liu Family melon patch to offer his thanks when he saw Liu Yemei, hoe in hand, weeding his two *mu* of rented land on the Canal Flats.

"Second Brother, how can I overburden you like this — not once but again and again." Wu Gou was overcome with shame.

"Fetching a few buckets of water and hoeing a couple of rows of vegetables won't kill me!" Liu Yemei said with a straight face and then added cuttingly, "You'd better go and worship your divine wife, and don't forget to kowtow and burn incense every morning and evening!"

Wu Gou was knocked speechless and turned home in

a burning fury. For the first time he raised his voice and quarrelled with Hua Sanchun.

"You ought to learn a lesson from Sister Mei, you shouldn't be so damned lazy, indulging yourself all the time and not doing a stroke of work."

"I know you're looking to see how green the grass is on the other side!" Hua Sanchun stretched out her fingers and lightly tapped Wu Gou's temples. "Eating from your bowl and looking into the cooking pot." She pursed her lips until you could have hung an oil bottle there; tear drops sparkled in her eyes, her expression was of one who has been grievously wronged.

"You . . . you . . . ." Wu Gou was too gentle and cultivated, all he could do was heave a long sigh.

But Hua Sanchun was all smiles again. She threw herself into Wu Gou's arms acting like a silly, spoilt child.

That day, Liu Yemei walked through the door with buckets full of water just as an exasperated Mother Wu was quarrelling with Hua Sanchun.

"People have a sense of face like trees have bark. You don't lift a finger all day, don't you feel your face burn with shame, or the slightest twinge of conscience?" Mother Wu grumbled. "Liu Yemei isn't indebted to us and doesn't owe us anything, and she isn't our hired hand. . . ."

"She's casting a long line to catch a big fish!" Hua Sanchun said sharply, impervious to all reason. "I have to keep a close eye on her and be wary of everything she does. I have a brick bed the size of your fist and she's not going to take it over!"

"People speak like people and beasts like beasts. What kind of two-legged animal are you!" In her fury

Mother Wu had to clutch the door post to prevent herself from fainting away.

"Hua Sanchun, what did you say?" Sparks of anger shone in Liu Yemei's eyes as she threw down the water buckets and burst into the room.

"You heard — and what are you going to do about it?" With a look of cunning, Hua Sanchun stuck her hands on her hips and shook her head until her earrings jangled. Liu Yemei jumped at her and grabbed the side of her mouth, but Hua Sanchun was not willing to submit, and scratched and bit: five long scratch marks were gouged in the back of Liu Yemei's hand and three teeth marks were left imprinted in her shoulder. This roused Liu Yemei to a primitive passion, and like an eagle swooping on a rabbit or a cat pouncing on a mouse, she dragged Hua Sanchun out of the house and threw her on the ground punching and kicking, shouting at her as she did: "Are you going to take that back? Are you going to take that back?"

Despite the beating, Hua Sanchun still raised her chin defiantly and shouted, "The Liu Family brat wants to take over my nest."

The blood surged to Liu Yemei's face and seizing up a blunt hatchet from the corner of the yard and bringing over a grindstone, she pressed Hua Sanchun's chin down on the stone, pinched her neck to force out her tongue and raised the hatchet. "Now do you take it back or not? I'll cut off your tongue to feed the dogs!"

Hua Sanchun's courage left her. Speaking with great difficulty she repeated over and over, "My dear sister, I . . . take it all back. . . ."

Liu Yemei threw down the hatchet, averted her face and left with a belly full of grievances and nowhere to air them. She walked home sobbing and when she reached the melon patch wiped away the tears that covered her face and sat stupefied by the cooking stove, lost in thought.

Across the Canal Flats, smoke from cooking fires curled upwards into the sky and dispersed in the gentle evening breeze. From the shady, willow-lined lane drifted a voice, now high, now low, sobbing and shouting.

Among the melon rows, Liu Shaoqing straightened his back, and hand behind his ear listened intently. The sounds were coming closer.

"That Liu girl is a thieving minx. . . ."

"Yemei!" Liu Shaoqing was shocked. "It sounds as if Hua Sanchun is cursing you!"

Liu Yemei listened. Sure enough it was Hua Sanchun shouting abuse at her from the lane. Her anger surged up like a firecracker shooting flames through the sky and she screamed in fury, "I'll skin her alive!"

"A gentleman uses his mouth, not his fists!" Liu Shaoqing barred his daughter's way and went out to meet Hua Sanchun.

Hua Sanchun, with hair dishevelled, came tottering down the road leaning on a willow cane. The moment she caught sight of Liu Shaoqing, she sank down and began to wail loudly, "Uncle Liu, your Yemei wants to take over my nest, just now she was trying to kill me with a hatchet. Plead with her for the sake of your niece, beg her to think of my kiddies even if she despises me, take pity on my children and save my life."

"Sanchun, no venomous mudslinging here," Liu Shaoqing looked stern.

"My good uncle, you're neither deaf nor blind, don't

tell me you're completely in the dark. Have you slept so much that your brain is addled?" Hua Sanchun's voice was thrill, a cold smile on her lips. "It's been more than a couple of days that Yemei and my kids' dad have been carrying on like a creeper wrapped round a tree."

"Hua Sanchun, there are gods three feet under the ground, we can slit our chests and open our hearts to them." Liu Yemei was filled with hatred and shame, and unable to find a word to say in her own defence, wished she might die on the spot.

Liu Shaoqing once more barred his daughter's way. Swallowing his disgust with an effort he said coldly, "Sanchun, go back home, from today on our families will have nothing more to do with each other."

"Uncle, thank you for your kindness," Hua Sanchun said mournfully, bowing and scraping.

Neither father nor daughter could eat a bite of their dinners and both retired early; the melon patch lay in darkness and a waning crescent moon showed faintly through the branches of the willows.

"Uncle Liu, Second Brother Yemei!" Wu Gou stood outside the willow fence, his breath coming in short gasps. "My worthless wife has offended you with her evil tongue. I've come to apologize."

"Wu Gou," Liu Yemei parted the curtain of willows screening the back window of the melon hut, revealing her torso. With a melon knife she cut off one corner of her jacket and threw it out of the window. "I'm breaking our blood pact. The relationship between us is severed."

"Uncle Liu! . . ." Wu Gou knelt on the ground.

But no matter how he begged and pleaded, no reply came from the silent hut.

He knelt until the moon sank in the west, then returned home where he remained seriously ill for many days.

8

In November 1935, at the instigation of the invading Japanese, the traitor Yin Rugeng marked off a region in the eastern part of Hebei Province as his private empire, named it the Jidong Anti-Communist Autonomous Government and enthroned himself at the Longevity Palace in Tongzhou. He then issued a decree making all the Canal Flats within fifteen *li* of the city government property. After separating the fertile from the barren, he divided it up into strips and patches and bestowed it upon his relatives and imperial officials. The square-shaped Canal Flats at Liuxiang were rich and fertile and the scenery was as pretty as a picture, so it nominally became the property of Yin Rugeng's three-year-old daughter, as a little rouge for this gracious young lady's cheeks. The Liu Family melon patch formed the outermost tip of this patch of rouge, so the property that had belonged to the Liu Family for three generations changed its name to Yin, and father and daughter only had to supply grain each year to their new mistress, they also had to pay rent.

Liu Yemei's blood boiled with an anger that couldn't be repressed. Sobbing with fury she shouted, "We'll boil the melon seeds so they won't shoot. We'll make sure not a blade of grass will grow on this ground."

Liu Shaoqing shook his head gravely. "One seed in the ground brings the thousand to the storehouse, we can't grieve heaven and harm reason."

But Liu Yemei remained unreconciled. "Then we'll spindle the seedlings so the melons won't set, neglect the plants so that the melons are small."

But Liu Shaoqing got angry, and slapping his thigh retorted, "And won't that ruin the reputation our family has preserved for generations?"

"Don't tell me you're going to calmly and quietly turn yourself into a good-for-nothing lackey." Liu Yemei lost her temper with her father.

Liu Shaoqing heaved a long sigh. "A real man has to know when to knuckle under and when to fight back."

He still worked as if he was tending his own melon patch. His sweat splashed on the flower petals, and his painstaking care reached every tiny melon tendril, putting to good use the secrets handed down from his forefathers and his own unique skills. His melons were ripe a solar term before anyone else's and tomorrow he would open the melon garden and put his melons on the market.

To a melon grower, opening the selling season is like holding a wedding. A wealthy plantation owner would call in a fortune-teller to select an auspicious day, prepare joss sticks, candles and paper horses to sacrifice to the gods of heaven and earth, arrange a splendid feast and respectfully await the arrival of his distinguished guests. Although their poorer counterparts were not so fastidious, they would still look through the calendar for a lucky date so as to ensure a good market. The grower would wash his face and comb his hair, put on his neatest clothes and the moment the rosy dawn glow appeared over the eastern mountains, would open the gates and let off a long string of firecrackers.

At the sound of the crackers, the earth would stir and melon eaters come from all directions; the swiftest footed and first to arrive would become the noble personage who would declare the garden open. The master of the melon patch, a picture of smiling amiability, would bow and scrape and lead his guest to the melon hut, bid him take a seat on a rush cushion and place a table before him. Then he'd bring forth his prize melon for the distinguished guest to admire. This noble personage, wanting to play along to please his host, would recite a happy verse or say a few auspicious words.

What melon growers feared most was for a widower, a widow or an orphan, or someone with no children, irregular features or a maimed limb to open his melon patch, for that would bring an unlucky year.

What they welcomed was someone with exceptional luck to open the garden. These people could also be divided into several ranks: A newly married official or a young wife whose first baby was a precious boy were both distinguished persons of the highest rank, they would fill the garden with unbounded joy; but the most welcome visitor would be a bare-bottomed little boy clad only in a red pinafore and head shaven to leave just a small patch of hair shaped like a flat-iron. In the eyes of the master of the melon patch, they were prosperity-bringing cherubs sent by the old god of wealth.

Each year for two weeks before the garden was opened, father and daughter went through every row of melons, searching through the leaves of every melon plant for the king melon. What it took was keen eyesight. The dark green rollers rambled in disorder over the whole ground, the huge watermelons like sets of identical twins — all of identical heights with shoulders of equal widths, it was impossible to tell the difference between them; one had to have exceptional insight into the art to be able to pick out the "lord of the dragons". Once the melon king was appointed, although it didn't leap to heaven in a single bound, it was nevertheless raised high above the melon masses. The character "happiness" in red was pinned to its body and it was padded beneath with a circle of rushes. A willow twig was inserted in its side holding a red-cloth market sign — a splash of red in a sea of green that drew one's immediate attention. At this time Liu Shaoqing and Liu Yemei had to take extra care in watching the melons, patrolling the rows several times at night and never letting their eyes wander during the day. If the melon king was stolen, it would be the disappointment of the year.

But everyone knew that Liu, father and daughter, had formidable fists and feet and watched the melons closely. No one would dare to provoke an opponent so far their superior, so the melon king had never once been stolen.

Although tomorrow was the day for opening the melon patch, Liu Shaoqing had been summoned to the Canal Flats police station just after noon, and since the melon patch was no longer theirs, Liu Yemei had no heart to watch the melons, so she sat in the melon hut engrossed in weaving mats and baskets, only raising her head to give the melon patch a cursory glance when her neck became sore.

She was already twenty and still unmarried. The Liu Family incense had to be kept burning, so she couldn't marry and join another family. But the men who were willing to change their names and live under her roof were either morally unsatisfactory, or she didn't like the look of them. She'd rather remain a stay-at-home spinster than become a fresh flower stuck in a heap of cow dung. She ought to become a mother, but a lone flower can't produce seeds. Once she had dreamed that a tiny boy like a green leaved musk-melon had squirmed in her arms, calling her mama in his soft, pampered voice. A careful look at him and she discovered it was Wu Gou's son Moyu'er. In her shame and embarrassment she woke with a start, heartbeating wildly, and no matter how she tried, was quite unable to get back to sleep. After that, whenever she saw the mischievous little Moyu'er, she would blush deep red, but seemed to feel that an invisible thread tied Moyu'er to her heart strings.

She'd had no contact with Wu Gou's family for several years now. Hua Sanchun gave birth to a son every year, just as the melons grew ripe each year under Liu Yemei's care. Traces of fish-tail wrinkles had already crept quietly to the corners of her eyes, but she still cherished her good looks. She only concerned herself with Wu Gou and had no time for her children. In winter they would huddle together on the heated brick bed like a brood of chickens, never leaving the house. In summer they became wild birds skimming through the skies, playing all day long in the wide canal.

Sitting in the melon hut, Liu Yemei had almost finished weaving two willow baskets to sell for a few coppers at the local market. She'd run out of willow strips, so she jumped down from the melon hut to fetch a few more bundles from the stack of firewood under the house. As her feet touched the ground, she inadvertently glanced up and suddenly discovered that the willow twigs supporting the red pennant among the rows of melons had disappeared. In fright and fury, she raced across to find out what had happened.

Following the ridge along the boundary of the melon patch, she saw a narrow hole the size of an irrigation outlet — too small to have been made by a brawny man — had been squeezed through the willow fence. She looked at the ground, and there, sure enough, were a row of little footprints. On tiptoe Liu Yemei followed the path they led in among the melon ridges. A brief search and under a thick layer of melon leaves she discovered a little boy naked as the day he was born, fast asleep and still biting on a *mian* melon. It was Moyu'er.

Liu Yemei couldn't prevent herself from laughing out loud, but quickly covered her mouth for fear of waking the child. She slowly squatted down to look at him and the more she looked, the more she loved him. The more she looked, the more her heart ached, thinking of her dream.

Moyu'er suddenly opened his eyes, squinting in the bright sunlight. When he saw that it was Liu Yemei squatting at his side, he hastily closed his eyes again, pretending to be asleep.

"Moyu'er, are you hungry?" Liu Yemei's voice was quiet and gentle, her heart aching.

Moyu'er nodded his head, then immediately shook it vigorously. "I'm already full."

"There's nothing to eat at home?"

"There's been nothing in the pot for several days."

"What about your papa?"

"The police bastards are after him. He ran away."

"Ah!" Liu Yemei's heart jumped in fright and the colour drained from her face. "What about your mama?"

"Mama's sitting in the corner crying, she wants to die."

"What about grandma?" Liu Yemei asked anxiously.

"Grandma sent me to beg Aunty Liu for something to eat."

"Why didn't you ask me then?"

"I . . . was scared you wouldn't give me anything, so I wriggled into the melon rows and stole some melons. I ate . . . and ate . . . and fell asleep."

Moyu'er was not yet six, but he was even brighter than his father had been at his age. The dark shadows that lay between adults cast themselves on his little heart. He indistinctly knew that between his family and the Liu family lay a knot of enmity that could never be untied.

Liu Yemei wept. She got up, fetched a woven willow basket from under the hut and piled it high with *mian* melons, saying, "Moyu'er, give these to your grandma and little brothers to eat."

She hoisted the basket full of melons onto her back and led Moyu'er homewards. When they were almost at the entrance to the village, Moyu'er called, "Aunty Liu, I'll call mama to come and meet you!" then raced off home at top speed.

Liu Yemei put the willow basket on the ground, then turned and went. She had no desire to meet Hua Sanchun.

When she got back to the melon patch, Liu Shaoqing had just been released from the police station and was sitting gloomily in the melon hut smoking. Hearing his daughter's footsteps, his voice rumbled in his throat, "Wu Gou's run away."

"I've just sent his family a basket of *mian* melons," Liu Yemei said despondently. "You don't know why those sons-of-bitches police are after him?"

"When enemies meet, there's hatred and jealousy aplenty." Liu Shaoqing took a couple of draws on his pipe before continuing, "Can you guess who the police chief is? It's that boss's son that we sent packing, Tang Sanyuanzi."

"Old enemies are bound to meet!" Liu Yemei was consumed with fury. "It was him that had you sent for so he could pick a quarrel, wasn't it?"

"He pressed me to tell him where Wu Gou is, but how should I know?" Liu Shaoqing grunted in disgust. "And even if I knew, I wouldn't tell him!"

"Where has he gone?" Liu Yemei's heart was heavy.

Liu Shaoqing called his daughter to his side and put his mouth to her ear. "Tang Sanyuanzi said Wu Gou has joined the Communist Party's Jingdong* Society to Fight the Japanese and Save the Country. He taught his students martial arts and plans to lead them to join the Communist Party's Jingdong People's Self-protection Army."

"Really?" Liu Yemei half believed, half doubted.

Liu Shaoqing gave a rare laugh. "Wu Gou may be a scholar, but he has a bigger heart than either of us,

* The name means "east of Beijing".

think of him learning martial arts these past few years, perhaps he's not just putting up a front."

"If only he would bring his troops back to the Canal Flats to shed some blood!" Liu Yemei was crazy with delight. "The two of us will join his band."

Liu Shaoqing was just about to open his mouth when Moyu'er appeared with the empty basket, shouting for Aunty Liu. "My grandma says thank you."

"It's nothing to thank me for." Liu Yemei was all smiles. "Go back and tell your grandma and when you've finished those, come and pick some more."

"My mama . . . also told me. . . ." Moyu'er stuttered, "to thank you."

Liu Yemei scowled. "I didn't give her my melons to eat, so I don't accept her thanks."

"She didn't eat a single one. . . ." Tears filled Moyu'er's eyes. "She said . . . she's been unfair to you in this life, in the next life she'll come back as a cow or horse and repay your kindness."

Liu Yemei's heart filled with warmth. She said quickly, "Tell your mama from me that she mustn't worry." Then she went back into the melon rows, picked two huge *mian* melons no smaller than the melon king and entrusted them to Moyu'er. "I'm sending these specially to your mama, none of you are allowed to eat any part of them."

"OK." Moyu'er answered, but knelt down and knocked his head on the ground in a deep kowtow.

"Good-for-nothing!" Liu Yemei pulled him up. "Where did you learn to act like a beggar?"

Moyu'er lowered his head, rubbing his little hands together nervously. "When I was just leaving, mama told me to kowtow on her behalf and beg you to forgive her and take good care of us little brothers."

Liu Yemei gave a start, then stood for a while, dazed, dully watching Moyu'er as he disappeared into the distance.

9

In the depths of the night, Moyu'er returned.

"Aunty Liu, my mama's disappeared!" Moyu'er stood under the willow curtain at the back window of the melon hut crying piteously. "Grandma sent me to beg you and Grandpa Liu to look for her."

Liu Yemei, sleeping in the inner room on a rush mat on the floor, had been roused by Moyu'er's calls. She hadn't had time to question the boy when she heard Liu Shaoqing leap up from his bed in the outer room with a bitter cry, "I've been so careless. Damnation!"

Liu Yemei threw a jacket over her shoulders and went out asking, "Papa, can you guess what's happened?"

"When I was called to the police station, I saw Tang Sanyuanzi and that cripple Jia Erhaba drinking together, I should have anticipated that they'd set about Hua Sanchun." Liu Shaoqing beat his breast and stamped his feet, stricken with remorse.

"I'm just afraid we're going to be too late." Liu Yemei became flustered.

She carried Moyu'er into the melon patch and put him into the hut. Then father and daughter set off along separate paths, plunging into the vast, dim, moonlit depths of the Canal Flats in search of Hua Sanchun.

It was almost dawn when, in a grove of willows interlaced by tiny streams, they found two bodies. One was Hua Sanchun, the other was Jia Erhaba.

After Wu Gou had fled, Hua Sanchun had once more heard the long whistles coming from outside the courtyard wall. She had never imagined that after so many years the big boss would still not let her go. She was a proud woman, so she didn't go to the melon patch to find the Lius. She took a grip on herself and sent Moyu'er to return the basket and send Liu Yemei a few heart-felt words. When Moyu'er came back from the melon patch with the two *mian* melons, she was so moved that she wept. She forced herself to eat half a *mian* melon Liu Yemei had sent her, and then hiding a pair of scissors in her clothes, set out to fight a lone battle.

She had crossed over the small bridge and followed the branch of the canal. She had not gone far when suddenly, from behind a lone grave, out leaped Jia Erhaba.

"Sanchun, I must congratulate you. You are going to become a widow!" Jia Erhaba leered at her. "The boss's son has been made police chief. Obeying the orders of the Anti-Communist Autonomous Government, he's going to catch that man of yours and kill him on the spot. Kill first and report afterwards."

"There's a lucky star shining over Wu Gou's head. Tang Sanyuanzi needn't imagine he can catch him." Hua Sanchun's eyes flamed with fury. "And if he does catch him, then in the same year, in the same month, on the same day, I shall die too."

"It's out of your hands." Jia Erhaba's face was vicious. "The boss's son has given you to me. Marry a rooster you follow a rooster, marry a dog you follow a dog, marry a shoulder pole you have to take it on your own shoulders."

Hua Sanchun stamped her feet in fury, leaving two footprints in the ground. "Everyone has a place for living and a place for dying. I'd rather be buried right here."

"Fine!" Jia Erhaba rolled up his sleeves. "First I'll kill you, then I'll kill your nest of spawn. It's called wiping out the whole family and leaving no one to cause trouble later on."

A cold shiver ran down Hua Sanchun's spine and her body swayed, but as she steadied herself on her feet an idea flashed into her mind. Half laughing, half crying, she said, "Jia Erhaba, you've got me between the devil and the deep blue sea. Alright, I'll marry you. I'll go with you."

"Empty words mean nothing, I won't just take a glib promise." Jia Erhaba began to drool in anticipation, preparing to make a move.

Hua Sanchun dodged to one side, but gave him an enticing look. "The sky can be our curtain and the earth our bed. First I'll play wild love birds with you."

They pushed through patch after patch of brambles, climbed barren hillock after barren hillock, and crossed narrow streamlet after narrow streamlet. With death in her heart, Hua Sanchun was seeking life. She found courage and self-confidence.

By the time they entered a grove of willows in the midst of the network of streamlets, they were already two or three *li* from the village.

"Sanchun, the *fengshui** is good here, we'il enter the marriage bed right here." Jia Erhaba opened his arms to embrace her.

Hua Sanchun had been on guard for a long time, now she threw herself into his arms and stabbed the scissors deep into Jia Erhaba's abdomen. Jia Erhaba reeled over backwards scrabbling wildly with his hands in an effort to pull out the scissors, but after writhing briefly in agony, his legs stretched out and his eyes closed. He moved no more.

Hua Sanchun's hands and feet went icy with fear. She stood petrified, lost in a trance.

"Well done!" Someone patted her on the shoulder. "You were the sweet morsel in my mouth. How could I let you be carried off by that mangy dog?"

Hua Sanchun turned her head with a start. Behind her stood the demonic form of Tang Sanyuanzi.

"Tang Sanyuanzi, if I kill you and die too, I'll still be one up!" Forgetting she was now empty-handed, Hua Sanchun leaped on him and fought with all her strength. She scratched Tang Sanyuanzi's face to a bloody mess and fought to bite his throat. But she died under Tang Sanyuanzi's knife.

Hua Sanchun lay on the dark grass, the dawn light covering her like a brocade quilt, touching her colourless cheeks with a pink glow. It was still a lovely, charming peach blossom face.

"Sister-in-law Sanchun!" Liu Yemei wailed. "You sent Moyu'er to me with words within words. I was so blind!"

---

* The geomantic location of a place supposed to have an influence on one's fortune.

When Liu Shaoqing carried the news to the Wu family, Old Mother Wu took a child on her back and one in her arms and led the rest to the police station to bewail her grievances.

The police station was in a temple in a neighbouring village. It was staffed by a regional inspector, a police chief and two constables. The regional inspector was in hospital in Tongzhou, being treated for V.D., so the little office was in the hands of Tang Sanyuanzi. He ordered that Old Mother Wu and Hua Sanchun's children be locked up in one of the small temple halls and personally visited the scene of the crime to inspect the bodies, record the details of the murder and prepare to break the case.

Just after midday, Tang Sanyuanzi arrived at the melon patch followed by a constable with a gun slung across his back. He kicked open the wooden gate and shouted, "Liu Shaoqing!"

"Here!" Liu Shaoqing, with a drooping lotus leaf over his head, rose up from among the melon ridges and came forward rubbing the dirt from his hands.

"Old Mother Wu has reported that her daughter-in-law Hua Sanchun and an unknown man are lying dead in a willow grove on the Canal Flats and you and your daughter saw them with your own eyes. Is that correct?" Tang Sanyuanzi put on a cocky, officious air.

"Correct." Liu Shaoqing replied in a single word.

"After an examination of the corpses, I have concluded that this is a case of adultery and murder." Tang Sanyuanzi nodded his head complacently, making himself quite repulsive. "This was a pair of adulterers who went to enjoy the spring wind on the Canal Flats in the middle of the night and met with a murderer. He died for a lovely woman, what a way to go!"

"Crap!" Liu Yemei leaped up from where she had been weaving a cape in the melon hut, her face red with anger. "Hua Sanchun was not that kind of licentious woman."

The weather was burning hot, so Liu Yemei was only wearing a short sleeveless coarse white cotton blouse embroidered with a few flowers and a little shirt of woven willow strips thrown over her shoulders. Tang Sanyuanzi's crafty, piercing eyes roved hungrily over her body until her flech crawled and she hastily covered her bosom and turned her head away.

"My dear girl! How could you understand the sufferings of a woman keeping an empty house alone?" Tang Sanyuanzi nodded his head and bowed, inching his way towards her. "In cases of the murder of adulterers, the murderer is nine times out of ten the husband of the loose woman, who turns violent to avenge himself, so the murderer who took two lives on the Canal Flats last night must have been Wu Gou."

"That's even worse crap!" Liu Yemei grabbed the still unfinished green woven cape and wrapped it round her body, then turned back to argue, "Wu Gou is a scholar, gentle and refined. In all these years he's never lifted a finger against Hua Sanchun, how could he have the guts to murder her?"

"My dear girl, Wu Gou has joined the Communist Party. Don't you know?"

Liu Yemei still argued back, "You've hounded him until he can't even seek refuge in his own home. How could he go home to murder anybody?"

"Wu Gou hasn't gone far." Tang Sanyuanzi put on

a smiling face, but his eyes glowed with a vicious light. "This Canal Flats has rushes and brambles, graveyards, melon huts and willow groves. He could be hiding anywhere."

"Don't give me the 'dagger hidden behind a smile'."

"The lady has a really formidable little mouth." Tang Sanyuanzi laughed drily. "This murder case hasn't been cracked yet. You and your father personally saw the bodies, so you're involved in it. I must trouble you to come down to the station and make a statement."

"I'll go with you!" Liu Yemei jumped down from the melon hut.

"My dear girl, you've made a mistake!" Tang Sanyuanzi feigned a stern countenance. "Soft, pampered girls can't rashly leave their boudoirs. Liu Shaoqing is the head of the household. Come with me!"

Liu Shaoqing calmly and collectedly left a few instructions with his daughter: "Take the water melon king and exchange it for a catty of wine. We'll drink it when I come back." Then bare-chested and shoeless, the drooping lotus leaf still on his head, he followed Tang Sanyuanzi.

Liu Yemei was astonished. Her father usually never touched a drop of wine. Only at Mid-Autumn Festival and New Year did he drink at all, and then only a tiny cupful drunk drop by drop from the tip of a chopstick. Why did he suddenly want to drink tonight — and why did he want a catty? Papa's mind was like an ancient well — impossible to guess its depth and impossible to see to the bottom; he must be grieved and want to drown his sorrows in drink.

Her heart in a knot, she quickly took the wine calabash from the wall and then went in among the melon rows and picked the melon king still emblazoned in red with the word "happiness". She heaved it onto her shoulder and took it down to the canal bank. In the shade of the willows on the canal bank, there were often pedlars doing business, soliciting custom from fishermen and boatmen who stopped there to eat and drink. Liu Yemei quickly made a bargain with a small vendor and in addition bought a bag of chopped entrails for her father to eat with the wine.

After locking the wooden gate, Liu Yemei moved restlessly around the melon hut with no heart to watch the melons or even to finish weaving the green cape. The night drew dark and there was still no sound of her father's footsteps. As the moon rose above the tips of the willows, she pushed aside the willow curtain and leaned out of the window gazing into the distance. But there was not even a hint of her father's shadow.

Burning with anxiety, Liu Yemei paced endlessly around the melon hut.

"Ai! Something's gone wrong!" she cried out involuntarily and frightened herself into a cold sweat. Papa must have been thrown in prison, locked up in the police station by Tang Sanyuanzi. She clenched her chattering teeth and from under her rush mat pulled a knife that gleamed in the darkness with a cold brilliance. But suddenly she heard a flying stone hit the roof and roll to the ground. Her heart began to beat like a drum. Could someone be coming to plunder the house, knowing that she was there alone? She grasped the knife firmly in her hand and dodged to one side of the open window. The moment the thief put his head into the room, he would lose his neck.

As the third stone rolled to the ground, someone outside the willow fence called softly, "Uncle Liu, Second Brother Yemei!"

The voice was so familiar, so kind, so gentle. . . . A brilliant flame leaped in Liu Yemei's heart. It was him!

Outside the melon garden, an unexpected guest stood in the moonlight. It was Wu Gou.

10

Wu Gou grasped the willow curtain with both hands and swung in through the window.

"Elder Brother!" Liu Yemei could scarcely speak through her tears. "Sister-in-law Sanchun met a cruel death. . . ."

"I only found out at dusk." Wu Gou forced back his tears. "Tang Sanyuanzi has announced in every village that as long as I give myself up, he'll release my mother and the children."

"Where have you been hiding these past few days?"

"In the homes of my 'comrades'."

"What are . . . comrades?"

"The brothers and sisters who've joined the Anti-Japanese Society to Save the Country, and living or dying stand together!"

"I want to join too. . . . Are you willing to take me?"

"If you and Uncle Liu join up, the dare-to-die corps of our Jingdong People's Self-protection Army will be even stronger."

Liu Yemei sobbed. "After Sister-in-law Sanchun died, Tang Sanyuanzi still smeared her name. You must avenge her!"

"Sanchun may not have emerged from the filthy mud unsoiled, but I believe her heart was pure." Wu Gou pulled a gun from his belt. "I've brought a dozen comrades to force our way into the police station at midnight. We'll finish off Tang Sanyuanzi and rescue mama and the children."

"Tang Sanyuanzi tricked my papa into going too — and he hasn't come back." Liu Yemei said, "Where are your comrades?"

"They're waiting amongst the rushes."

"Quick! Bring them in to eat some melons."

Wu Gou was about to grasp the willow curtain and swing out when they heard the sound of a drunkard lurching along the road to the melon patch, singing obscenely:

"On the seventh day of the seventh month,
A girl in red went to visit her aunts.
She met with a flower picker on the way
And he took her to a corn field to romp and play."

"Tang Sanyuanzi!" Liu Yemei cried out.

"Don't panic!" Wu Gou's eyes were as cold as starlight. "The two of us can settle him."

"Little Liu Maiden . . . come and open the gate." Tang Sanyuanzi crashed his head against the wooden crossbars.

Wu Gou signalled to Liu Yemei and she answered in a sleepy voice, "Who is it?"

"Your . . . dream man. . . ."

Liu Yemei was about to scream a shower of abuse at him when Wu Gou clapped a hand over her mouth and whispered, "Lure him in."

"Oh, it's Police Chief Tang! If you want to eat some melons, you'd better wait for my papa to come back."

"Your papa . . . won't be back tonight." Tang Sanyuanzi broke open the gate and stumbled into the melon patch. "He's afraid you'll . . . be lonely . . . by yourself. . . . He begged me to bring you a mauser to keep you company."

"Trick him into coming into the hut." Wu Gou whispered urgently in Liu Yemei's ear.

"Police Chief Tang, don't . . . don't come into the melon hut. I . . . I haven't got my clothes on yet."

"That's . . . that's . . . convenient." Clinging to one of the supporting pillars, Tang Sanyuanzi climbed up and rushed straight into Liu Yemei's dark room.

As he plunged in, his head hit the wall and he fell to the ground, biting the dust. Wu Gou sat astride him and took away his weapon.

"Hey! Who are you?" Tang Sanyuanzi's fear sobered him up.

"Wu Gou," Wu Gou shouted. "Why did you lock up Liu Shaoqing? Confess!"

"I was going to . . . convict him of murder, then take his daughter by force, play around with her . . . then make her a flying falcon. . . ."

"Son of a bitch!" Liu Yemei spat at him and put the blade of her knife against his neck.

"Who killed Hua Sanchun?"

"It was . . . it was . . . it was Jia Erhaba."

"Liar!" Liu Yemei pressed the knife lightly so that it cut through the skin.

"Ahhh!" Tang Sanyuanzi screamed in agony like a pig being slaughtered. "It was Hua Sanchun who first killed Jia Erhaba, then tried to kill me. Only then did I . . . quite against my will . . . kill her. . . ."

Liu Yemei trembled with fury like a reed in a hurricane. Tears of distress flowed down her cheeks like rain and she cursed him, "You vile murderer." Her wrists involuntarily pushed downwards and off rolled Tang Sanyuanzi's head.

Wu Gou and Liu Yemei carried Tang Sanyuanzi's body between them and threw it in the canal.

"I'll go and call the comrades to come to the bank." Wu Gou walked to a patch of rushes close by, clapping as he walked.

From the rushes along the wide canal that shone silver under the full moon came a reply.

Liu Yemei turned back to the melon patch, but caught sight of shadows moving through the darkness under the willows and heard the disordered trample of feet. She dodged behind a clump of willows and squatted down to take a look. It was her papa, Liu Shaoqing, supporting the old and leading the young, coming home.

"Papa!" With a sob in her voice, Liu Yemei went to meet them.

"Yemei, did you get the wine?" Liu Shaoqing shouted excitedly.

One hand twisted behind him held one of Wu Gou's children onto his back, the other held another of Wu Gou's children against his chest. Several paces behind came Old Mother Wu, hobbling on her bound feet, drawing a child along in each hand.

"Papa, you've escaped with Old Mother Wu and her whole family!" Liu Yemei laughed with tears in her eyes.

"The words grate on my ears!" Liu Shaoqing looked annoyed. "I killed two constables in a row, then went to the rescue of Mother Wu and all her little kiddies. Now I'm returning victorious to my palace and I want to drink a calabash of victory wine."

"Papa, you'd planned this all along!" Liu Yemei darted forward to support Old Mother Wu. "Elder Brother Wu Gou has gone to the rush pool to call his men to the bank. In a minute you can have a big reunion."

"Quickly go and pick some melons to serve the guests!" The usually quiet Liu Shaoqing let off a stream of continuous gunfire. "The moon is so round, the moonlight so beautiful. Tonight we'll open up the melon patch!"

Father and daughter settled Old Mother Wu in the melon hut and quickly disappeared among the melon ridges.

Liu Shaoqing rolled up one great water melon after another, happy as a lark.

One by one, Liu Yemei picked *mian* melons white as white jade and yellow as gold; smooth, round and full bodied. Then she picked *mian* melons like painted faces of Beijing opera characters, melons with wry expressions and melons like simpletons, all quite ridiculous looking and delightfully charming. As she picked and picked, a faint ache suddenly tugged at her heart. Her heart was tied by a thousand invisible threads to the melon plants in this tiny garden. It would be hard to leave their poor family home and this warm earth! They would leave today and next year they would see no garden full of melon plants, the ground covered with melons. The melon hut would collapse and fall into ruin, be buried under a tangle of brambles.

Who knew when they could return?

Liu Yemei sniffed and couldn't hold back her sobs as she said to her father, "Papa, when we've beaten the Japanese and driven out Yin Rugeng, we'll come back home and grow melons in peace."

"If only I might live to see the day. . . ." Liu Shaoqing raised his head and gazed at the moon, emotion welling in his heart and a deeply thoughtful expression on his face. "In chaotic times like these, if my skills are to be carried on when I'm gone, I can't just rely on an only daughter, I must pass on your grandpa's melon growing secrets and all your grandma's martial arts skills to some people outside the family."

Liu Yemei gave a start. "You've suddenly found the courage of a lion. Would you really dare to break the strict family rules?"

Liu Shaoqing gave an ingenuous laugh. "Yemei, grandpa and grandma both loved you dearly. They're sure to grant whatever you request. Lay out a table with melons and that calabash of wine, and offer it as a sacrifice. Tell the old folk what I'm going to do and beg them to have mercy on me!"

Liu Yemei smiled through her tears.

Translated by Rosie Roberts

Literature with a Local Flavour

I was born on February 29, 1936 in Scholar Village, Tongxian County, on the outskirts of Beijing. A small village of clay sheds and thatched cottages, it nestled under green trees around an ancient canal. At that time, there were only a dozen or so households there.

Though the name "Scholar Village" suggests there should have been a great number of intellectuals living there, this was not so. Originally, it belonged to a Qing nobleman and its first inhabitants were his serfs. Later, that piece of land was part of his daughter's dowry. People flocked there from all parts of the country and settled along the sandy banks of the canal and subsequently the village was founded. Most of the villagers were tenant farmers, boatmen and trackers. Some went to Beijing and Tianjin to earn a living as coolies. From 1644 to the establishment of the People's Republic in 1949, a period of over three hundred years, no school existed there. The majority of the villagers were illiterate, with the exception of a few who attended a school in a neighbouring village for two or three years. I was their first intellectual.

Three years before my birth, my village was occupied by the Japanese. In 1942 it was liberated by the Communist-led Eighth Route Army. As it was surrounded by dense woods and bushes, anti-Japanese county and district and guerrilla leaders sought cover there. Though I was only six or so at the time, I joined the anti-Japanese children's corps.

My earliest cultural influences were primarily the folk tales told by my mother, the villagers and storytellers, as well as popular operas, ballads and folk art. These delighted me, taught me a great deal and stimulated my youthful imagination.

I was just thirteen years old at the time of Liberation in October 1949, yet I had already begun publishing my writing in papers and magazines. At fifteen, I decided to write about my birthplace, describing the locality and its customs and the fate of its inhabitants. In the past thirty years, I have produced three novels, twenty-four novellas and about a hundred short stories, all about the countryside around the canal, apart from one about a university student. My heroes and heroines are the peasants and their children.

I studied at Beijing University where I was taught by eminent scholars. As one of the first generation of post-Liberation writers, I was guided by many well-established literary figures. In 1956, I became a member of the Chinese Writers' Association and a professional writer.

My recent work, mostly novellas, falls into two categories. One describes the historical events that occurred in my childhood, such as "Catkin Willow Flats". The other concentrates on local rural life, such as "The Budding Lotus". The character of Manzi, the little rascal in "Catkin Willow Flats", for instance, was in large measure based on myself as a child. My memories of childhood are vivid. Snaring birds, fishing, catching crabs, stealing melons, reading picture books, teasing brides, that coloured apron-diaper. . . . They still remain fresh in my mind. I see myself as a boy romping round the village, in fields and around the canal banks and ferries. I am not alone; my old chums and many, many others appear in my mind's eye. I know their personalities and speech well. I believe that the creative impulse is stimulated by specific living characters. In order to write realistically, a writer must grasp and accurately record the speech of his characters.

While writing, I have thought a lot about literature that has a strongly regional flavour and have published two collections of essays entitled *Literature and Locale* and *Native Literature and I.*

Translated by Song Shouquan

刘绍棠中篇小说选
熊 猫 丛 书

《中国文学》雜志社出版
（中国北京百万庄路24号）
中国国际图书贸易总公司发行
（中国国际书店）
外文印刷厂印刷
1984年第1版
编号：（英）2—916—25
00190
10—E—1760P